DIVORCE
POOL

www.mascotbooks.com

DIVORCE POOL

For more information, please contact:
Mascot Books
620 Herndon Parkway #320
Herndon, VA 20170
info@mascotbooks.com

Cover Art by David Wiersch
Special Thanks to Margaret Schreiber

Library of Congress Control Number: 2020910315

CPSIA Code: PRV0820A
ISBN-13: 978-1-64543-398-9

Printed in the United States

This book is dedicated
to the profound joy of
the bubble bath.

DIVORCE POOL

PHILIP BUCKMAN

PART ONE

THE WAY WE WERE

nly gluttonous entertainment exists. No one can escape the screen. The screen is not nature nor fully urban or technological. The screen is faces. Solace is a half-pound Cheez-fry and a cola. There are seventy-five thousand strains of Mary Jane and a Za Shak on every corner. At every table, domestic or fine dining, a digital silica display is within view. From the middle class up, people have dozens of them. Some are lucky enough to have viewing units installed in lavatories of plush mats and linoleum. The faces will find you everywhere, and celebrity status is as relevant as politics or money.

The constant prods into the outside world make all art irrelevant. Human creativity is spent on ad design and silly games about the famous. Content is God, and there are many ways to worship. Channel XY has Brock Russell's *"Who's A Jerk?": Hollywood Insider #1*. On Cinetime Alpha, *Wardrobe Hero* is a hit. Tens of millions keep a cult-like following of *Comedian Roommates*.

On most programs, contestants are quizzed on pop culture. Common folk can achieve stardom, merely based on fandom. The cycle is repeated and spun once again, every day of the week. Returning champions make the cover of *Adult Bop* magazine and haunt the nightly news. Game shows beget spin-offs, which in turn spawn new trivia knowledge. Production crews work tirelessly on computer graphics and flatulent sound effects. It is crude, sexualized, and grotesquely tongue-in-cheek.

The most popular games cross-market for their sponsors. They sell monstrosities like the nacho-flavored soft drink. The screens are equipped with 3-D effects, neuron buzzers, and aromatic viewing. These technologies hawk the product and invite new flesh to participate in the game. Consumerism is the lottery system, and UPCs are the ticket. Proof of purchase can be a chance at fame and fortune. Winners are congratulated on the screen. It is a long-lived tradition, a pastime more beloved than baseball. Game shows have become our Colosseum.

Some people are keen enough to devise their games. They do so without purchase or registration of intellectual property, just like the old rituals of kindergarten play. Inevitably, many tend to focus on cash wagers. Gambling involves anything and everything with odds working on a wide range of factors. Payouts represent a sizable chunk of the American economy.

Ghettos and gated communities alike swarm with players, putting money down on arguably insignificant topics: Which hair color will Bono choose for his meeting with United Nations? Will Mariah Carey renegotiate her contract with Palacio de Caesar? Will anyone in the Boston Celtics seek gender reassignment? There are millions and millions of games every week. Who will place the star on the giant Thunder Oak at Rockefeller? Which series in the *Law & Order* canon will be canceled in the fall? A quick search of discussion boards will yield a hundred thousand results. Some people build careers on cheap bets and speculation.

Celebrity recreation, or Celeb Rec, is a network of household industries. Like all American enterprises, some cheat and some become addicts. In most cases, it is innocent fun, like an office potluck or a bingo game at the American Legion Hall. It can be a form of bonding or a pathway to murder. Short bets are based on immediate events, while long bets take fads, trends, and ideas into consideration. People would place a wager on the apocalypse if given the chance.

In one such Celeb Rec game, four people from distant corners of the Southwestern United States met once a year. They placed bets, worked odds, and collected on past bets. It had started as an infrequent and sporadic hootenanny, a gathering of old friends, which were a hard-won accessory in late-era capitalism. The game began in morbid fashion. It was a gamble on celebrity deaths. Everyone already worshiped fame, and the element of sacrifice seemed like the obvious next step. Aiming for shock value, they called the game Death Pool.

The idea was simple enough: meet up for New Year's Eve; catch up with one another; spend New Year's Day planning the list and working out the odds; live your life as planned while the lunar cycles pass; regroup to see if anything sticks. Young celebrities would garner favorable odds. Likewise, the payout for baby boomers was low and hardly worth wasting one of six picks. But in Death Pool, everyone got six picks. No more and no less.

Obscurity would also increase the payout, as would primacy. Tabloid research would help find important clues, such as who has been suffering from depression or received a recent diagnosis. Sometimes the effort would involve frantic queries from the hotel partition AI:

"Sulo, does Bob Dylan have cancer?"

"Ishtar, who are the current contestants of '*So You Think You Can Adrenaline Sport?*'"

"Laszlo, perform a triangulation of reported divorces, bankruptcies, and rhinoplasties."

Sometimes they would meet in Albuquerque, sometimes in Denver. Their preference was Las Vegas, but that only happened once. It was on the inaugural run of Death Pool. In Vegas, they truly felt as if they were the sickest Celeb Rec fucks on Earth, Nero on a hoverboard, an AR-15 in each hand, and Roc with one-hundred mouths. They threw beer bottles at Drumpf Tower while paper lanterns floated into the sky. They laughed and teased one another. After a pitcher of rose brandy and a pack of menthol Dromedaries, the four friends slept like seasoned drunks. They would wake the next morning, anxious to run odds and to pick someone to die.

FORTY-SOMETHINGS HARDLY HAVE AN INTEREST in such endeavors. In America, decrepit individualism feeds the ego. There is frankly little time for any project outside of the nuclear family, if you're lucky enough to have one. The self is the altar upon which we sacrifice the other. We conquer the competition, make a million, and move on. It is a wonder that anyone is capable of friendship in the United States.

The screen is one's daily loaf, and true friends are still commonplace.

Nonetheless, people yearn for companionship, plain and simple. The desire for camaraderie affects their decisions in cryptic ways. Self-interest is not an invincible force, regardless of what the stock market says. Connectivity is an act of self-preservation. It is a wonderful island in a heap of trash, and kinship is the life vest that brings us to the shoreline. Thus, in spite of the world around them, the four friends made time for one another. Their connections were tenuous, but intact.

History played a vital factor. They had spent their earliest years in Los Angeles in a neighborhood commonly known as Historic Filipinotown. Each had a standard childhood, played out entirely before the atrocities of '93. The eighties saw health food fads and machismo movies. Human contact hadn't been dashed by the Internet. The screens, and by extension the faces, were forced to follow rigid schedules sans auto-blush and panoramic videoshoppe augmentation. The screens had not yet acquired an inherent power over us, but the fiber-optic cables were being laid.

Esther and Muhammad were bicentennial babies. Geo was the youngest, and Clea was one year his elder. They attended Zheng He Elementary and Belmont High School together; their mascots were the Admirals and the Sentinels. Major milestones were collectively experienced. First kisses were talked about with corresponding shame and support. They watched Spielberg films, built forts, fought, and smoked weed in littered alleyways. They hated Soviet scum and listened to Shalamar on the radio.

Each lived on different lengths of Temple Street. It was the lifeline to every destination: the 101, the Dodgers, Huìshēng Park, and eventually, the punker shows. In their earliest interactions, Esther's mom would tuck them into a hatchback Toyota for arcade time and gelato. On unsupervised afternoons, they would sneak into the transient camps of Skid Row to make friends with the homeless children. Truth or Dare was a regular.

Long walks were also common, especially in the spring. They zigzagged through various neighborhoods with cans of soda and bags of candy in tow. Geo would throw rocks at stray cats, and Esther would reprimand him. Clea loved to tag her name on stop signs with a permanent marker. In those years, graffiti was the only proof of one's existence. She was unable to think of anything clever when her mother passed away. The day after the tragedy, she was joined by her friends while mourning on the beach. On the walk home, Muhammad found a patch of wet cement and wrote "*Mama Zamora*" with a stick.

For films and stadiums on a whim, Geo would usually spot everyone for ticket fare. His allowance cast a shadow on his friends, a minor demonstration of the wage gap that plagued the nation. Once the VCR was within grasp, the Simmermanns held movie nights, Sundays after dinner. One time, after playing spin the bottle at Clea's Bat Mitzvah, they watched *Rocky I* and *Rocky II* back-to-back. Arguments about the virtues and failings of heavy metal were common, with the exception of Megadeth, who were eternally infallible. They were drawn to, and eventually withdrawn from, skating culture, settling on a subscription to *Thrasher*. They hung out with older kids. Back then, parents granted a greater swath of freedom compared to the helicopter guardians of today.

There was camping in the San Gabriel Mountains every other weekend in the summer. They snorted breath freshener spray because Xi said it would get them high. Handheld consoles were played under the bridge until the AA batteries were bled dry. The boys measured penises, and the girls compared breasts. Adolescence wasn't wholly awkward, as many romantic comedies would have you believe. It was experimental.

There were other milestones as well, like the DMV and virginity. Being drunk for the first time was an especially meaningful and messy bond. They opened up the fuel that built the pyramids, spilling guts on love, life, God, and war. On that intoxicated night, Geo stumbled while taking a piss, smashed his forehead into a porcelain vanity, and unconsciously emptied the rest of his bladder onto his flannel blazer. His nose was broken, and his liver screamed for assistance.

Luckily, Clea had a strong preference for dirt weed, instead of the coconut-flavored vodka stolen by Esther. She cleaned Geo's face and chest. Esther helped tend to him as well. Afterward, she called Mrs. Simmermann, who was a nurse, for advice. Clea and Esther were always the responsible ones. Geo spent the weekend recovering from alcohol poisoning. His parents were upset but thankful for the friends that looked out for him.

Booze followed them to basements along 2nd Avenue, where they thrashed like airborne mullet fish. Muhammad's parents used to play at Sake-a-Dance-Dance and knew of every house venue popping up and coming down. House shows helped them navigate the complexities of being social: sarcastically requesting "Freebird," flirting with bands on tour—some of which were too young to buy alcohol, and flaunting their status as ardent patrons of cheap malt liquor.

Esther formed a three-piece band in '91. She made T-shirts and recorded a four-song demo. That was a great year with Anarcho-themed festivals that taught courses in self-defense, Knox gelatin caking up the hair, and roasting in leather jackets under the sun in the City of Angels.

It was during those years, sweating at some punk or techno show, that cemented their future relationships. The bonds formed sturdy and strong, even though they required incentives like gambling and fascination with the macabre to remain intact over the years. When the four friends were faced with leaving LA for college and careers, they promised to meet every year to celebrate shared experiences. They hoped to create new ones as well.

GEO WAS THE FIRST TO cash in on Death Pool when he listed Anton Yelchin and George Michael in '14. Yelchin scored decent odds on obscurity and unbridled youth. Geo was a *Star Trek* fanatic since the eighties. Perhaps as homage to the Russian-American ancestry of his father, he loved Chekov. The reboot of an alternate-universe franchise was on his mind when he finalized his list the year prior. It was a crapshoot, and so was George Michael, for that matter. It was odd how George Michael sang the song about Horus Mass, and then died on Horus Mass. Esther also earned seven hundred that year for picking David Bowie.

They all hated Geo in '14. They missed Prince dearly, and they hated Geo for cashing in on all the lost talent. There was precedent for such feelings, as it is an American custom to despise any deficit between personal and peer status. Keeping up with the Joneses, or the inability to, always preoccupies the mind. In any case, Geo was the richest of the four.

At a certain point in his life, he could have been considered an oil man. In reality, he was more of a bank man. His college years led him down that path. After making many friends at UCLA's Anderson School of Management, he was offered a lucrative opportunity to make boatloads of cash. Feeling ripe for wanton exploitation, he was tasked with devising a method of sharing bank account data, specifically in a way that could monitor the balances and transactions of the nation's poorest people.

The algorithm was difficult work. He spent many late nights drinking espresso at the twenty-four-hour pancake trough, editing and reworking the numbers. Due to the hushed manner in which his group operated, he could not ask for help from other mathletes. Finally, after a solitary and stressful month, it was conceived. Now he just needed a mechanism to attract victims, a Venus flytrap of sorts. He rested, shaved his face, and applied for a small business loan.

By the age of twenty-eight, Geo had established a string of pay-by-check gas stations. They targeted those living on the biweekly dole. He advertised the gas stations as a service for the disadvantaged, hanging posters in bus stations and in the Office of Social Security. He used marketing tactics similar to those employed by payday loan vendors. The ads featured a special mascot, a winged fairy godmother who could fill your tank with a whisk of her wand. Once his business began attracting customers, he pampered them with free coffee and clean restrooms. Eventually, his experiment would extend into cities along the Mexican border and deep into the Bible Belt.

To be fair, Geo genuinely helped his patrons. It was a form of short-term assistance. Unfortunately, the process was also meant as an act of brazen data mining. Personal checks contained all of the information needed for the scheme. Thus, obtaining the routing and account numbers was the easy part.

Building a network of banking associates was also an easy part. It was all easy. The demand for reliable fuel was strong. As a rule, those most concerned with gas prices and mileage tended to live on tight budgets. Now anyone could write a check, even postdate it, to commute to their shitty job.

Account data was shared with the team of bankers, and with Geo's four regional managers. Using Geo's fancy algorithm, the banks kept a tab on purchases and ATM withdrawals. It was transactional surveillance. They would wait patiently. Sometimes they would wait weeks, even months—long enough for the patron to forget the debt. Then, when balances dipped below the amount written on a previously-tendered check, they requested the funds. They called the process "NSF Farming."

This was when the cash cow produced milk. The chain of gas stations, appropriately named "Geo's Check-and-Go," had a stringent policy on bounced checks. Non-sufficient funds incurred a fifty-dollar charge. A half-dozen banks, actively scheming with Geo, agreed to pay the transactions and the penalties, charging their own NSF fees after the fact. Geo and the bankers quickly became rich. Eventually, the franchise expanded, and fresh speculators secretly enlisted in the effort.

Geo was a home-grown celebrity, filming comedic ads, and using giant, inflatable animals when pushing a special promotion. His commercial demeanor effectively masked any personal intent to swindle. To cover his paper trail, his earnings were channeled into multiple offshore accounts, housed in various nation-states throughout the Caribbean and the South Pacific. He married a former Ms. Texas named Mishelle and settled in a wealthy suburb of Houston.

Four years passed before anyone had noticed any ill will. Most people paid the fines without second-guessing the origin. For some, the fines amounted to a month of groceries. Any effort to address management was slowly lost in a sea of call centers. Those who didn't pay up were subject to collections and adjustments to their risk profile. Finally, a credit reporting agency, noticing a sharp spike in FICO damage, caught wind of the entities responsible, and an investigation was launched. Geo's empire was heavily scrutinized, and after seven months of research into the matter, Check-and-Go became a prominent theme in the news cycle.

The culprits bribed every angle of the legal system. Therefore, the trial was swift with guilty verdicts from a dozen associates, including Geo himself. Everyone was caught in the act, but no one went to prison. Geo was forced to liquidate his holdings, and the corporation was dismantled. The immediate and televised concession of his company seemed to quell most of the public outrage. His accumulated assets were left untouched. Within a year of the trial, he secured a position as a financial consultant. It was a common tale. Anything short of rabid cannibalism, and the American elite were generally left unscathed.

So, with the wave of celebrity deaths that occurred in '14, Geo had cashed in on two of his picks. Half-expecting him to write off the bet, his friends sullenly authorized credits to his account. It didn't seem fair. No one complained at length. After all, it was part and parcel of Death Pool's charm as a game of chance.

In '16, Muhammad made a laughable two hundred bucks when he guessed Tom Petty's death. Old rockers never make for favorable odds. In '17, Clea made a cool grand for predicting Ben Affleck's end. He suffered a massive heart attack. Another Batman movie was on the horizon, earning her an extra payout. At the time, Death Pool was becoming a loved tradition for the four friends.

For a while, it felt like the teenage years, but without the pimples. The connections were rekindled. The extended weekends brought release from the stresses of adulthood. The friends reminisced about loved and hated teachers at Belmont. They provided armchair therapy to one another. They bitched about lovers, spouses, and exes. They sang at karaoke clubs, especially after learning of Clea's love for impersonating Sinatra and Sade. They binge-watched documentaries and argued about the Drumpf administration. It felt good to hash out the past in the present and to be happy with the results. The Celeb Rec game was a catalyst for their continued friendship. It would not hold their interest for very long.

After '17, there was a two-year drought of winners. The six slots doubled to one dozen in an attempt to keep interest. Then, without prior consultation, Esther decided not to attend in '21. It was obvious that the game was rapidly losing its appeal. There were so many other games occurring in hometowns and hookah bars. And why bother playing with no apparent reward? In a society easily bored, Death Pool had become hardly worth the drive or flight.

One day, in the last stretches of a spring morning, Clea fixed her eyes on a screen. It was playing a live feed of a wedding for some European monarch.

The groom echoed Adonis—nothing but bronzed skin and muscles. He was a well-known model from Madrid. The bride publicly kept a long list of failed relationships. Clea had heard rumors of the upcoming union. She had a tendency of chuckling at every mention of it. She took a deep swig of her budget Moscato.

Under her breath and to herself, she mumbled, "I bet they get divorced within a year."

The words escaped from her lips and into the atmosphere. An idea was forming. It was becoming certain: Death Pool had to end. It would be reborn into something new. Jackpots would be handed out once again in the company of friends. In the streets of all Hollywoods, the only thing more predictable than death was divorce. Without any explicit effort, a new Celeb Rec sport had flashed across Clea's mind. Rushing to her home phone, she called Muhammad, Esther, and Geo, and asked about plans for the upcoming New Year's Day holiday.

II

It's just an unplanned project, I tell myself. It's not like I would be doing anything else. The parents are broke, and I am bored. I'm one month into summer break and five days before my allowance. I groan under my breath. Hopefully, this thing works. I haven't seen many quarters ever since Mom and Dad started talking about the recession. Not even after cleaning the house and the backyard. What is a recession anyway?

I've been rifling through all of the stuff in my stepdad's garage for over an hour. *Thin-gauge twine, check.* The older kid at Ochoa's Arcade called it a means of delivery. I'm trying to remember his words. *What did he say about making the knot as tight and small as possible? Tweezers to tie the twine, check.* Finally, I find a drawer full of nuts and bolts. I can see some washers buried in the back. Are they the right size? I find one that fits the bill. *This is exciting.* My hands are getting sweaty. *Let's hold it up to a quarter. Perfect!*

"Cool beans," I whisper, bragging to myself.

I look down at my black arms, and they are sprinkled with sawdust and grease. I am wearing my favorite yellow shirt. Hopefully, it's not ruined. I take a quick chug from a lukewarm juice box. It is apple juice, and the box has a picture of Muscle Moth and the Power Triplets.

Now the twine must be tied to the donut-shaped washer. This is the hard part. *Take a deep breath, Muhammad.* This must be how surgeons feel when they operate. I am beginning to remember the step-by-step instructions. The knot must rest within the inner lip so it won't chafe the coin deposit slot. Make sure to have all of the dangling threads trimmed. Get the perfect amount of slack. *Popeye, Luna Policia,* and *Hot Dog Restaurant;* I can't wait.

The petrol shop on the corner has a few new titles as well. If I get this right, they will all be mine. I dream in 8-bit. *This slug is gonna reach those dreams.*

DAD WAS PISSED WHEN CARTER won re-election. "America's first female president," he used to say. He always tries to scare me with stories about the hydrogen bomb, saying that Carter is unable to protect us from invasion or missile strike. I don't really understand what the Russians have against us. Perhaps it is the fast food, milkshakes, and Ferraris. Dad loves to explain how the Russians get jealous about regular, everyday things.

"Imagine a world without toilet paper," he once told me.

He is always upset. Not at me or Mom, but at everything else. He is upset with the Soviet Union. He is upset with Reagan for losing the race in '78. He is upset with Los Angeles for being so big and dirty. He is upset with the punk scene and with the friends who chose to stick with it. Most of all, he is upset with couples. Whenever we visit Griffith Park, he makes a point to poke fun at "cuddlers" on benches. He makes guesses about couples breaking up. Most couples, according to Dad, break up within a year.

When I was five, he started working at the Hyperion Treatment Plant. It was his first job after the divorce. At first, he was thrilled. I remember when we watched *Planet of the Apes*. He was so excited, telling me how the movie was filmed near his work. He made good money at Hyperion. Before Hyperion, he could hardly rely on the occasional offer to play Sunset Strip. With the new job, he could focus on quality time with his son, and he could finally give up on late-night gigs.

"Muhammad, don't grow up to be a musician," he once told me.

I don't think he believes in love anymore. I don't know enough about love to say for sure. One time, I asked him if he wanted a girlfriend, or if he would ever get married again. His answer was a quick shrug. His excuse is his work. The plant makes Dad smell like farts. At night, he strips off his overalls before coming into our one-bedroom apartment. He blames the fart smell for being single. It's not bad once you get used to it. I doubt pretty women feel the same. I don't think he really wants a girlfriend. To be honest, I don't want to share the apartment with anyone else. In any case, it would be nice to see him hold hands with a lady. Sometimes, I can tell when he is feeling lonely.

On my weekends, we look through old baby pictures, and his face frowns at the ones with Mom. They never told me anything about the divorce. They are saving that for when I am older. Many of my friends have divorced parents, so I don't think about it too much. Tamara Chen has divorced parents that scream at each other. Tiffany Hernandez has parents that call the police on one another. I guess I am lucky to have parents that are on speaking terms. On holidays, we all eat at the same restaurant, and laugh like nothing ever happened. On my weekends, Dad and I eat macaroni and cheese.

"That shit is fortified with vitamins, so you can grow up with big muscles and get a lady," he once told me.

MOM HAS BEEN MARRIED TO Larry, my stepfather, for almost two years. Sometimes she spends more time with him than she does with me. I don't let it get me down. At home with Mom and Larry, I act very serious. I do the homework and the chores that boys my age are told to do. I save the fun stuff for Dad's house. I would never mention this fact to my custodial parents.

I think that Mom sees Larry as a true soulmate. Tamara and Tiffany have similar stories about their parents meeting new boyfriends and new girl-friends. They tell me it's a phase, and that it will pass. Mom and Larry met in Xiào Chǎng, at a Rodney Dangerfield show. I remember how Mom was so happy that year. The same year that Dad was in the hospital for depression.

We moved in with Larry the following summer, and for the first time in my life, I had my own bedroom. It was a great change, but I couldn't help but feel a little guilty. I could tell that the situation made Dad jealous, not because of Larry, but because Larry had nicer things. In Mom's eyes, Dad was a mistake. Sometimes, even though I know she doesn't mean it, she treats me like a mistake.

Larry and my Dad are very different. Larry's house is very clean and modern. Larry collects postage stamps and rare coins. He is a big deal at the Museum of Contemporary Art, making final decisions on featured artists.

His life in the world of art was part of Mom's attraction to him. He is a tall and handsome Native American. He has never mentioned his tribe. Perhaps he doesn't know. Most of the coastal tribes were gone over a century ago.

Larry is nice, but he tries too hard to be cool like Dad. His jokes suck. He dresses nicely, and his tattoos haven't faded. He never gets angry, which seems weird for a grown man. Most men look angry to me.

I feel safe living in Larry's house. There is no graffiti in the alleyway. There is no broken glass on the sidewalk. The only adventurous thing about Larry's house is eating non-halal foods. Sometimes, he brings out his clarinet, to practice major and minor scales. Larry never misses an opportunity to mention the time he saw Dad play at Al Cid when they both were students at Cal State.

I was too young to ever see Mom or Dad play. Mom's band was called Nixon Babies, and Dad's band was called Bile Rocket. Nixon Babies was mildly successful. From what I've heard, Bile Rocket was a huge influence on the Caliphornia thrash of today. I remember when Metallica gave them a shout-out in cassette liner notes. Mom and Dad used to tell stories about their five-week tour in '76. They lived in a van together and met Darby Crash in Reno. They always bragged about one night when cops in riot gear broke up a basement party in St. Louis. The riot gear might have been an exaggeration. I love to see pictures from those days, when both parents wore jeans.

Mom still brings me to all-ages shows whenever she can find them. She gave up punk rock when I was born, but still talks about her old friends with love and respect. Dad quit Bile Rocket before I could walk upright. Mom called him a bad fit for the scene, blaming his beliefs as a conservative Muslim. I think she misses being a well-known name in Los Angeles. Dad sure as hell doesn't. He blames his music for losing Mom and his life in general.

"Does it look like it will work?" I am asking for advice from the tall boy with a denim vest and red peach-fuzz on his face.

"Yeah, I think so. It looks like good work. Just make sure that old man Ochoa isn't looking whenever you use it, or you'll be banned for life," he answers, chewing on a wad of grape-flavored gum.

"He's too busy looking at dirty magazines." Ochoa Arcade's owner always sits in a small office at the corner of the gaming floor.

Giggling through his purple-stained teeth, he mumbles, "Good luck." He turns away from me to chase down some girl that he obviously has a crush on. I should probably learn his name. Most boys in middle school aren't so nice to eight-year-olds like me.

Before leaving me to test the slug, he adds, "There are some new kids here. They seem to be about your age."

"Thanks." I am ashamed to be one of the runts that hang out here.

I can see them huddled around *Missile Frenzy*. A girl with short hair is playing, and from a distance it looks like she is struggling to get past level four. Surrounding her are five younger kids, which makes me feel less worried about my own age. The girl with short hair is wearing a crisp, clean Def Leppard shirt, which is one of many bands that Dad likes to make fun of. She looks about my age.

I make my way to the long-awaited sequel of *Mr. Don't*, not because I want to play the game, but because it sits out of Ochoa's view. Fumbling through my left pocket, I sneak the slug out. I release the torque from the twine with two fingernails. Once it is uncurled, I carefully look back over each shoulder. No one is watching, and I nervously place the slug at the lip of the coin deposit. I say a quick prayer to Allah and drop it into the game. The screen switches from its default demo and instructs me to begin. The slug works, and I grin from ear to ear.

To avoid suspicion, I will play a few levels of *Mrs. Don't*. It's not that great and less colorful than the original. The power-ups are a cool addition. Emeralds double your speed, and peanuts give you the ability to breathe fire. Nonetheless, it is boring. I check to see if anyone in the arcade is looking. Ochoa has stepped out for a cigarette, and I feel comfortable walking among the other titles. I glance over at the short-haired girl. She is finally past level four. Her pile of quarters is almost gone. She is really pretty. Instead of playing *Octagon Prison*, I decide to introduce myself. For some reason, I am not held back by shyness.

As I approach, I can hear the six kids talking. It sounds like they want to order a pizza from Glory Stash, the cheap restaurant on the other end of the strip mall. The short-haired girl does not look ready to give up on her game. I walk up to the group and stand there. They are arguing about toppings and do not notice me. I clear my throat and step forward.

"Hi. My name is Muhammad. Do any of you go to Zheng He?"

The younger white boy answers in a snarky tone, "We all do."

"You're still in kindergarten, Geo. Quit acting like you're a big kid," snaps the older white boy.

"It looks like you are kicking ass on *Missile Frenzy*. I've never been past level four." This is a lie. Just last week, I reached level nine, the one with the red and orange artillery. Larry had bought me the handheld version for my birthday.

"Yeah," she replies.

"Uh, who's your teacher?" I ask.

Silence. The short-haired girl is losing the last of her infantry. After a few seconds, one of younger girls responds, "Mrs. Krint."

This one seems interested in talking with me. "Krint! I had her last year. Does she still do the jump rope competition?"

"Yeah, she does! I got second place this year." She beams with pride.

"Will you all please shut up? You're screwing up my game," the short-haired girl complains.

I look down for the pile of quarters, and it is gone. She is on her last credit. Without shoving anyone, I move toward the console. I am careful not to bump the short-haired girl while she plays. She is close to finishing the level, but does not have enough ammunition to defeat the rival army. I will not mention this to cover my earlier lie. I watch her wiggle the controls and give a sigh when her command center is finally destroyed. She looks defeated as the continue prompt flashes. I check for Ochoa. He is busy reading the newspaper in his office. I show her the slug. She looks confused and unimpressed. I drop the slug into the coin slot, and her army is replenished.

A quick smile lights up her face. "Thanks, man."

"Whoa! How did you do that?" asks the older boy.

"Top secret," I answer with a low voice, impersonating a suave spy.

"Well, it is nice to meet you, Muhammad. My name is Chadley." He gestures to his side and adds, "This is my younger brother, Geo. Do you live near here?"

"His dad used to play in Bile Rocket," the short-haired girl says before I can answer.

"Cool," Chadley says, understanding the reference.

The youngest girl looks at me and says, "I am Clea. This is my sister Nefe, and this booger is my brother Yoshi. Chadley and Nefe are boyfriend and girlfr—"

"Shut up, Clea! We are not," Nefe interrupts.

"It's nice to meet you all." I look over to the short-haired girl. "What's your name?"

"Esther Marigold Hawass," she answers as she begins level six.

III

Not explicitly comprised of hooves or bones, but containing remnants of nearly every local genus, the trash golem spans over twelve-hundred square miles. A mass of various matter, it exists in flux, influenced by the cycles of night and day. At night, the gelatin hardens, marked with chunks of non-biodegradable flotsam. It looks like a ribbed Bundt mold with aluminum and Styrofoam in lieu of fruit. It makes a sound when struck, resembling a quivering saw blade or a muted gong.

It holds weight. Many have proven it. During the short days of winter and depending on the temperature, Gel Lago stays solid after dawn. This is when migration occurs among animals and analysts. There is always evidence of light foot traffic. The tracks lie in the malleable waste, wiggling and wobbling, like one of Jeffy's detours in a *Family Circus* strip. At daybreak, everything liquefies, accompanied by a wretched odor. The footprints are smoothed out and settled as if they never existed.

Some critters thrive in the tailings of this ancient garbage. At one end, bioluminescent worms nibble at the slime. What makes them glow? Is it the chemicals, the melted lipsticks, pesticides, and artificial taco flavorings? If that were the case, we'd all be gelatinous by now. What about the fumes? One might be quick to blame smog and dirty ozone. But these are only pieces in the puzzle. This living stretch of the American Southwest is an amalgamation of many factors.

In Bhopal and on the fiery Cuyahoga, many chemicals can be removed. Spill and leak sites can be purified. Flirting with nukes has no such luxury. The Cold War. The race into Earth's orbit. Mining for atoms and fracking for petrol in the same pile of dirt. It's a wonder that the cities still thrive. Some regions of the world are utterly inhabitable.

The quotes from Los Alamos are laughable in retrospect. Oppenheimer did not envision this back when he cited the Bhagavad-Gita. Bikini Atoll was his nightmare come true, his destroyer of worlds. With heartbreaking ease, we relocated all of those natives and bombed their homes. We starved them while the white boys dined on MREs, Mai Tais, and smoked ham. It was a matter of national security, and we knew little about fallout or radiation sickness. Shoot first, ask questions later. It's a miracle that this logic never translated into a more aggressive brinkmanship.

For the United States to flex its atomic muscle, it needed a worthy gymnasium. The oceans and atmospheres of the South Pacific would do, for a while. We broke the Van Allen belt, if only for a few moments. *Aurora Borealis Tropicanis*, it was dubbed. The last giant squid was blown to smithereens. Hopefully, we didn't miss our chance to find Atlantis. We would blow up the moon given the opportunity. The Soviets almost did, after all. A missile gap was fabricated for the general public. Production increased along with necessary tests and observations. It felt like the radium crazes of a generation earlier. If the results are not immediately seen, they must not exist.

Eventually, sending troops and goods from Hawaii became expensive and tiresome. We needed a new farm for our mushroom cloud. The Aloha State itself must have been considered as a viable substitute. For reasons unknown to the layman, we didn't choose it. Too many exotic fruits. Sugarcane to feed our fat bodies. The ghosts of Pearl Harbor. The desire to keep our vacations intact. The newly-taken state just wasn't an option. And so, we brought the madness home.

We brought it to the American Southwest. In the few places unspoiled by Manifest Destiny, we stuffed that missile gap like a Thanksgiving turkey. No Roman emperor could have ever foreseen a militarization like that of the Mojave Desert. Our battle with commie scum justified the means, legitimizing the possible end of days. Pontificating and proliferating, one in the same.

Everyone watched stock footage of dummy villages burnt askew. The beauty pageants, blue curacao cocktails, and B-movies are all symptoms of our fascination with the atom. Then we peered into the walls of the Grand Canyon. We found high-grade uranium and were driven insane with the prospect of policing the entire world. Navajo men pushed the element, processed the element. Some of their families were given cleft palates as a consequence. Landowners made cold, hard government cash, merely for sitting on some yellowcake nest egg.

And so, the region between Reno and Las Vegas, dripping with isotopes, was seen as the epicenter of the Atomic Age. Secrets were kept under lock and key with only a few drifting past the sand dunes and cactus gardens into our science fiction and our nightly news. No wonder folks peddled theories about alien technology and mind control. The conspiracy became legal tender, even as elected officials held our undivided trust. In fact, they never lost an ounce of support in the process. As long as we could stomp the Muscovites, nothing else mattered. It was simply patriotic to allow the veil. Ironically, the veil did not cover the tests themselves. One could watch a blinding detonation from Adirondack chairs, poolside at the Golden Nugget.

Above-ground testing continued into the sixties. The emerging defense industry swallowed everything west of the Rockies. Populations spiked, and cities sprawled. Fortunes were made, and homelands were desecrated. The Southwest became the catalyst of pasty, American values: the BBQ, the surfboard, and campgrounds dotted along fresh interstates. Continuous warfare was an afterthought.

And we forgot about Bikini Atoll. Now that the madness was home with us, we embraced it like a pet cancer. We never asked ourselves the important questions. What did the tests do to the oceans? What had become of the islanders, left destitute and covered with sores? What had become of that Polynesian mess after it was blown to smithereens?

CONSIDER THE BOMB'S UNIQUE FINGERPRINT, drawn across so many blue skies. To some, the mushroom cloud resembles a human brain. Rocket trajectory is like a spinal cord, attached to the curvy, cerebral mass above. The bomb itself, a symbol of Man's mastery over the physical realm, the brimming power of self-cognition. Neurons fire off, and a causal relationship is implied. The splitting of atoms is an act of testing some grand and cosmic nervous system. Mutually assured destruction is only the development of muscle memory. We are merely building pathways. Perhaps we should revise the Cogito to say: "I think, therefore I destroy." As a condition of entropy, the physicist Ludwig Boltzmann once spoke of a brain, a self-aware entity that exists only under extreme thermodynamic imbalance. One billion sticks of dynamite should fit the bill. No rest until the weapon can tear through the universal fabric. It's the only way to protect us from communism. Dangerous thoughts lead to dangerous actions. The brain was and is our closest approximation of what enables thought—not to mention thinking about thoughts and thinking about thinking. Big Bang, Boltzmann's brain; it is all about coming into consciousness, honey.

Enter the mushroom cloud as a phallus, the old prototype of idol worship. Servicemen rally around ground zero, anticipating the smog-laden lingam, like satyrs in heat. Their girlfriends and mistresses wait at the base in drab, olive tents. Are they not permitted due to top-secret status, or is it an effort to avoid offense on prudish sensibilities? In either case, the exercise seeps eroticism. No deliberate design could have foreseen the shape of the smoky discharge, rising and rising. Take ammunition, for example. Missiles and bullets are phallic. It doesn't matter if they're built in Berlin or Aberdeen. The thought process merely caters to aerodynamics—function superseding fashion, in any likeness to the obelisk. But the cloud was like sex in action, rising and swelling at various intervals of intensity. First, the blinding light, metaphorically representing the orgasm. A seed at its base, climbing upward, post-detonation. Trails of smoke, twitching like a spent vas deferens. Fallout is an ICBM's ejaculate.

Or perhaps the space-time continuum is an eternal homage to the womb. We are star stuff in an oven. The swelling cloud is less destroyer, more creator. Invert the mashed potato texture of that thin, earthbound cord. It is a passage, dark like the night sky, pushing diamonds and other space junk. The fetus takes in all things through its navel, even the sticky remnants of quasars. All entities begin when their domes breach the ether. Narrow and elastic, the canal is wet with the spit we call Newtonian physics. We crawl out and into our planet of birth, using bodies as a balancing beam, an anchor, leverage in general. Every addict, lawyer, lover, and bully lieutenant; we all emerge from that almond. The bomb was meant to take away, but it can also give. No army on earth can kill Creation herself. The military-industrial complex has nothing on Mama.

And so, Gel Lago squeezed through the opening, through the yoni in the Pacific, and sat unseen for years. Part atmosphere and part saltwater, it fed on the residual radiation left by the testing grounds. Gel Lago was a mind. It was the mind of a child, but a mind nonetheless—an intangible half-skull of unstable molecules. Right away, this daughter of Bikini Atoll felt a sense of neglect. It yearned to be touched by other living things; not to establish emphatic connection, but to be fed. Contact with the slime was the first stage in its digestive process. In this fashion, a tropical ecosystem was taken as the child's first meal, and the waters became sterile. A crib for a baby the size of a school bus. With nothing left, no meat, and no growth to suck upon, the newborn cried out and received no response. The US left it to starve like an absent father leaving home for a pack of cigarettes, never to return.

No teat to nurse from, Gel Lago grew hungrier. Rudimentary antennae probed for more radiation to feed on. Early in the Atomic Age, it wouldn't have to look far. At that point in history, the supply was endless—a truck stop buffet with dessert bar and soda fountain. Unfortunately, Gel Lago could not access the cafeteria from the perimeters of its ocean home. All of the immediate food had been sucked up. It would have to make an effort at mobility. Shaking itself from the coral sprawl wasn't too difficult, and once free, the blob set out on an adventure to find sustenance. An amoebic caravan, wandering and lost, seeking its kin.

At once, its radar exploded with hot spots. Edible isotopes were being stashed somewhere in the extreme northeast. Gulf streams, however, restricted any movement in that direction. Gel Lago would have to rely on the tidal flow. First, it hitched a ride on the East Australia Current, and slowly moved past the northern shores of New Zealand. Next, it traveled eastward along the Antarctic Circumpolar Current. Just shy of the Falkland fork, it made a detour up the Peru Current and alongside South America. The process of reaching the American continents had taken well over a decade. Land-based power plants called out to the starving entity, forcing it to eat residuals of the South Pacific.

Before reaching the Galapagos, the jellied monster was jerked back into the deep waters, pulled westward by the South Equatorial Current. For over twenty years, Gel Lago skirted the hemispheric boundary. It consumed sea life on occasion, but its belly cramped and squirmed for atomic waste. This was the loneliest stretch of the journey. The creature, by human definition, wept. It wept until the Spice Islands were within vision. The Kuroshio Current swept the mass northward and into well-traveled whaling routes. Feelers stood erect in the direction of post-war Japan, in the direction of Russian silos. The atmosphere felt like echoes of home. Perhaps, if it could only find a chunk of land to beach itself upon, it could finally settle down after a long and grueling road trip. Sadly, there would be no opportunity to feast; not in Japan and not in the U.S.S.R.

Tailgating on Kuroshio, the mass was hijacked by the North Pacific Current and, once again, made a transit across the lonely ocean like a drugged gastropod. This time it would have some company. Three generations had passed since the birth of Gel Lago, and the forces of consumerism left a footprint upon an unoccupied and borderless territory. When humans kept landfills at capacity, other methods of disposal were necessary. The oceans became undeniably gross. They became littered with rubbish with the toys of toddlers and the toys of men in a mid-life crisis. Before garnering the attention of the scientific community, the Great Pacific Garbage Patch circled clockwise like a clogged toilet being flushed.

Polymers melting like butter. Rust-lined aluminum. Bleached condoms, both used and unused. The stench of a mile-long cardboard corridor mildewed through and through. Barnacles chewing on cans of *Aqua-Net* brand aerosol. Bobbing red bags, stewing with the bio-hazardous leftovers of a broken healthcare system: bone shavings, rotten molars, colostomy bags, lipids, and sinews. A pressure cooker heated by sunlight from above and geothermal bubbles from below. To Gel Lago, starved and committed to a venture yielding no fruit, the trash islands were an edible obstacle. Massive sections of the waste were incorporated into a rough exoskeleton. The entity grew and grew as it approached the Americas for a second time. Its frame buckled under the weight of trash being partially digested. The chemical residues, man-made and toxic, boiled like goulash during the summer months. The warmer conditions flattened Gel Lago, spreading it across acres of saline.

In its first act of metamorphosis, it receded and hardened in cold waters. This was apparent as it traveled further and further north. The solidification was a new sensation, granting a faculty akin to muscle strength. In the winter seasons, movement accelerated, almost unfazed by the strong current underneath. The potent source of radiation that inspired the slime to leave home so many years ago was being detected once again. It was coming from the American Southwest. With newfound energy, Gel Lago made a drastic effort to reach land.

'07 WAS A HORRENDOUS YEAR with many sources of fear and disappointment. But the beaching of Gel Lago, just south of Juneau, took precedence in the twenty-four-hour news cycle. By early March, it had fully emerged from the Pacific Ocean and started a long crawl toward the familiar scent of a proliferating war machine. The ordeal echoed sentiments from the classic movie *The Blob*, originally filmed in the fifties and remade in the eighties. It was natural to assume the monster was alien, whether borne from a meteorite or a crash landing. By the time it was moving full-throttle past the Yukon, and people could see it up close, the general public knew that they were complicit in its creation. The smell, the crinkling sound made while in motion, the particles of packaging; there was no doubt in the collective mind that humans were responsible. As Gel Lago moved south throughout the month of April, it left behind a trail of irradiated mucus, contaminating the countryside.

Vancouver was the first major cataclysm of impact and digestion. Luckily, Gel Lago's position was heavily monitored, presented to the audience as any other reality television show would be. This exposure led to effective evacuation plans. Other cities were put on high alert, with the possibility of mass exodus. There were few casualties.

By May, the gelatin freak had reached the Canadian-American border. As a function of protocol, artillery was sent. It had no effect and spawned no defensive maneuver. After a week at the firing range, the military finally gave up. In Gel Lago's broken mind, the camouflaged soldiers seemed like some distant relative who only visits on Horus Mass.

Seattle and Portland were left scathed, but not entirely ruined. Half of Oregon is still in recovery. Salt Lake City, abandoned for weeks, did nothing but alter the pH of the entity. Mormons and punkers alike had fled for Arizona, Colorado, and New Mexico. Some westerners didn't feel safe until crossing the eastern banks of the Mississippi River.

Finally, the creature could taste the radiation being produced by the defense establishment. The Nevada test site was its target. The stronghold had fortified itself in anticipation, but many fled, especially after the threat had passed through the outskirts of Reno. Those who remained would suffer a slow death as the beast ate. Their deaths were arguably painless, due to a paralytic contained within Gel Lago's flesh.

The journey was coming to an end. At last, the jelly returned to a state of homeostasis. Like a dog nesting into a warm corner, it settled into the new home. Here, it would have enough food to last for nearly a millennium. Thus, in the first weeks of June '07, after years and years of searching, the ooze rested.

That summer, in the heat of the desert, Gel Lago flattened into a viscous pool. The semi-liquid form of its loosened body spread out across even larger swathes of land. To the naked eye, it resembled a lake. Thus, the moniker was given. Warning signs and barbed wire were placed around the living lake. By autumn, people got bored of the breaking news announcements, and Gel Lago was left alone for the most part. Curious researchers pitched tents on its banks. The US Military ended all exercises in the region. Consensus assumed it to be harmless. The waxing and waning mold was only interested in eating. It was seen as neither ominous nor friendly. It was just there. It has been there ever since.

THE QUESTION REMAINS: WHAT MAKES the small worm glow a dim chartreuse? It is the essence of everything American. It is the penultimate form of patriotism. It is the United States as malevolent policemen of the world. It is the end of days, an omen of judgment coming soon. It is orthodox Judeo-Islamic wishes come true.

Once part of our reality, Gel Lago was appropriated as a facet of the national culture, on the same standing as Elvis or Denzel Washington. It was loved in a uniquely weird way. The screens focused on it, studied it. Celebrities filmed home movies with the creature in supporting roles or merely as an enchanting background. Now, the blob is just another face. People either become obsessed with it or ignore it entirely. One thing is certain: its existence is a mystery. No one knows the origin story of where it came from or why it is here. No one knows that it began in Bikini Atoll.

The cleanup continues in places caught in its homeward-bound path. Most places will never recover, but the Southwestern States are still quite beautiful. National parks, interstates, and the occasional wildlife refuge are regularly visited. In fact, US-95 skirts the western edge of Gel Lago, but the route can only be driven in winter months. Summer is too warm, and the lake spreads out over random patches of asphalt, requiring new tar every autumn. More than ten years after landing in Nevada, the creature is as commonplace as the highway itself.

IT IS ALONG THE SOUTHBOUND stretch of US-95 where two old friends, Muhammad Liu-Miller and Clea Socorro-Zamora, carpool in a Nissan Sentra rental. They are headed to Phoenix to see Esther Marigold Hawass and Geo Simmermann for the first game of Divorce Pool. It is early on New Year's Eve.

"I can't stand Dave Matthews Band. They sound like elevator music fronted by a singing Adam Sandler," Clea said in a pissy and exhausted tone.

Muhammad briefly smiled and reminded her, "That was the deal. I had to pick you up in Oakland, so we get to listen to my shitty college memories." They chuckled as Clea reached into her satchel for a slim, menthol cigarette.

"I thought you quit last month," Muhammad said, scorning her as friends do.

Turning red, she explained, "I did five years without tobacco, and I hate that vaping shit. Those fools are gonna die before I do. Besides, I will get back on track after all of the fun in Phoenix."

"Are you excited to see the crew?"

"Yeah. Well, I am really excited to see Esther. A year is always too long to go without seeing my Marigold. I hope she has new exercises for me. My sciatic nerve has been driving me crazy. And I'm always happy to spend time with you, Mo." After pausing to light her cigarette, she continued, "To be honest, Geo can be kind of an asshole. Every time I see him, he does something that drives me up the fucking wall."

Muhammad noted, "He's the same as he's always been. We've never held it against him before, right?"

Clea attempted to clarify, "Sure. He's part of the crew. But with all of the vultures out there trying to make a quick billion, it's hard to think that he's one of them. It's not the same as when we were growing up. He's changed."

"At least we can hit him up for money whenever we need!"

"And let him bring it up every time we WallChat? No, thank you."

"I gotta say, I'm pretty impressed that he has stuck around with Mishelle for so long. If it weren't for her, he'd be a total monster."

Clea took a long drag from her cigarette, inhaled deeply, and blew the thick smoke out of the corner of her window. "For sure, duder. I'm more surprised that she hasn't left him."

After a few moments of silence, Muhammad joked, "I bet you're glad I don't listen to that contemporary country or that aggro-pop that he's into."

"Oh, Yahweh! That would be the worst road trip ever!"

After laughing for a bit, Clea broke in, "Sometimes, I get the impression that Mish really hates Geo to the core. She is an absolute angel, but I can't believe that she would stay with him for any other reason than money. And as much as I gossip about Geo, I wouldn't want him to be in a loveless marriage, where he's just some breadwinner."

"Yeah, but what else would he provide? Surely, not tenderness. It's the type of relationship he'd be in with any other woman."

Exhaling another long drag, Clea answered, "I suppose so. Remember how pissed we were when he won all of that money in '14?"

Muhammad's face turned slightly sour. "Three months' worth of rent."

"Well, maybe we'll be the winners this year, Mo. I have a particular talent for seeing through the bullshit when it comes to couples," Clea said matter-of-factly.

"I've already got a good idea of who I'm going to pick. Should be pretty decent odds if it comes true. With enough luck, I'll get those three months of rent back." Muhammad paused, craned his neck to the left, and pointed toward the roadside ahead. "Here comes Gel Lago."

"I never get tired of seeing that shit," Clea jested as she took a final drag from the cigarette. Scraping the red-hot cherry into an empty can of Royal Crown, she waited until the blob was within a few yards and flicked the burnt butt into its side. The roar of the wind rushing into the window muffled any outside sounds. The friends did not hear the quiet slurp of a carcinogenic cylinder sinking into green flesh.

"We will get Geo this year," Clea said with confidence.

IV

Mr. Rabinowitz is the worst. He is pacing from one end of the room to the other. I can't tell if it's anxiety or poor map placement. Jennie thinks he's cute. He's thin and pale, and his beard makes him look like a serial killer from *Unsolved Mysteries*. The very thought of physical contact with him makes me nauseous. *What's the use in learning this crap anyway? This is a US history class, not some AP world history elective. I'll never use this in real life. I can't imagine sitting in an interview, being asked about the spread of Islam in Asia.*

He startles me, "Did I lose your attention, Clea?"

"No, Mr. R. I was just editing some of my lecture notes."

"Very well. In review of our last lecture, Islam had rapidly developed in China due to the influence of the Khanates. The Delhi Sultanate was also instrumental in missionary work north of the Himalayas. You see, early in the fourth millennium, Taoism and Buddhism were in decline, and the teachings of Muhammad appealed to the sensibilities of the Ming Dynasty. In addition, many bureaucrats were eager to incorporate elements of Islam into the official Confucian canon."

I'd love to shoot a cannon at Mr. R. He is so boring. His wife, Belmont's principal since last year, was a total bitch when I was caught smoking weed in the catwalk above the auditorium. She paraded me through the cafeteria as an act of shaming. She's not the only one. All of the teachers and staff treat me like shit.

Mom tells me not to stress it, but it's hard not to feel offended. Mom always gives the same explanation: They're only putting in enough years to secure that sweet Caliphornia State pension. She wants me to behave, to let the abuse roll off my shoulders, and harden myself. One day when I finalize a scholarship, I can tell them all to piss off.

"Clea! Perhaps you would like to finish the lecture? Apparently, you have already learned everything I have to teach you and are content with day-dreaming two days before midterms," Mr. Rabinowitz snaps in frustration.

"Actually, Mr. R., I was wondering if Islam was accepted by all classes in Chinese society or if it was only practiced among the elites."

"If you will recall the information from yesterday, you'll remember that it was limited to Nanjing and a few border provinces," he answers. "Check your notes for all of the details."

"Thanks, Mr. R." I know how much he hates it that I've aced every one of his stupid exams.

"Now, it is the overthrow of Nanjing that is instrumental in the end of the Yuan dynasty. Once emperor Zhu Di is in power, there is an effort to increase military campaigns against the Mongols. Zhu Di, also known as the Yongle emperor, openly attacked Mongolian culture and language. There was a particular concern among his administration that traditional Buddhist values were being eclipsed by the growth of Islam. Defeating the Mongols served the dual purpose of territorial expansion and limiting religious conversion. The costs for the proposed wars and the building of ambitious works surged. The construction of the Forbidden City, the new imperial capital in Beijing, was just one of many examples of the exorbitant funds required to implement the plans of the Ming dynasty.

"This is where we left off yesterday. In short, the Yongle emperor needed to find new sources of revenue. Outright conquest did not do enough to meet his lofty goals. After years of difficulties, Vietnam was finally taken, but the process of doing so was a huge drain on state funds. Similarly, the campaigns to drive Mongolian forces back into the north were incredibly expensive. China was forced to ask how it would fund further projects, especially with an agenda to take new territories. The immediate answer would be the expansion and re-establishment of trade networks, an effort that came to be known as the 'Ming treasure voyages.' These expeditions, east into the

Pacific Ocean and west across the Indian Ocean, were led by the man you all know and love, the naval admiral Zheng He.

"Before reaching adulthood, Zheng was a trusted professional in almost all matters relating to the fledgling Ming Empire. He was raised a Muslim and understood the rich history of the Khanates. In fact, some of his ancestors were players in the old Yuan-Mongol alliances. Captured after the fall of Nanjing, he was castrated and subsequently drafted into the imperial army. After proving his worth as both a military strategist and imperial adviser, he quickly became a court favorite, especially after Zhu Di assumed the throne.

"Zheng He had the full support of the emperor and was given free rein to drive eastward, past what traditional maps had charted. The hope was to establish lucrative trading posts that would enrich the imperial coffers back home on the mainland. After two voyages, the plan seemed to be paying off. Large stockpiles of nutmeg and clove from the Moluccas and cinnamon from Ceylon were brought back. These spices fetched absurd profits from European and African traders. After forging many international alliances, Zheng He was trusted in all endeavors.

"On Zheng's third voyage, an attempt was made to sail past Sumatra and into uncharted waters. In October of 4112, he reached the northern shores of modern-day Australia, finding Papua New Guinea in the process. After consulting his senior officers and his vast collection of maps, Zheng He agreed that the vessels had reached unknown civilizations. The admiral was now faced with a decision: immediately return home and relay his discoveries to the imperial court, or attempt to use the new territories as a base for further exploration east.

"He chose the latter and established small farms and trading posts for supplies and barter. Zheng was very polite and cordial with the Aboriginal leaders, demanding very little other than information and temporary shelter. The natives of Oceania, in the eyes of a Ming-era eunuch, were decidedly African. Thus, he did not want to offend the sensibilities of powerful African empires with any effort at conquest or religious conversion. Once satisfied with the new alliances he had garnered, he set off eastbound into the sparse waters of Polynesia."

Okay. I should probably write some of that down. I know the general story, but I've never heard any of these specific details. Everyone knows the legend of Zheng He's discovery of the "New World." The fact that we're even discussing him is ridiculous. We have a day to celebrate him. We used to solve word puzzles with the various names of the junk he navigated as early as fourth grade in a school named after him. Mom calls him a monster. Really screwed over the natives with germs and whatnot. I guess that's the one thing I like about this class. They don't sugarcoat everything when you're in high school. My teachers in elementary and junior high honored Zheng He as a glorious hero who brought civilization and Islamic thought to the ravenous barbarians. To be fair, they had been living here for quite some time and were doing just fine.

Mr. Rabinowitz continued, "The admiral would begin to lose hope. Only a few islands were found between Oceania and the Americas. First, he established vast farms on Vanuatu and recruited as many natives as he could from the tiny archipelago. He did this in an arguably peaceful manner. On Vanuatu, he gave the expert mariners instructions on how to reach the continents of the west. A temple was built in his honor and is still maintained today.

"His next discovery would be the small, volcanic formation of modern-day Horutimati. That island would prove to be useful but only as a means to navigate back home. There was no indigenous population, and fishing yielded nothing of substance. With no natives to employ or conquer, the landform was taken as an official colony of the Ming. After resting on Horutimati for a day or two, the admiral left several men on the island to search for reliable food and shelter. He gifted them with a sturdy junk in the likely event that they needed to return for supplies. Zheng then forged on eastward, convinced that something significant waited for him in the far corners of the ocean.

"Then, on April 21, 4114, he spotted a large stretch of sandy beaches and hillsides. Zheng had found what would soon become known as the American continents. Landing midway between the old settlements of Zacatollan and Acapulco, he befriended several chieftains and immediately sought to establish relations. They gladly exchanged goods and attempted to learn the languages and customs of one another. Gifts of jade and obsidian were exchanged for gifts of porcelain and silk. Eventually, Zheng He and his men were informed of other settlements. They were told that any lasting diplomacy would have to involve discussions with the regional kings and tribal leaders.

"According to many accounts, including his own, the admiral had a dream on the 4th of May in which he was visited by the Prophet. By his own recollection, and I quote: 'Muhammad told me that I would be punished by the fires of hell unless I returned to Allah wholeheartedly and without reservation; to cast away the belief systems of my homeland, as they are filth and excrement; to pursue the way of my ancestors, of my childhood, the righteous avenue which calls on me to walk straight and with purpose. I am tasked with the overwhelming duty of bringing the sacred teachings of the Qur'an into these godless lands. Destroy all idols and annihilate anyone standing in your path. The anger of the sword and the patience of the Prophet will guide your hand. If you die in the process, the seeds of a glorious reformation will be watered with your blood. You embark upon a jihad like no other, and the stakes are nothing less than the eradication of our sacred task. Allah is with you, and so am I.'"

Whoa! That's some heavy shit. I wonder if—

"All right, class. Tomorrow we will continue with He's role in the Aztec Empire and discuss the siege of Tenochtitlan. I will end the class with a brief review. Remember, the midterm exam is on Friday, and you can use a three-by-five index card for notes. Hopefully, you have taken sufficient notes over the last week. Have a nice day."

As I stuff my composition notebook into my backpack, covered in Sepultura and Slayer patches, the bell rings, and we are dismissed for lunch. I have a turkey sandwich and two oranges.

"I just picked up *Street* *Fighter II Turbo* last weekend. Let's meet up at my place after dinner," said Muhammad, lugging his bright orange book bag across his torso. I am happy to see him for the long walk home. He is joined by Geo and Esther, and I can see Yoshi running to catch up with the group.

"That's the one where you can play Vega, right?"

"For sure, dude. I've been kicking serious ass with Balrog," Muhammad brags.

Yoshi wraps his hand around my bicep and shouts, "Slow down, squirt!"

"You know, I hate it when you call me that," I mumble, trying not to be seen by Hubert Ortegon, the skater boy that I have had a crush on since sixth grade.

Esther checks the perimeter of our route for some unseen threat. After a few seconds, she calls out to Yoshi and Muhammad, already shoulder-to-shoulder, "The coast is clear!"

"Hey, sweets," Yoshi exclaims as he grabs the hand of his boyfriend.

Muhammad smiles and seems to be skipping on air.

"I don't think I'll ever get used to that," mocks Geo.

"Then walk with a different crew."

Hoping that no one notices my own discomfort, I jokingly add, "I can't believe that both of my siblings are gay." With that, I shoot a goofy stare in Esther's direction, who is being her silent, usual self. She smiles, and I am relieved to deflate what would normally be tension. I am honest with myself but not vocal like Geo. It was a shock to see my brother and sister come out, even secretly and among friends. After all, I am a product of the eighties, which wasn't kind to homosexuality. The nineties aren't doing much better with a mile-long list of Melissa Etheridge puns. It was a bigger shock to discover that my siblings were dating close friends of mine in a clique that had been established since our elementary years.

"Let's make a plan and set a time. Can any of you make it to my place tonight for a little tournament?" Muhammad asks the group.

Esther answers first, "Sure."

I am itching to try out the new characters. "I can be there by 7:00."

"I'm gonna Sonic Kick all of your asses to the curb," said Geo. It is true that he was always the best among us in the original versions.

Yoshi is stalling in his reply and finally asks, "Are you still nervous about me coming over? I feel like I have to walk on egg shells whenever I'm there."

"You know my mom would be fine if she ever found out, and Tariq seems to be more open-minded than Larry ever was. We should be fine. It's my dad's house that we have to worry about. He would kill me if he ever found out," Muhammad remarks with a tinge of sorrow.

"All right. If the console is at your mom's, I can dig it. I can be there after dinner, probably 6:45." The two young men exchange rapid and noisy kisses upon cheeks, chuckling and blushing in the process.

"Then it is settled, let's all aim for seven. I can pick up a bag of Queso Curls from Djinni Mart on the way," I declare with enthusiasm. At the corner of the street ahead of us, a figure is approaching. I can see Yoshi and Muhammad quickly release their hands from one another, until it is certain that the figure is that of my older sister. Nefe picks up speed and embraces Esther with a tight hug. They engage in a long and wet kiss.

"Hey! I heard there's a clearance sale on carpets over at K-mart," Geo jokes with the tact of a sedated baboon.

"Fuck off, Geo." I chide him while playfully beating him across his back.

AFTER WALKING MY FRIENDS HOME, I reluctantly head to my father's house. It is his night for dinner, and I can feel my muscles tighten with anxiety. It is a defense mechanism, whatever that's supposed to mean. Esther recently told me about defense mechanisms, something she had learned in her AP Biology class. I don't quite understand on a technical level but fully comprehend on an emotional level.

I ascend the green stairs of my father's porch and can hear his favorite norteño record playing in the living room. As I open the door, I am saddened to find my pink, ceramic unicorn shattered on the laminate flooring. It was a Horus Mass gift from Mom. I can smell vodka and cigarettes. The broken memento and the sickening odors lead me to believe that my father is in one of his moods. I tense up even tighter and enter the living room, where he is perched in his vermilion recliner, watching O.J. coverage with the sound muted. It doesn't surprise me that he roots for Simpson and that my mother roots against him. The story reads like a facsimile of the relationship they once had, just shy of his full wrath or her murder.

"Hey, Dad," I manage to squeak out in fear. I wish it wasn't my night with him.

"Dinner is in the fridge. You can heat it up in the micro," he says.

I am quaking but eager to get the question out and over with. "Is it all right if I go to Muhammad's tonight after dinner? I can be home before 9:00."

"What? My time with you isn't good enough? You're just like your mother. Nothing is up-to-par to your standards. Everything is shit to you, including your night with your father."

"I can stay home if you want to spend time with me."

"Are you suggesting that I don't want to spend time with you?"

"No, it's just that you seem to be—"

"Don't fucking assume what I want, Clea," he interrupts.

"Sorry, Dad." After so many years, I've found it easiest to apologize even when there is no reason to. I sneak off into the kitchen to find what I've already assumed is a Kid's Cuisine with brownie dessert. I stopped eating those years ago, but he doesn't care as long as he can tell Mom that I've been fed.

"I accidentally dropped your unicorn earlier. I was trying to reach an old photo album. You shouldn't have placed it so close to the edge of the shelving unit," he explains without emotion or shame.

I know better. He is telling the truth about the photo album. He always looks through them for reasons to justify his lifelong anger. The unicorn was just another casualty of his reminiscing. I am surprised he hadn't smashed more in his solitary tantrum. Maybe he did. Maybe he smashed other items, cleaning up the majority of his mess, and leaving the splintered unicorn for me to find: a symbolic reminder of his disappointment with me in general.

"That's fine, Dad. I'll clean it up after eating."

He grunts in what can only be an affirmative response.

The microwave is loud as it spins and cooks my shitty meal. The noise muffles the crooning, falsetto voice of the Sonoran man who leads my father's favorite band. The brownie bubbles. It looks like what my brain feels like. I was too young to remember those PSA commercials, where an egg cooks and reminds the viewer of the damaging effects of drug use. In this fashion, my brain boils. I am angry. It is simultaneously a liberating and frightening feeling. Liberating, because it is hidden from Father. Frightening, because it comes from him; a hereditary trait of unhinged rage passed onto me.

I take a deep breath in through my nostrils. This is a technique learned from my stepdad, my true father figure. He used to joke about a short fuse, hiding among my other personality traits. He joked until I started breaking my toys on purpose. He joked until I squeezed my Genesis controller into bits, lacerating my palms. I bled onto my tie-dyed bean bag. After that, he made a serious effort to teach me methods of quelling my anger. He even proposed therapy to Mom, who wasn't thrilled about any treatment not covered by insurance. His best advice was to count to ten. I have done this ever since. I am doing it now.

The microwave dings, and I remove the scalding tray from the oscillating glass disc. By now, I am an expert on TV dinners and know that I should let it cool for a few minutes before peeling back the cellophane. I used to burn my hands when I was younger. I've always cooked my own meals when I'm at dad's house. Sometimes, when he's too drunk to stand up, I'll even cook for him. He likes the El Hombre Hambre Salisbury steak with mashed potatoes. I decide I'll pick up the unicorn while I wait for the food to cool. Turning around, I see my father standing in the corridor.

"Why don't your brother and sister visit anymore? Have you been pitting them against me? This is supposed to be my night with them, too, and I haven't seen them for over a month," he yells into the beige kitchen, lit by fluorescent rods.

"No, Dad. I would never do that."

The veins on his forehead bulge and he screams, "Bullshit! You and your mother have it out against me, and now Yoshi and Nefe are in on it, too." He grabs a coffee mug from a nearby table and throws it at me. I have developed pretty quick reflexes from similar outbursts in the past, and I easily dodge the mug. It shatters on the cabinet behind me. He begins to walk toward me.

Something inside of me breaks under the pressure of his presence. I snap, fully and without any boundaries. This is the seed of anger, passed on by the patriarch's ancestors, and I am letting it grow in a split-second reaction. I can feel my blood rushing. *Is this the defense mechanism that Esther spoke of?*

Surely, I am protecting myself from an external threat. He is the threat. Any further action is entirely warranted. I would stab him in the neck, if I were closer to the utensil drawer. In spontaneous reflex, I grab the Kid's Cuisine entree, still piping hot, and throw it in his general direction without aiming. The platter hits him squarely in the face and empties its steaming contents onto his drunken profile.

"Fuck! I'm going to fuckin' kill you, you ungrateful twat!"

He clears the mess from his eyes, and I assume that he is temporarily blinded. I am genuinely fearing death and feeling my adrenaline rise. I have never attacked him verbally or physically. This is uncharted territory. I do not doubt that he would take my life, and I must either fight or escape. I don't feel comfortable fighting him, mostly because I would kill him given the chance. As he approaches, stumbling and screaming, I make a quick dash past his left flank into the living room and to the front door.

He loudly hisses at me, "Come back here, you bitch!"

I push the door open and quickly shuffle down the stairs. I run as fast as I can in the direction of the Simmermanns. They are the closest house that I can take refuge in. They are also avid gun aficionados, which makes me feel even safer, given the circumstances. I am crying, hyperventilating, and sweating profusely.

By the time I reach the Simmermann's porch, I can hear the percussion of my heartbeat in my eardrums. Knocking loudly on the intricate French door adorned with a giant fleur-de-lis, I look back to see if my father has followed me. It seems like hours waiting for someone to answer. I really hope someone is home. Finally, Geo answers the door, and his eyes widen with worry. I've never seen him display any form of empathy before this very moment.

"What's wrong, Clea?"

"Can I please come in, Geo? I just need to calm down."

"It's your Dad. I can tell. I can't believe that bastard. Did he hit you again? We can call the cops, if you'd like," Geo reassuringly tells me.

"No, I just need to get out of sight, somewhere safe."

"Come on in."

I AM IN GEO'S BEDROOM. It is Navajo white and decorated with Dodger's fanfare. The '86 championship pennant is framed with tickets from game two. His bed cover is clean and wrinkle-free. A poster hangs above it, listing different fighter jets of the US Military. The stealth models are presented by tanned women wearing black bikinis. On Geo's bedside table, a copy of *The Hobbit* rests next to a winding alarm clock. I have the same alarm clock with glow-in-the-dark numbers and hands.

After nearly an hour of uncontrollable sobbing, I have finally calmed down. There's been no knocking at the door, no incessant phone calls. It's very possible that my father just gave up and went back to the bottle for comfort. I wonder how badly he's been burned, if at all. *Mom's gonna be pissed that she has to modify the court order again.*

Geo pokes his head in and informs me, "There's some dinner downstairs if you want some. I can also bring it up here. Vegetarian lasagna and Caesar salad. I think that's kosher, or halal, or whatever you're into." He smiles warmly, trying to get a laugh in this very serious moment.

"I'm starving. Could I eat in here? Your family won't be offended, right?"

"That is absolutely fine. I kind of clued them in on the situation without saying too much. After all, you've come here after his episodes before. I'll even join you."

"Thanks, Geo."

He leaves me, and I can hear his footsteps as he descends the carpeted stairs. I hate that my father has put me in this situation time and time again. *He got what he deserved. Why am I regretting my actions?* It was self-defense, obviously. I guess I'm worried he'll try to hurt someone close to me. *He's too chickenshit for that.* I'm always the easiest target, being the youngest sibling.

I need to think about something else. Maybe Geo and I can head over to Muhammad's for some Super Famicom after dinner. The footsteps are now coming up the stairs. The door creaks open, and Geo is holding a dinner tray. It holds a massive slice of lasagna, and I am reminded of my favorite comic strip, *Garfield*. What a weird train of thought.

"Here you go," he says in a gentle tone.

"Thanks. This looks way better than Kid's Cuisine."

He laughs, which makes me laugh for the first time in what seems like years.

"So, you threw the food at his face? I gotta say, Clea, you're a badass. He must be furious. Do you think you'll ever have to go back there?"

"Given the circumstances, I highly doubt it. He has a way of crafting these elaborate stories whenever he's in front of a judge. But I don't think he'll push for any joint custody after this stunt. Something tells me he'll just brush it off and be his regular self, whether I visit or not. It's not like he's ever shown any real interest in me, Yoshi, or Nefe. It's almost as if he argues about visitation as a mere statement of his legal right to demand it. His kids are just an afterthought."

"Damn, that's rough. Well, good riddance." He holds up his Capri Sun, motions for me to do the same, and adds, "To a life without Mr. Socorro, the fuckhead drunk. Cheers."

We bump pouch drinks and slurp from tiny, yellow straws.

I eat without speaking for most of the meal. Once I have finished most of my lasagna, I ask Geo, "Do you still want to go to Muhammad's at 7:00?"

"Sure. That sounds like a great idea. Let me finish my plate, and we can pack up." He takes a huge bite and chews it.

"Thanks. I could really use a distraction. I'm super nervous about telling my mom what happened today."

Geo wipes his face with a paper towel and sets his plate on his bedside table. Then, he looks at me with a face I've never seen him make. He scoots closer to me on his queen-sized mattress and gives me a side hug. Suddenly, but softly, he places his hand on my thigh. Then, without warning, he moves his face in my direction. *Holy shit, he's gonna try to kiss me.* I push him away and turn my back toward him.

"I'm sorry, Clea. It's just that you are so stressed out and—"

"Geo, this isn't the time. Plus, I've told you before I don't like you in that way."

"But we've fooled around before," he states defensively.

"I know. I just don't think it's appropriate. I just had a physical altercation with my father, for fuck's sake!"

He lowers his head and gives a convincing pout of shame. "I am so sorry, Clea. It won't happen again, I promise."

I am furious with him in a way that I've never felt before. Perhaps his house is not a safe place to be. I ask myself: *How many times has he been kind, just to get something he wants further on down the line? What a piece of work. To think he would pounce on this opportunity, just hours after a life-or-death situation. Oh shit, now he's crying. Are they real tears, or are they staged?*

"It's okay, Geo. Please don't cry. It just makes everything even more awkward."

"I'm just really embarrassed. I hope you don't hate me."

"No, Geo. I don't hate you. Let's just head over to Muhammad's place."

"That sounds good," he says, wiping snot from his nose.

THE BUSINESS WITH DAD, AND now the business with Geo, made me completely forget about the Queso Curls. I'm not gonna talk about it, and I have asked Geo not to mention anything. We arrive at Muhammad's house and are greeted by his mother, who is holding a huge glass of white wine while she chews on a sausage appetizer. After swallowing the pork treat, she invites us in and informs us that the others are waiting upstairs. She makes a remark about how pretty I've become and how fast I've grown. This is a ritual among parents, especially once adolescence begins. To be fair, adults are quite keen on the insecurities of high school. It's a giant popularity contest. Regardless of my shitty day, it feels nice to be complimented.

"Thanks. That's really sweet of you."

She takes a large gulp of her Chardonnay and returns to a television program already in progress. It's probably the O.J. story. All adults are fascinated with the O.J. story as of late. He hasn't even gone to trial yet. Geo and I head upstairs and into Muhammad's fart-soaked room. Our friends look up as a nonverbal greeting. We are given high fives as we make our way across the bedroom. Nefe and Esther are engaged in a battle between Chun Li and Blanka. Nefe always cheats with Blanka's electricity, mashing the "Y" button until her opponent is knocked out.

Yoshi yells with excitement, "Kick her ass, Esther!"

"Hey! You're supposed to cheer for your sister, knucklehead," Nefe sneers back.

"I can't wait to kick both of your asses," Muhammad adds. He leans back on his bed and is embraced by Yoshi. He wears Yoshi's arms like a blanket. It is young love that can't be expressed anywhere else in this house or anywhere else in this city. My newly-estranged father, my stepfather Feng Mian (whom I openly call 'Dad' with love and approval), and even my mother; they would all disapprove of Yoshi's preference for males. They would probably call it a phase, but I know better. He's always been into boys. One of these days, they'll just have to face it.

Esther and Nefe are another story. They argue and get jealous. They avoid each other in groups, and never go on dates. They aren't interested in the freedom to cuddle in public. Truth be told, they are more like fuck buddies. They are only interested in the physical aspects of the relationship. Part of me wonders if Nefe is even a lesbian. If my parents were to call it a phase, I'd probably agree with them. Esther, on the other hand, is just Esther. She could like boys or girls; I'd never be able to tell. She has never dated any boys, but it wouldn't surprise me if she did. One time, she admitted that it would be easier for her to come out than for Muhammad or Yoshi to do the same. Society has accepted lesbians on the basis of sex appeal, while gay men still get beaten in public.

"Damn you, Chun Li! I was so close. All right, who's next?" Nefe asks.

I raise my hand. "Can I cut in?"

"Of course you can. We've all gone a few rounds already," Muhammad answers.

"Sweet."

As I am choosing a character, Muhammad asks the question I've been dreading.

"Did you have to go over to your Dad's today? I thought Wednesdays were his for visitation."

Geo looks over at me and then abruptly interrupts any response, "Yeah, and guess what? Kid's Cuisine again!" The others laugh, because this is an inside joke among us. I imagine it might be funnier from now on. Geo is being sweet and I will allow it, regardless of his gross attempt earlier.

Yoshi notes, "I hate those damned dinners almost as much as I hate him."

"Yeah, brownies as hard as a brick! And those nasty, little nuggets of corn, all buttered up and salted." It feels good to laugh with my friends and my siblings. I pick Sagat, who, according to the official story, had trained both Ken and Ryu. The scar on his chest is apparently from a Dragon Punch, placed by one of the two disciples, a mystery that Capcom has left for the player to figure out. I am fighting Esther, who is returning as Chun Li in the flashy streets of Las Vegas. I've always wanted to visit Las Vegas.

"Get ready for an ass beating," Esther jests.

"You talking to me?" I am doing my best De Niro impression.

I have almost forgotten about the episode with Dad. It is here, with my friends, that I feel safest. Geo may be a creep sometimes, but he is my favorite creep. I've known him since we were in kindergarten. Esther, while distant, always has good advice and a shoulder to cry on. Muhammad, I would say, is my best friend. He may be a few years older than I am, but we've always been on the same wavelength. At times, he is more of an older brother to me than Yoshi. I don't know what I'd do without these friends. I hope that we always stay in touch, even in adulthood. Man, Sagat is really hard to control. I can't seem to execute his special moves.

"Clea, your dad is on the phone," Muhammad's mom calls from the stairwell. Her tone is one of concern. I freeze with fear. Geo is looking in my direction with worry in his eyes.

She clarifies, "Sorry, honey. It's your stepfather. He really needs to talk to you."

The fear partially fades away, but I am still nervous. *Did my biological father contact the custodial parents and tell them some crazy story about how I've flipped my lid? Well, I was gonna have to tell them anyways. Let's rip the bandage off.* I pause the game and excuse myself from the bedroom.

"Be right back."

I walk downstairs and meet Muhammad's mom in the kitchen. She hands me the phone and I place my ear to the receiver. I softly speak, "Dad?"

"Clea." Silence and then sobbing. I've never heard or seen him cry.

"Um, I can explain. I was trying to . . . I didn't mean to—"

"Clea, your mother has been in a terrible accident. I don't know how to describe it. I guess it was a head-on collision. On the 110. Clea, I need you to come to Good Samaritan right away. It doesn't look good."

"Is she going to live?"

He starts crying again and answers, "I don't know. It happened this afternoon."

I am holding my breath. "Okay, Dad. I'll have someone drive me over."

"I am so sorry to tell you about this, honey. I love you."

"Love you too, Dad."

This is the worst day of my life.

V

"ast time I was in this armpit of a city, it was during Ramadan, and the temperature reached one hundred eighteen. All of the air-conditioning in the world couldn't convince me to live here," Clea noted as she and Muhammad waited in the elevator, clutching at their baggage. The northern wall was made of stainless steel, embossed with the Clarendon logo. The other three walls were screens tuned in to season nine of *Insanity Chef.* "At least February is relatively nice. Gotta love saguaros, too. Some of them are centuries old. Did you know that?"

Muhammad shrugged and answered, "I've heard about it."

The Clarendon Hotel was a well-known landmark in Phoenix. Its centralized location made it easy to visit a variety of attractions, including two art museums and a dozen venues. The modernist hotel was decorated with brightly-colored tiles, bejeweled fixtures, and a general hipster vibe. There are local legends surrounding the hotel, which claims to be haunted. Every room was equipped with standard utilities, such as wall units and land lines. Muhammad and Clea were pleasantly impressed as they left the elevator and made their way to the adjacent suites. As in past years, the rooms were reserved in advance by Geo.

Phoenix was a good choice for Divorce Pool. It was a cheaper city, compared to most. Planning anything in California or Texas would cost a year's salary. Not in Phoenix. Food and drink were in high supply and a major source of tourism. Muhammad had already plotted some of the cheap eats at his home kiosk.

"The voice message said that two fourteen and two fifteen are on the southeast corner," Muhammad reminded his friend. As Arizona does not observe daylight savings, the sun is setting, minutes shy of 6:00. The rays of light peek through the courtyard, making the hotel grounds look like an old, tube television with the tint turned high. Looking up into the sky, Muhammad was greeted by an orange and purple Sonoran sunset. It looked like the colors of a Phoenix Suns jersey or an impression of the Arizona state flag, with secondary colors instead of primary.

"Nice of Geo to spot us for the rooms. Let's make sure to cover dinner and drinks," Clea said, unfazed by the panoramic view above. She continued, "I could go for a margarita. Tons of salt. Are you going to be a good Muslim this time around, or are you going to join us in being lecherous?"

"I've made my peace with having a periodic bender, especially when I'm with you degenerates." Muhammad laughed loudly, and Clea joined him in the exercise of self-deprecation. He pointed at a corner resting above a stairwell. "There it is."

Fumbling for the card key, Clea approached the vividly painted door. "Just a second." In an awkward fashion, her right hand migrated to her left-side pocket. She felt the plastic rectangle mixed in with various coins and sighed with excitement. "Let's check it out, dude."

"You lead the way."

She inserted the card, and before being given the green light that signifies safe entrance, the door swung open. Looking up, they saw a familiar face. Geo stood there dressed in an ugly polo shirt. It was stone-washed and colored in Adobe-style with the word "Sedona" written across the front in turquoise, Papyrus font. Underneath the text, a solitary Kokopelli stood in side profile, blowing its flute. It was apparent that he had spent a few extra days in Arizona prior to the first run of Divorce Pool. Geo finished his tourist outfit with floral-print board shorts and neon flip-flops. He loudly welcomed his friends, "Hey, fuckers!"

Muhammad embraced the fashion disaster. "Geo! It is good to see you, friend. How have you been, and where did you get that nightmare of a shirt?"

"Can't you read?"

Clea interrupted, "Come here, you shithead." She joined the two men in a group hug and felt genuinely happy to be with the old crew again.

The skunky smell of dispensary-quality weed lingered in the air. From the leather recliner perched in the far end of the room, Esther's voice called out, "Hey."

Clea released her grip from Geo and rushed into the room to smother her stoned friend. "Esther! I've missed you so much." After squeezing for half a minute, she looked up at Esther's face. "You're looking great, honey. How do you do it?"

"Unlike you, I quit cigarettes in college. Drinking adequate water helps."

Everyone exchanged greetings and engaged in socially normative small talk. Clea brought her luggage into the other room and found a restroom to clean up after a long drive. Muhammad, already standing in what was deemed the "men's room," put his suitcase on the bed and started unpacking. When the friends were finally settled in and acclimated to the suites, they all sat down together and started scheming about where to go and what to do. The hotel was already crawling with activity, as other guests were gearing up to celebrate New Year's Eve and New Year's Day to celebrate the start of 4723, Anno Huángdì.

THE RESTAURANT WAS GAUDY AND carried the scent of freshly-made tortillas. Clea finished her first margarita, quickly glanced at her checking ledger, and prompted the server to bring her another. She was happy to elaborate on the road trip to Phoenix and the heavy traffic of Interstate 10. She had been talking about work and was interested in hearing about the career paths of her closest friends. So much can change after a year.

"I've explained this to you a thousand times, Geo. My nonprofit facilitates reparations payments for a variety of claims. Take slavery, for example. A simple DNA test determines which ancestors were held as slaves. If the database finds a match to families that 'owned' the ancestors, then a request can be sent for financial reconciliation."

Geo confusedly asked, "And they willingly make the payments?"

"Not all people do or can. I'd say that we have a success rate of forty percent. Sometimes, it's less a matter of money. Some people ignore the request altogether. Some offer apologies to the affected family, no payments involved at all. It's an effort to make all parties feel better. Our contracts use clear language. None of it is legally binding."

Muhammad took a break from his enchilada platter to give his opinion. "Don't you think it would come across as racist to assume that blacks need the handout? Not to mention, you're making a bet on white families being better off."

"Yeah, but that's the reality we live in. Inherited fortunes are a continuing legacy of white supremacy in America. And it's not just reparations for slavery. We are also paying out on the Tuskegee experiments and the federal settlements from the Simpson riots," Clea explained and then suddenly froze with embarrassment.

Muhammad cleared his throat, took a deep breath, and reassured Clea, "It's fine. I can talk about it without breaking down like I used to."

After a few moments of uncomfortable silence, Esther commented, "This is becoming a pretty heavy conversation. Perhaps we should talk about something else. No offense, Clea."

"None taken."

Esther asked, "What are you up to these days, Mo?"

Muhammad was looking at a screen on the far wall when he responded, "If you're looking for an appropriate conversation to have during dinner, my job is the last thing you'd want to talk about."

Geo giggled and inquired, "Are you still working as an endo tech?"

"Yeah. Our clinic has finally started offering fecal transplants."

Clea tilted her head with a look of pure disorientation. She asked, "Did you say *fecal* transplant? Like . . . shit?"

Muhammad looked absolutely amused. "Yeppers."

Now Geo was leaning in for more information. "I'm game. I've gotta know. Why would anyone want to have a shit transplant?"

"It's gonna gross you out."

Geo doubled down and demanded, "No, it won't. We can handle it, right?" He looked at Esther and Clea, who both gave affirmative nods.

Muhammad surrendered to the request, knowing in his heart that this wasn't the standard dinner with a prudish family, hell-bent on etiquette. He explained, "There are diseases, like ulcerative colitis, in which the mucosa of the colon is prone to infection. These people do not create the same enzymes in their stool as someone with a healthy digestive system. Stool donors act as a way to provide those enzymes. So, I take a sample, mix it with saline in a medical-grade blender, and apply the transplant via colonoscopy. That is all I'm willing to discuss while eating."

Esther was fascinated and let out an audible, "Whoa."

Clea added, "What a fucking trip. I hope they are paying you good money to do that, Mo. I would ask for a handling fee for every sample." She laughed to herself.

Muhammad was already tired of discussing his life. He asked Geo, "What fortunes have you been making, friend?"

He replied, "I'm afraid that my ventures are not dinner material, either."

No one bought it. Geo was a true suit and utterly unable to do anything that would get his hands dirty. The bar had already been set high with fecal transplants, and no one accepted his non-disclosure. Perhaps Geo could not talk about his career. That only made the curiosity cut even deeper. His three friends looked at him, pressuring him to open up and spill the beans. Finally, he broke. "I am still a consultant. Lately, I've been working with a company that wants to produce smartphones."

Clea was taken aback. She posed the question, "*Personal* smartphones?"

"Yeah. Handheld. Just like the ones we used to have."

Muhammad quickly remarked, "You were right, Geo. That's definitely not a discussion to have over dinner."

"I told you so!"

Esther looked displeased at this revelation and said, "How does that make you feel? I mean, there's no way you could find investors to support such a dangerous business plan."

"You would be surprised, Esther. The thought is that everyone has forgotten about '07. It's been a generation since that nonsense."

Esther angrily replied, "It figures. With a fuck like Drumpf in power, anything goes these days. It makes me fucking sick. You're dipping your hand into the potential murder of millions, Geo."

The table was silent. A nerve was struck. Socio-economic differences and political differences came to a head like a pressurized zit. It was times like this that the friends realized how different they were. Adulthood had forged drastically different paths among the four. Clea's second margarita was brought, as well as a fresh round of chips and salsa. She calmly took a sip and suggested, "Let's grab the check and hit the bars. We can make a note to not talk about work."

"You should try out my new salve. It burns a little, due to the capsaicin, but it works really well on lower back pain," Esther explained to Clea while fiddling with her gin and seltzer.

"Thanks, Esther." Crouching over the rosined bar, Clea looked over her shoulder and wondered, "Where did the boys go? Geo's song is up next."

"I saw them buy a few Swisher Sweet singles earlier. The fruity ones that smell like a fucking brothel." The women laughed and continued to sip on drinks while commenting on the peculiar tastes of grown men.

Then, without prompt or cue, Esther stared off into one of the many screens placed throughout the ranch-themed watering hole. She focused on a scripted newsreel. The beginnings of crow's feet, evident on her face, tightened as she read the words, cascading vertically down the massive wall unit. Her fingernails tapped neurotically on the rosin. Clea gently placed a hand on her shoulder, knowing that her close friend was of anti-authoritarian, anti-establishment temper. She was certain that the stress was related to the recent election, if one could call it that. She made an attempt to change the mood. She asked, "Are you reading the lyrics on the karaoke screen?"

Esther broke from her spell and fibbed. "Uh, yeah. I've always loved Neil Diamond but have never bothered to learn any of his words. Quite beautiful."

She took a sip of her drink and continued, "I wonder if Geo picked another shitty country song. He loves that patriotic bullshit."

"Toby fucking Keith. No, he and Mo are gonna do a duet, something classic. They told me about it without revealing too much. Speaking of which, here they come."

Muhammad and Geo walked toward the bar, stumbling along the way. With a silly grin smeared across his face, Muhammad raised his hand for a series of high fives. Over the poorly-composed backup track of "Cracklin' Rosie," he yelled, "I'm getting a little bit drunk over here!"

"Yeah, buddy," Geo proudly exclaimed.

The two women made sour faces at them. A fresh round of beverages was ordered, and the men maneuvered into vacant, upholstered bar stools. Clea wanted to continue the act of catching up on personal lives and relationships. She asked Geo, "How are things with you and Mishelle? Are the kiddos leaving for college yet?"

Geo answered, "I'm not that old, you goober. Millie is finishing up on her freshman year. You'll remember, she is the oldest. She is on the volleyball team and is kicking ass in her French elective."

"And Mish?"

"Oh, things are great. She's my bread and butter. We just celebrated our sixteenth anniversary. Spent a week on Lake Tahoe. We did the Gel Lago tour too. It was the first time she had seen it."

Muhammad interrupted, "We drove past it on the way here."

"I think it is fascinating," Clea added.

Esther laughed and started, "A long time ago, heading home from a sales trip, I pissed on Gel Lago. Oh my! It made this smelly steam that stuck with me for two days." The four chuckled at the lowbrow tale.

Geo continued gushing about his marriage, "I'm thinking of asking her to renew our vows this summer. She would be keen on the idea. We would go to Ottawa, where we originally honeymooned."

Clea's face tightened with a giant smile. "That's sweet, Geo. I'm always impressed with your relationship. Most marriages end in divorce, and it is refreshing to see love work out." There was an uncomfortable and sugary tone to her compliment.

"Thanks, Clea." Geo lowered his brow and raised his drink.

"My ex-husband has already been divorced a second time. Personally, I don't know if I'd ever find the courage to ever get remarried with the high dropout rate."

The karaoke DJ boomed over the loudspeaker, "Next up, we have Geo and Mo! Give it up, ladies and gentlemen!"

The two men looked excitedly at each other. For a moment, they looked like the close friends they had once been. It was a tender display of male affection. It reminded Clea of a time, many years ago, when Muhammad had stood up against a bully who taunted and teased Geo for living in an upscale house. She encouraged the two, "Go get 'em, boys!"

Geo was beaming as he called on his singing partner, "Come on, Mo. Let's kick some ass. Do you remember how to do the harmonies?"

"You bet your sweet ass I do."

They headed to the raised stage and stepped onto cheap, checkerboard flooring. The karaoke prompt transitioned to the song title: "Pretty Woman" by Roy Orbison. It was one of Muhammad's favorite songs, sung by one of Geo's favorite artists. The DJ handed them two microphones while a Motown beat filled the dancing area, four-on-the-floor with snares in-between. The riff came in, cutting itself off in anticipation for the first two rounds and finishing in golden oldie glory for the next two. The two men harmonized in perfect tune, exchanging glances at each other, and then, at the audience, *"Pretty woman, walking down the street . . ."*

The crowd gave a round of applause. Esther and Clea joined in by whooping and hollering. Once the clamor subsided, Esther turned to Clea, cupped her hand to her ear, and whispered, "You know he's full of shit, right?"

"Who?"

"Geo," Esther replied, returning to upright position.

Clea could read her friend quite well, but she felt the need to play innocent. She asked, "What do you mean?"

"The whole bit about his happy marriage." Esther paused, sipped deeply from her tumbler, and continued, "Their relationship is in shambles."

Clea looked unconvinced. "How so?"

Esther gazed down into her drink. She was deep in thought, as if she were about to make a drastic decision. She made a quick note of the karaoke lyrics, seemingly to judge whether or not she could go into a round of gossip. It became obvious that she was hiding some secret: one that she had either promised Geo to keep, or one that she was keeping from him. After what seemed like an eternity, she looked at Clea and asked her, "Can you keep a secret?"

"Sure, Esther."

"Mish and I are having an affair," she said bluntly.

Clea was floored. She took a deep breath in through her nostrils and asked for further clarification, "What do you mean?"

"Remember back in 4721, when I canceled on Death Pool?"

"Yeah."

"Well, I was actually visiting Houston . . . to see Mish."

"Was that the first time?"

Esther looked slightly ashamed as she answered, "No. Many years ago when I took that huge road trip to visit all of you. It was after Gel Lago and the smartphone nonsense. Must have been '08 or '09. Do you remember? I was checking in on everyone. When I came to visit Geo, it was the first time I met his wife. We really hit it off. I could tell she was into me. I was pissed about Geo becoming another soulless suit, not to mention all of those times that he moved in on you. His selfishness made me feel justified, like it was an excuse to take something that I wanted dearly." She began to tremble. "I know Geo is an old friend. Sometimes, I can't help but despise him. He's become everything that I hate about this stupid fucking country. He is a creep." A tear fell down her cheek.

"Damn."

"But that doesn't mean I don't feel bad about it."

Clea shuddered at the thought of it all. She quickly ordered a round of mezcal, and said, "So, you've been doing this for over a decade? I just can't believe it. Geo must know something. Surely, he's caught onto you."

"If I were a man, he'd probably be more suspicious. Geo thinks he's the man of Mish's dreams, and that she would never consider a woman for a lover. Don't get me wrong. He is the jealous type, but he's also clueless. Perhaps, he would have caught on, if he wasn't busy cashing in on pyramid schemes and speculation."

The mescal shots were brought to the table. Clea downed hers and signaled Esther to do the same. The song was ending, and their brief conversation would have to continue another time. Sparse applause echoed through the bar as the two men handed the mics off and stepped down from the stage. Glowing with pride, they approached Esther and Clea, who donned fake smiles like nothing had happened. Geo cut in-between the two and ordered a trendy microbrew.

He asked, "How did we do, ladies?"

VI

ne by one, they rose, groaning like zombies and nursing their hangovers. Clea was the first to wake. She made her way into the washroom, poured a plastic cup of water, and set it aside for her morning medications. Unable to find her purse, she briefly panicked, wondering if it had been left at the bar. After Esther's revelation, she was in a bit of a rush to return to the Clarendon. Her head ached, and her clothes carried the distinctive smell of menthol Dromedaries. Aiming her eyes on the base of a viewing unit, she finally located the teal bag.

The pill container was packed with many antidepressants. Using her thumbnail, Clea pried the hatch open and emptied the day's ration into her palm. She swallowed the pills and began collecting her mind for the day. Locating a remote, she started the viewing unit, muted the volume, and looked through various e-mails. Nothing new had come through because all of her co-workers were also on vacation for the New Year's holiday. There were no personal messages, which was mildly disappointing. She was expecting sweet texts from Freeman, the interior designer who had frequented her bed for two months. With a defeated frown, she assumed the worst and opened her briefcase for a fresh outfit.

Esther grunted, supported her body on both elbows, and yawned loudly.

"Happy 4723. What a way to start the year," Clea said with fake enthusiasm.

"Fuck off," Esther replied.

They laughed and got dressed for their day. As the sun began to peek in through vertical slat blinds, they remembered their discussion from the previous night. Pulling an orange blouse over her shoulders, Esther pleaded, "Please don't mention anything to Geo."

"I wouldn't dare."

BY 9:00, THE "BOYS' ROOM" had ordered a platter of breakfast burritos. Muhammad was practically green with sickness. With a large jug of water waiting for him on the nightstand, he dismissed the greasy meal with a waving hand. He cuddled underneath the downy blanket and waited for the pain to subside.

Meanwhile, Geo brought out a pack of graphite pencils and several pads of paper. It was time to go over the rules of Divorce Pool. After agreeing on the general structure of the game, the friends could check out of their rooms, meet elsewhere, and place their bets on the doomed relationships of the year. Clea started the conversation and suggested, "There should be six picks . . . by which I mean six couples. Just like we did with Death Pool."

"That sounds like a solid plan," Geo remarked. Raising his voice, he added, "All in favor?"

Ending with Muhammad, the four responded with, "Aye."

Geo jotted down the rule as if to set it in stone. Then, he placed the writing accessories on the nightstand and took a bite of his burrito. Each burrito weighed nearly a pound. Chewing his food and dropping remnants on his starched collar, he then asked, "Are there any relationships that are off the menu? Anything that's out-of-bounds?"

Esther replied, "As long as they're famous, I think it's all fair game."

"Okay." Another erratic note scribbled down.

Muhammad pulled the covers from his head and inquired, "Does that include political figures?"

"I would certainly hope so," answered Geo. "I think that we should reserve one of the slots as a special pick, something that increases payout. Kind of like a star quarterback in a fantasy football league. Our number one player. It will increase payout, let's say, tenfold?"

Clea shook her head in agreement. "Sure. That sounds swell." She was starting to feel uncomfortable, hiding things from her old friend. She knew that Esther didn't want to burden her with keeping secrets. She recalled her conversation with Mo from the long drive in, bitching about Geo and his general demeanor. It made her feel sick with shame. She also remembered the many times that Geo hit on her, like a snake-tongued chancellor, always toeing the line between friend and lover. It was all so confusing not knowing whether to feel pity or wrath.

Esther cut in on these thoughts. "All right, what factors should we use in working the odds? I think that we should consider public image. A couple that openly discusses their boundless love, kissing when cameras are looking, sharing vacation photos with the world—that would certainly deserve a bump in payout."

Geo disagreed. "Sure, but wouldn't the weakest relationship count on such a phony facade?"

Without being too obvious, Esther and Clea shot a glance at one another. His marriage to Mishelle was a prime example of his argument. "Okay, you've got a point. But surely our perception of a strong relationship is a minor detail that deserves attention," Esther explained.

"Absolutely. I think anniversary and birthday celebrations can be drawn on. Relationships that cherish such things are generally solid."

"Agreed." Esther shouted in Muhammad's direction, "Do you agree, Sleeping Beauty?"

He simply poked his arm from the pile of blankets and gave a thumbs up.

"What else?" Geo was eager to move on to the selection of potential divorces.

Esther quickly responded, "Longevity is key. Doubled odds for every five years married."

"Doubling seems a bit weak," Geo said. "Let's triple the odds for every five years married. Hollywood chews them up and spits them out pretty quickly."

Clea was fast in objecting. "Five years isn't that long. Let's double the odds for the first five years, then triple them at ten, and quadruple them at fifteen, so on and so forth." Clea knew that five years, even for the most volatile of companions, was an easily-served sentence.

"Sounds good."

Clea added, "Are we to adjust for inflation?"

Geo considered this and answered, "I think it would add to the excitement of the game to do so." He looked to Esther, who nodded her head in agreement. He added the rule to his notebook.

Muhammad finally rose from his crypt of bedding. He commented, "I like where you guys are going with the length of the marriage, but perhaps we should think about couples that have been hitched for less than six months as well. Double or triple?"

They chewed on the suggestion for a moment, and Geo said, "If they are married for less than a year at the time of the divorce, then odds double. I don't see how we could predict anything shorter than six months when the game lasts until next February." He was writing rapid-fire in his notes. Then, in what seemed like a friendly jab, he added, "What about same-sex couples?"

The other three knew that Geo had overcome most of the homophobic tendencies of his past. His comment was merely an attempt to be concise in drafting the rules. Plus, there was a tiny bit of shock value involved in a culture that worshiped the hetero and the square. The dissolution of a same-sex marriage garnered special attention. They each nodded and agreed on doubled odds.

Things were wrapping up, if only because checkout time was approaching. A few minor details were worked out. The highest stakes in the game involved the murder of a spouse. That was a long shot but deserved consideration. Another cash cow was a long-lived marriage, breaking apart to facilitate the return to a past lover. One assumed rule was the strict guideline of fame, notoriety, or fall from grace. The forerunners must have a relationship with the screen. They could be newbies or American legends, but they must have been in front of a camera at some point in their life.

With guidelines now established, they packed up their belongings. Geo went to the reservation desk and finalized their paperwork. He tapped his foot and answered questions, watching a saucy talk show on one of the wall units. Most of the screens were meant for hotel-related services and advertisements for local attractions. He thought about the days of Death Pool when the group would hunker down in rented rooms for nearly a week, sampling all of the restaurants and drinking at all of the bars. Those days were gone. The others waited for him in the parking lot. Clea smoked, and Muhammad desperately tried to rehydrate. The real fun was just beginning. Now, they would all make their picks for Divorce Pool. Afterwards, they would catch a movie before flying and driving out of Phoenix.

IN THE EARLY AFTERNOON, THEY hovered over hamburgers in a sock hop-themed diner. Their mood was a weird mix of sullenness and anxiety. Tattooed waiters whisked through the dining quarters, and a jukebox played doo-wop hits. The scene was a juxtaposition of eras; antique-looking black-and-white televisions on display along with silica screens mounted on every wall. One screen featured a panel of talking heads arguing about some inevitable constitutional crisis. Captions scrolled along like the karaoke lyrics from the night before. It was rare to see political discussion as most people preferred cheap celebrity banter. Patrons all throughout the diner were wishing for a year of fortune, making resolutions that would easily be broken. Dead paper lanterns littered the streets outside.

The lunch was accompanied by details of personal life, forgotten in the lecherous fun. A few last details were worked out for rules and regulations. During these final deliberations Clea fidgeted with her napkin, looking distressed about something. In her mind, an idea was gaining speed, much like when she had conceived Divorce Pool. Ready to write down their picks on specially-formatted sheets, Esther decided to put forth her decisions first.

"My top pick is Lindsay Lohan and Dave Grohl. Since they were married just last month, my payout will double if they get divorced by July. My tenfold bonus stands regardless."

"Very nice," Geo said. "And your other picks?"

"Mario Lin and Moma Rodriguez. The Altmanns. The Chens. Zac Efron and Lucille Nakamura. My last pick has a contingency. I predict that Alec Baldwin will leave his current wife and return to Kim Basinger. I will commit five hundred dollars to the pool."

Muhammad was impressed. This was a solid list. He commented, "Wow, Esther. Way to make our first round exciting. That's a pretty decent wager too."

She smiled. "Thanks. Do you want to go next, Mo?"

"Sure. I am curious if my top pick might get another bump in odds. I choose Donald and Melania Drumpf. Surely, that is unlikely enough to warrant an extra double bonus." They all nodded in agreement. He continued, "They are definitely divorce material, but the optics for either one of them would be enough to discourage the effort. Sure would make for a fascinating news cycle! Anywho, my other picks are as follows: Neil Degrasse Tyson and Ariana Grande, the Koplins, Ellen Degeneres and Portia De Rossi, the Liangs, and the Durants. I will commit two-hundred dollars to the pool."

The group was giggling with excitement. They were genuinely having a good time. After the plates were taken from the table, they ordered a round of coffee. Clea doodled on a pad of paper and tapped her fingernails on the side of the bench seat. She was visibly nervous, but the others did not notice in the adventurous spirit of the game. She passed the opportunity to give her picks, giving her turn to Geo.

He began, "My primary pick is an attempt to get some odds on longevity. Annette Bening and Warren Beatty."

Esther reeled with disbelief. "There's no way in hell."

Geo defended his decision, explaining, "If I remember correctly, I'll get an increased payout for the sugary way that they always praise their relationship. In all honesty, I'd hate to see such an American power couple break their union. It would be more devastating than the Drumpfs, in my opinion. If they split, I want to be the first to make a profit on it." He paused and hastily scribbled their names onto his sheet. "My other picks are the Duke and Duchess of Gloucester, Mary Ann Jennings and Kiran Applegate, the Bauers, Corey Feldman and Courtney Anne Mitchell, and finally, the McGillicuttys. I will commit one thousand dollars to the pool."

The waiter brought the coffees and passed them out. A Paul Anka song played on the tinny speaker system overhead. Knives and frying pans created a sharp din in the background, mixing in and out of the crooning singer's voice. The screen above the restroom entrance played a recap of Anderson

Cooper and Michelle Wolf at Times Square, ringing in 4723 and clanking flutes of champagne. The game of Divorce Pool was a manifestation of every face. Faces influence so many discussions and interactions in the United States. These four friends were no exception. Clea thought about the insanity of it all as she stirred creamer into her mug. She was thinking about Esther's confession; she was also thinking about winning.

Geo's voice broke her train of thought. He asked her, "What about you, Clea? Surely, you've been mulling over it ever since you thought of the game. We've got nearly two thousand in the pool, and I'm sure you can commit a pretty penny as well. Who are you going to put your money on?"

She took a long sip of coffee and held it with two hands. She took a deep breath and said, "I'm going to shake up the rules a little bit. We can discuss whether or not it is fair, but remember, I am the mind behind Divorce Pool. I would think that I'm entitled to a small tweak." Setting her mug down, she continued, "My primary pick is Geo and Mishelle Simmermann."

PART TWO

THE WAY WE ARE

VII

I t is difficult to imagine Mecca through the smog on air advisory days. My eyes squint at the rising sun. Early on a Friday, the radio is tuned to KPCC and playing at low volume. The war in Afghanistan is a year old, and Horus Mass is later this month. I am attending my last semester at Cal State, completing my bachelor's in nursing at the ripe age of twenty-six. Today is an easy day. I have an obligatory history class and have not been scheduled at Dr. Zaidi's clinic. I will study for final exams and loaf around.

"Glory to my Lord, the Most High."

I stand up and gather my prayer rug. Coffee drips from a Hamilton Beach on the kitchen counter. My tiny Thunder Oak, made of dyed PVC, rests in a corner of my studio apartment and is adorned with icicles and mementos. Dad never celebrated Horus Mass, saying it conflicted with his hardline beliefs. I am a little looser in my interpretation of God. I can't help but feel giddy during the holiday season, watching people gifting, gambling, and covering every hot drink with cinnamon. The traditions of Yule and Saturnalia are fascinating.

4700 has been an interesting year. The Y4.7K scare passed and was never a threat to begin with. Computers cycled the date without a hitch. The D.C. sniper has been apprehended. Young men, many of whom look like me, are being shot by the LAPD, but that's been going on for decades. The Lakers secured the championship and drove the city bonkers. K-mart has filed for bankruptcy. I guess I'll buy bedsheets from PanMart like everyone else.

People are still affected by 9/11. Imams and Rabbis make various pre-dictions about living in the end times. President Bush is loved by his conservative Muslim base, and hated by progressive Jews. Images of American cavalry, fighting the Taliban on horseback, inspire a strong sense of patriotism throughout the country. We are winning the war on terror. Not everyone is convinced of our advantage in the conflict. Some say the war is an omen, a signal of worse things to come. Many folks believe that Los Angeles is the next big target.

Generally, I am broke. Tuition rates have doubled since the nineties. I used the last of my inheritance to pay for my first two years. Paying for the rest has been an exhausting endeavor. With the degree program winding down, I can probably quit my second job, but I'm not sure if I will. The rent keeps increasing. Demand for nurses is stagnant.

The radio lists headlines at the top of the hour. "From NPR news in Washington, I'm Jacoby Patel-Johns. Israeli troops have broken up a refugee camp in the Gaza Strip. Tanks and helicopters entered the camp, provoking a firefight that has killed ten people and wounded dozens of others. A general strike has been called for in Venezuela, halting the country's petroleum production. The strike is organized by opposition to the presidency of Hugo Chavez. Cities in the Midwest are bracing for a powerful blizzard. Some areas predict over a foot of snow. Market futures are mixed."

I walk across my tiny unit and sit on the edge of my mattress. Justin is sleeping soundly, cuddled in my lavender comforter. I set his coffee on the nightstand and sweep a blonde lock from his forehead. We have been dating for nearly a year, which is an eternity compared to the other short-lived relationships of my early twenties. No one seems interested in commitment these days. I am not sure if I want a life partner, either.

He wakes as the weight of my body shifts the bed. With watery eyes, he looks up at me and takes a deep breath. "Hey, sunshine. Is there coffee?"

"Right here." I kiss his cheek.

"Yum. You're the best, Mo," he comments as he reaches for the hot mug.

"Did you sleep well?"

"Oh yeah. Like a rock. Would you hand me my pager? I was on call last night. I want to make sure I didn't drop the ball."

I find it lying on an embroidered doily and hand it to him. He looks at it with concern, and then rests his face in relief. "Must have been a dead night."

"I have to leave here in a few minutes. There is cereal in the cupboard and milk in the refrigerator. Will you make sure to lock up when you leave?"

"You got it, handsome."

Justin really appeals to my vainest tendencies. He sits up, and I lean over for a deep kiss. I am vaguely turned on as we breathe into each other, his hand squeezing my inner thigh. I break from the spell and wish him a nice day.

"I'll see you either tonight or early Sunday morning," he reminds me as I walk toward the door and out into the hallway.

"Kisses, my dear."

"Kisses to you, my sweet Mo."

"THAT'S AN EXCELLENT QUESTION, CARLOS. In the last thirty years, Ford and Clinton are the only presidents that failed to win a second term. Ford was unpopular because of his pardon of Nixon, and people were eager to elect an outsider, someone unburdened by the political elitism of Washington," Mrs. Gbedemah explained. "Are there any other questions before we move on?"

The class was silent, and no hands went up. She continued, "Very well. As I was saying, Clinton lost his chance at re-election when he ordered the National Guard to suppress the Simpson Riots, right here in Los Angeles. Surely, this had been done in the past. Throughout American history, troops have been used to break strikes, as well as protect innocent people and property during dangerous protests. Why was Clinton's response a total failure? What was the federal government dealing with? How did everything go so wrong?"

"It is true that the guilty verdict led to a stifled economy, widespread looting, and several attacks on the police. It is important to remember, however, that the effort was highly organized. It wasn't anything like the King Riots. Minor events set aside, the movement was largely nonviolent. It was an attempt to bring the LAPD to account for decades of racial discrimination and violence. Businesses were shut down for weeks. Mail delivery was stopped by massive human blockades. Schools and universities were forced to send faculty home. You can imagine the power of the statements being made."

"The local government did not know how to respond to the overwhelming demands of the protesters. Trying to quell the anger, the city suggested a retrial of O.J. They couldn't fathom that the protesters were angry about so many other things: income inequality, access to affordable housing, institutionalized segregation, and the massive wave of incarceration affecting young, black men. Those orchestrating the riots and protests laughed at the offer. So, the city appealed to the federal government for assistance. It was inconceivable that the request would lead to the atrocities that followed."

I had heard this many times. The Winter of Death. The White Boot. Clinton's Folly. The disaster went by many names. I simply called it the year that I lost my parents. Being ex-punkers, they naturally gravitated toward a mistrust of government. Even my conservative father was quick to act. He would curse throughout the trial, explaining how he once had a run-in with Fuhrman. Every black man knows what it's like. I have been pulled over for spotty reasons.

My last years at Belmont were a rocky time for my dad and me. We had minor disagreements, most of which centered on religion and morality. One day, I came home crying. Being the great father that he was, he asked what was wrong. Yoshi and I had just broken up, and it was my first experience with heartache. At first, I tried to hide it from him. But he had a way of getting me to open up, and I spilled my guts. I came out as gay. He was the first person I had told. He looked at me in a weird way, stood up, and walked into another room.

We didn't talk for weeks. It was a devastating reality for him to accept. He even denied my confession, telling me that I'd blossom later on in life and properly get into women. The trial was the first thing that brought us together again. It was a bonding experience to discuss race, power, and justice in America. The verdict strengthened this bond even further.

The Simpson Riots were a way for my parents to return to the community. They led demonstrations and registered people to vote. They held hands during the human blockades. They interacted in ways I hadn't seen before, as if the context had energized their friendship. Part of me wondered if they might be falling in love once again. After all, Mom was no longer with Larry or Tariq. She complained about their shortcomings, many of which were opposite to Dad's charming presence and personality. I couldn't help but think that this was a rekindling of sorts. Sadly, those thoughts were innocent and naive wishes. They would never come true. There was not an opportunity for them to come true.

I remember everything so vividly. I was home playing the Super Famicom. I was enjoying a welcome break from the hubbub of street activism. Suddenly, an emergency broadcast signal blared through amplifiers at every end of the city. Over them, I could hear the shots fired, one after another. At first, I couldn't tell if they were coming from the troops or the protesters. I made the drastic conclusion that citizens were being killed by the federal government.

My fears were soon confirmed. I switched off the console and searched the channels for a local news outlet. I didn't have to surf for long. Even Nickelodeon was shut down for national coverage. I left the house and headed downtown to find my parents, but I was stopped by National Guard troops. They had put my neighborhood in quarantine, hoping to mask the madness occurring in the streets. Families throughout the block were gathered into khaki tents. AM/FM receivers were taken away. Esther had already left for college, but Geo and Clea had come to see me in the makeshift camp. They were my only consolation as the disaster played out. For three days, the firing continued. A week later, I heard that Mom and Dad were among the many casualties. I was given the opportunity to visit a mass grave. The authorities did not bother to identify the dead, because there were just too many bodies. It wasn't until four years later that the city matched the bodies with dental records.

Mrs. Gbedemah was wrapping up her analysis. "The Clinton administration would have done well to send federal investigators to assess citywide police conduct. That alone would have ended the riots. Instead, they sent armed soldiers, most of whom were as white as the policemen in question. This affair is, and will remain, the greatest injustice ever committed by the executive branch. It was a blatant abuse of power that will affect Americans for generations to come."

You're telling me.

WITH THE LOSS ON MY mind, I drive to Evergreen cemetery, where my mom and dad have plots. Their graves are on the same aisle but forty feet apart. I did not want to offend them by forcing them to share sarcophagi space. Each headstone is inscribed with a prayer from the Qur'an. I ache to speak with either of them. My morning class struck a nerve, and I don't know how to shake this feeling. Perhaps it is survivor's guilt. I could have been one of the five thousand people murdered that week. I would give anything to communicate a proper parting note; a poem or a song, something to let them know how much I loved them. I can only find contentment in the memory of a happy childhood. They provided me with everything, from self-confidence to morality.

A blessing from father would be particularly nice. Although we had hashed out most of the awkwardness, he never really told me his thoughts on homosexuality. In a selfish way, I would like him to see that it was more than a phase. My true self loves men and men alone. He was a good enough father to see past that shit, I just know it. But I can't help but want to hear it from his lips. Do we grieve merely because we are denied peace of mind?

I know that he would like Justin. Justin exemplified the kind of hard work ethic that my father cherished in other men. He would also be proud of my upcoming graduation from college. We could sing the Cal State Alma Mater. He would be happy to see Bush's son in office, regardless of the war. It would have been nice to discuss the piss-poor decisions of Clinton with him. He hated "Willie" mostly because he loathed Democrats but also because of the appearance on Arsenio, where the candidate blew on a saxophone, wearing shades like a schmuck. As an avid fan of science-fiction in general, he would have loved to see the Star Wars prequels. He would hate modern country music. He would hate the growing presence of the internet. There are many things he wouldn't like about this world, but I am certain that he would like Justin.

After reclining on Dad's headstone for a while, I kiss the granite block. "I love you, Dad."

I walk down the aisle to see Mom. Pain and confusion begin to cloud my thoughts. I had mixed feelings about our relationship, especially in the five years before her killing. I still do. She was always vocal in her criticisms of Dad, which forced me to keep secrets between the two of them. I despised being the interpreter of their power struggle, decoding the special language of ex-lovers. At least it ended differently. Her newfound activism and her effort to find common ground with Dad was a nice note to leave on.

But there were so many questions left unanswered. Quite honestly, I always wondered about her indecisiveness when it came to men. I would never fault her for it. My own love life hasn't been a long series of successes. Maybe I am still waiting for Mr. Right and haven't made up my mind about what he's like. But I would never push through the discomfort of a bad fit for the promise of something better. It was this method by which she used Larry as a crutch, as a bookmark for some happier chapter. Why torture yourself with an unhappy union when you're obviously interested in something more exciting?

She would never admit it to me, but I know that she was unfaithful to Larry. Too many late nights to assume otherwise. The timing was all wrong, as well. It wasn't too long after they had divorced that she moved in with Tariq. The sequence of events was too suspicious for me to grant her the benefit of the doubt. Larry was absolutely devastated, but he was a good sport when Mom found a new love. Tariq, on the other hand, was quick to make fun of Larry's squareness. I couldn't stand that machismo bullshit and despised my mother for being attracted to it. Tariq had a smooth style and a deep baritone voice but was void of character in general. Simply put, he was a tool. I might not have thought that Larry was hip, but at least he provided a safe and happy life for his spouse and his stepson.

I breathe deeply, and the cold air stings the bridge of my nose. I am losing sight of what should be a respectful visit. "Damn, Mom. I'm sorry."

Why am I so hard on her? Am I a closet chauvinist? Why do I blindly and unconditionally love my father while criticizing her at the base of her grave? Surely, she gave up many things for my benefit. It is the curse of prompt loss. The living beat themselves up over details that are probably moot points.

I am crying. No, I am hyperventilating. It isn't stopping, no matter how hard I try. *Fuck.* I press my head to the earth and grieve, holding none of it back. This has never happened to me. I am shaking and feel like I could vomit. A wave of understanding washes over me. I can compute the data, but my body is overloading. There is nothing to do but lie here and weep over my mother's grave.

She did it all for me—every maneuver, calculated and precise. Love is not enough when the American economy beats you down. No wonder she quit Nixon Babies. Punk rock, and its fascination with the wasted, was counter to the new reality of parenthood. It's quite possible that she loved Dad more than any other man. He might have been her soulmate, but he couldn't provide the life she demanded for her child.

She had to find another avenue. Larry was a good man, and she knew it. He was a good substitute when love had waned for the father of her only son. But I shamed her for leaving the man that I respected. It never occurred to me that she was acting out some sick ritual in which mothers must climb a social ladder for baubles and swing sets. So focused on my silly gaming habits, I assumed that she had lost interest in me. Every day, I pretended to be hurt over some lack of attention. The lack of attention never existed.

Lashing out at her was the only way to compensate for having to shuttle between two households. I had despised her. I never told her outright, but it was probably spoken in my actions. I despised her for being a divorced woman in a country that did not allow such things. I despised her for daring to carve her own path, under the watchful eye of Allah. I might have even despised her merely for being a woman. My early childhood was one continuous tantrum, and mother was the floor that I beat my fists upon. Only now, in this very moment, do I realize the folly of my ways.

I am beginning to catch up with my heartbeat. It rings in my ears, and I am reminded of the same rhythm, resting in my mother's womb. I can hear her now as I heard her in the crib, a long and soothing shushing. The amniotic fluid coming in and receding back. It sounds like an ocean in my mind. She is here to comfort me, in this, the most religious experience of my life thus far. Not even a sacred pilgrimage to the Kaaba could bring such light into the soul.

I raise my head and can feel the onset of a migraine. I have never cried so hard. Wrapping my arms around myself, I finally begin to calm down. This has been a revelation, and I am thankful. I softly speak into her headstone, "Mom. I wish you were around. It is hard to resist fighting with your memory. You were blamed for everything wrong in my life. I now know better. I know that you tried your best. Thank you dearly for your undying effort in making me a decent man. I will repay you in heaven with kisses and hugs until my fucking arms fall off. I love you with all of my heart."

Standing up, I feel true serenity for the first time in my life. It is Friday, and the afternoon is still young. I am eager to visit the mosque on 4th Street. There are some questions about God that need to be addressed. I jump in my car and drive off, thinking about Mom.

HAMZI GRISHAM IS THE IMAM serving the public on this brisk day. I have never seen him here before but have heard his name. The mosque is a very small and very clean outlet in a massive strip mall. I have been coming here ever since Dad died. He preferred the Islamic center on Wilshire, where I went as a child.

The work day has not yet ended, and the room is sparsely populated with people offering prayers and having discussions. The Imam does not look busy. I approach him, curious about my encounter at the cemetery. He looks at me with a kind face and greets me with a simple nod of his head.

"Good afternoon, Imam."

"Good afternoon, my son."

"I was hoping to discuss an experience that I had earlier today. It involves my mother, who is deceased. I would like to offer a prayer for her, but I am unsure if that is appropriate."

"Is she a disbeliever or worshiper of idols?"

"She was a believer at one time but had lost her way."

"I think we can arrange something. As long as we do not intercede with God's judgment."

I am struggling with the orthodoxy of my religion. *Isn't outright devotion enough?* "Thank you, Imam. You see, I visited her grave today, and I am certain that she spoke to me. To be concise, it wasn't words. I just felt like she was comforting me, the way one would comfort a crying child."

"I see. Communication with the dead is a phenomenon that has many examples throughout history. In those cases, it is generally agreed that the recipient was talking with God, and not with the spirit of one who has passed. I suppose the issue is up for debate."

"This is what confuses me. I have felt the presence of God before. This was somehow different, and more powerful. Every memory of her was distinct in my mind. I could see every hug, every argument, every conversation, all at once. She was forgiving me for my ill-treatment toward her. I know it. She was telling me that I was wrong about something but that it didn't matter, and that her love was unconditional."

"It sounds like you were holding on to some unsaid and unrealized guilt, my son."

"Yes, Imam."

He smiled and continued, "I do not doubt your account, and I do not discount your interpretation of it. However, it is precisely the type of personal burden that would warrant God's blessings and God's gift of a clean conscience. Let me remind you of the story of Ibrahim. Ibrahim, who has also been recognized as Akhenaten and Zarathustra, carried the guilt of his father's idolatry. This is a well-known story. But when did God reveal himself to Ibrahim? The question has been debated for centuries. It is like the chicken and egg conundrum. What came first: the truth of one God, or the lie of many gods? Did God reveal himself as a result of Ibrahim's guilt, or as a precondition of his guilt? Which came first, the monotheist or the drive to preach monotheism to others? Do you see where I am going with this?"

I am confused by the question and confused by the reference. "I apologize, Imam. Who is Akhenaten?"

"Pharaoh and convert to the glory of God. Akhenaten is Ibrahim. Akhenaten is Zarathustra. They are all one and the same. The pharaoh's conversion helped spread early Judaism throughout the African continent. Do you remember the legend? The roots of our great religion are tied to it. People tend to forget that Muslims and Jews share a rich history."

"How could three people be the same?" Dad used to talk about the Covenant but never went into such detail.

"Akhenaten carried the guilt of idolatry that plagued his royal lineage. Zarathustra carried the guilt of idolatry that affected the citizens of ancient Iran. Ibrahim carried the guilt of idolatry practiced by his father, Terah. Only God could ease their guilt. They are the same person, and they are not the same person."

"I understand the similarities, but I can't seem to grasp the connection of the three."

"Do you doubt the ancient alliances between the Egyptian pharaohs, the Persian monarchs, and the Judaic kings?"

"No, Imam."

"Do you understand that God speaks in times of personal distress?"

"Yes, Imam."

"Then you understand that God was your mother. God is everyone and everything. God had embodied the arms of your mother. You would not have responded to any other embrace. You would not have listened to any other voice. You would not have been open to any other communication. You carried the guilt of your past, and God responded."

"Thank you, Imam. I think I understand now."

"It is nothing, my child."

I motion my hand in a farewell gesture. He turns to speak with other attendees and answers other questions on faith. He goes about his business, discussing the eternal struggle between good and evil, and the people caught in the middle.

Frankly, I did not understand anything he said. He has a sweet, subtle demeanor and a voice that sounds like a lullaby, but he has not helped me in any way. I leave the mosque as confused as when I entered it. As I step onto the sidewalk, I look up into the sky and say a quick prayer to my mother. I do not care if it intercedes on God's judgment. She deserves my blessing and would love to hear about my new take on things. I will no longer curse her name.

VIII

"The slow murder that we perform upon ourselves is actually a blessing. Cancel or deny misery, and the parameters of joy will never be defined. True, we are wasted in this world. In pursuit of our grand selves, and it is art. It is the egg that becomes the ego, a costume or mask that suffices as a makeshift map, leading to an impression. Repeat this mantra in your mind:

I will cut off my limbs, as to never be in your way, when walking down a street.

I will staple my lips together, as to never offend you, or say your name in vain.

I will glue my eyelids shut, as to never glance in your direction, or barter your comfort for a sip of beauty.

I will peel my skin off, as to never feel companionship, when I offer nothing in return.

I will plug my nostrils, my urethra, my anus.

I will pull the eardrums from my skull, as to never overhear your secrets, spoken in a barroom or restaurant.

I will block the passage of my esophagus, as to never hog the sweet air you that breathe.

I will stifle my soul, as to never steal your slice of the pie.

I will pry my teeth out, as to never gnash them on trendy foods, or flash a tricky grin as a sales pitch.

I will disembowel myself, castrate myself, flagellate my shoulders to repent for sins not yet committed.

I will deaden my mind, as to never know clarity.

I will fill my lungs with phlegm, as to never sing a song that doesn't fit your genre.

I will shatter my pelvis with a sledgehammer, as to never dance again.

I will end my pursuit of knowledge, as to never be correct, when you yearn to be an authority.

But I will never take my life, a reminder of the price paid, for your lovely existence to thrive.

Once we can fully envision these commitments, the path will be seen. But the path is strewn with misery. Be prepared, my friend, for the joy found afterward."

The Tibetan bowl rings and I open my eyes. Maharaj Aten Mazda wears a calm and mysterious smile. My body feels light, and I am sweating. The heat lamps are powering down, and everyone is offered a complimentary bottle of water. The weekly meditation session has ended, and the doors are opening to let in cool, Marin County breeze. I gather my cell and stand up slowly, as to not get dizzy or disoriented.

Patrons take their turn thanking the leader of the session. The Maharaj is a freckled redhead with a sinewy frame. His long dreadlocks are pinned up with an eagle's feather, which seems to be laminated with some unknown substance. He presses his palms together and bows for each student. The room temperature stabilizes, and I can already feel my relaxed state washing away into my anxiety-ridden, default setting.

After the bulk of the group has dispersed, I decide to approach this special man. He has done so much for me in the last three months. I will try not to be self-conscious when I talk to him. It is important to avoid "projecting," as he calls it. Toweling off the last of my perspiration, I softly ask him, "Dear Maharaj, did you write that mantra?"

He responds with his heavenly tenor voice, "Why yes, I did. I certainly hope that you enjoyed it, without fear, and without doubting your potential to be non-obstructive."

"It was lovely, and no, I did not feel any fear. The experience was truly peaceful."

"The words are meant to saturate your spirit, my child. I humbly apologize for not remembering. What is your name?"

"Clea Socorro-Zamora."

"That's right. Clea. What a wonderful name. What does it signify?"

"My mother told me it was an homage to Cleopatra. My sister's name if Nefe, short for Nefertiti. My grandparents are some seriously orthodox Jews, in the vein of the African diaspora. You know, when the ancient Semites used to name their children after the converted pharaohs?" I am talking too much. I am being the antithesis of everything I've learned in this converted freight container.

"The culture fascinates me. I was raised in a conservative Muslim family and know little of the old African or European denominations."

"Then you probably know what I was dealing with."

He laughs and responds, "Certainly. Is your family of born-again fervor?"

Is he flirting with me? He doesn't seem to chitchat like this with the other students. Everyone else has left the room. No, he's too grounded to bother with petty things like that. Surely, he lives by his teachings. Hooking up with attendees seems an abstraction to the path. "No. They always make a point to differentiate themselves from the morality police. They generally shun any American influence on the faith. They are ardent followers of every word in the King James Tanakh."

"Wow, I wouldn't have guessed."

"Do you still practice?"

"Goodness, no. I gave away my prayer rug years ago. It would be impossible as a vegan to always worry about the standards of halal. I'd probably starve."

Was that a joke? I let out a forced giggle. "I'm sure."

"My upbringing made me who I am but also provided a framework for what I did not want to be. To be honest, it pains me to see so much of Allah in American politics."

"You're talking about those Tea Party types?"

"Yeah. The war on terror, the prosperity hadith, ammophilia, conversion therapy; it's all a nightmare."

"Agreed. At least we're done with Bush."

"Absolutely."

I pivot from the serious tone of our conversation. "That's a lovely potpourri that you're using. Is it homemade?"

"Yes. Thank you for the compliment. It is cinnamon, sage, and lavender. It is my first recipe."

"I like it," I need to end this. We are engaging in small talk, wearing our egos on our sleeves. Even the teacher is susceptible to temptation. But I am intrigued and lonely. I can't help but want the attention of his eyes. I could swear, they were walking up and down my torso, as we spoke.

Finally, he breaks in and asks, "Do you mix?"

"No. I don't have the time or patience for any of that. One of my best friends is an herbalist. She makes tinctures for her physical therapy practice."

"That sounds quite interesting."

"Yeah, she's a badass." He is stalling on something. Some question that he would like to ask but is unable. Perhaps he'd have to drop the guru shtick. I can see it in his face. It's the same look I get at 1:30 in the morning on any given weekend. The look of desperation. He is lonely, too.

He pulls his cell from jet-black yoga pants and asks, "I am thinking of adding an aromatherapy element to the class. Could I possibly get your number? Perhaps, you could refer me to your friend, or we could continue our thoughts on God at another time."

"That would be great." I am charmed but also disappointed. Scents and spirituality are just fronts for an ulterior motive. I've seen it a thousand times, and I am a magnet for such attention. Apparently, I give off the vibes of desperation as well. The instructor is trying to bed me. Maharaj Aten Mazda is just another fuck boy. *Why am I intrigued?* He is solid eye candy, but I had made a promise to myself to avoid such cheap and meaningless interactions. Oh, well. If anything, I'll have a few fun nights and save fifty bucks a month by canceling my membership to the class. We trade our devices and exchange information.

"Wonderful. It's been a pleasure chatting with you, Clea." He presses his palms together, closes his eyes, and bows deeply as a farewell to his most recent adventure in sexual conquest.

"Namaste." I am simultaneously blushing and foaming at the bit with annoyance.

He turns away from me, flips his towel over his shoulder, and walks to a messy pile of milk crates. I assume they hold paperwork and literature on New Age philosophy. Healers are all the same: self-absorbed and trite, especially here in the Bay.

Walking out of the freight box, the air feels crisp on my arms and neck as it brushes against sweat not yet dry. Unlocking my '97 Hyundai Sonata, I am eager to get home. My new job requires constant attention to my inbox. Work would be a refreshing distraction from my awkward encounter.

Starting the engine, the voices of KQED come in clear. Koji Atkins of affiliate station KTOO and Kret Plettiker of the National Weather Service are discussing breaking news. Plettiker explains, "It is about twelve kilometers out. Officials believe that it could reach the shore by tomorrow morning. Juneau residents are evacuating as we speak, and the word is out to coastal communities."

"Was there any identification of its movement prior to today?"

"I'm sure anyone would have just assumed it to be an extension of the garbage patch."

"And what about efforts to get closer? Do you have a team studying the mass?"

Plettiker groaned and took a deep breath. "The Coast Guard have a vessel circling the outer stretches. At first glance, it seems to be an oil spill. But it rises above the water in ways that would rule out such a theory. A team of divers went out this morning. They have not yet returned."

Sounds interesting. Must be a pretty toxic concoction to ask for evacuations. Hopefully, it's not some Chernobyl shit. At least it's in Alaska and not here. I am bored by the seriousness of it all. I turn the dial, but my favorite R&B station is covering the same interview. Koji Atkins updates the listeners, "For those of you just joining, we are covering the movement of an unknown material approaching the Pacific coast. Officials in Alaska and Canada have ordered citizens to move inland as a precaution. We will continue to bring you information as we receive it."

I shove a compact disc into the stereo. Wafer Sloth's *Riddle Me This, You Smell Like Piss*. I am caught in gridlocked traffic on Solano. I've got a few hours before daycare closes. I'll just pull into a Huffy Lewb for that oil change that I've been putting off. While considering my plan, my cell rings. It is Geo.

MY DIVORCE WAS FINALIZED OVER a platter of gravy tots. Now that I'm thirty, I can laugh at the youth of it all. Asnee leaning into the composite table with his elbows and shooting that silly grin. *What an asshole!* I had smiled back but only as a mask. In the tradition we helped create, a friendship was feigned between us. But I knew that I could never forgive him. I also knew that playing the game of smiles was the best thing for Horus.

Upon signing the papers, it was agreed that we would share custody. I would receive primary parental rights. He would be the non-custodial; the standard Tuesday and Thursday model, with every other weekend. He would get the Cadillac, and I would get the house. The market had just crashed, but the value of our two-bedroom in Berkeley hadn't been affected. In a way, I was content with the spoils of this romantic war. I could continue raising my son in the home he was familiar with. Asnee said it was a peace offering of sorts. The house, merely barter, for his deeds with my close friend and coworker.

Asnee's partnership with the law offices of Egert, Bach, and Hinojosa made the process easy. A short form was used, and neither party had to hire lawyers. Asnee would have won that game. He agreed to a child support order fixed at three thousand a month. He also agreed to pay half of all insurance premiums and to maintain the life insurance policy taken out with his son as beneficiary. To be close to both work and Horus, he bought a small house in Albany. He was to be out of my life. I remember asking myself if I was ready for that reality. So, what if I couldn't help but spill tears into the gravy? I needed to communicate that I was hurt, without jeopardizing the agreement.

He apologized, earnestly and with no agenda other than highlighting the fickleness of human nature. "It's all in the hard-wiring, babe. Don't take it personally."

We ride on jalopies called norms, preferences, and the status quo. They easily fall apart. All we can do is pick up the most expensive pieces and rig them into a new automobile. *Did you really expect to settle down into the standard nuclear unit?* Life had already proven to you that these conventions are unreal. Not just for yourself, but for everyone, including Asnee.

I can still remember our conversation. He looked up from his cream soda and began his long list of regrets. "I know I fucked up a good thing. I should have talked to you, at the slightest feeling of abandoning ship. Everything just moved so quickly. Good God, we graduated college and got engaged in the same month, Clea. You're everything I've ever known. But it's ripping me apart. The way I feel about Ephra. I never meant to—"

"Why did it have to be Ephra?"

He hung his head in his shame. "I—I don't know what to say. We've discussed this already. If you hadn't been so eager to introduce her into our lives . . ."

"Don't blame me for anything, Asnee. Did you not want me to make friends? What was I supposed to do? Be content working with her and going out on the occasional girl's night? Should I have kept her a secret?"

"I couldn't help myself. I love her. She loves me. And you won't accept any apology from her. She feels bad about it too, you know," he scoffed. "But now, she could care less about you, after all of the roadblocks you've put up."

"I am your fucking wife, Asnee!"

"Not anymore. Let's just finish this up, so we can cool off and continue our lives. It's plain and simple: I fell out of love with you, Clea. You're a good person, but I don't give a shit about the sanctity of marriage."

"Don't do this. It's not fair."

"Seriously, Clea. You're a good person. You deserve better. We are still young. You will find love again."

"Fuck off, Asnee."

I signed the last line on the court order and shoved the papers across the table. Those were my last words to him. I had ended an eight-year relationship

with the most simple and powerful words on Earth. He gathered the pile
and left me to finish the greasy, cylindrical nuggets, now soggy with turkey
drippings and cream. I shoveled my fork into them and slowly wept. Sodium
and oil are like the arms of a grandmother in times like these.

There were many nights during our separation and divorce that I felt like
my situation was unique. My pain was mine to own, and no other human
had felt it. Over the months, while he moved his belongings into Ephra's
storage, I realized the folly of my reasoning. The ritual of divorce is the most
American thing. It is the slice of apple pie, and it is Quetzalcoatl. Adam Smith
would be proud because it is capitalism. To the core. It is the experience that
binds us all, rejects looking for another not-so-perfect fit.

The ladder always presents itself in mysterious ways. *Why not love? Why
not the mirage of combined interests?* Clea thought of Geo and Mishelle Simmermann in an unconscious nod to the mythos of the sugar daddy and the
gold digger. Love is just a stepping stone to shared rents, shared mortgages.
To climb up is our mission. We are individuals, God damn it. Look out
for your ass or it will be handed to you. And I had played that game, just
chancing the rungs all along. He was a handsome lawyer, and his oyster was
everything and anything. *But not you anymore. You are not a pearl, and you
are not a consolation prize.* I lost the game; I let him take a mistress. I let my
guard down. At least I've got the house. And a beautiful son.

Fuck off, Asnee! How dare he and Ephra find happiness. I still have to
work with the cunt. She, Malik, and I are the founders of the nonprofit and
integral to its operation. And now I have to play the smile game with Ephra,
too. It is double duty. I am forced to watch her play the ladder game and
the smile game, back-to-back programming, like a Thursday night sitcom
block. Hopefully, the rumors are true. She's on her way out. Cue laugh track.
Surely, the shame should drive her from the outfit. I sure as hell will never let
her disrupt something that I helped create. *I will win that game. And I will
never trust another woman to be my close friend.* Esther is the only one. She is
the only woman who has ever had my back. Cue applause.

Enter swelling violins in a sad minor key. I had the audacity to make a
friend that was prettier than me, younger than me. *What a disastrous recipe.*

Who was the third wheel on any given outing? Perhaps Asnee was right to point out how I was playing with fire, how Prometheus didn't bother to leave the instruction manual. It is so painful to not know all of the details. I ask myself why and weave reasons without merit, but I've got to buck up. I've got no power over the results. Cue saxophone that signifies a life lesson well-learned. It sustains on a dissonant note, and the dream sequence comes to an end.

A car horn wakes me from my brief memory. The cell continues to ring. I give the car some gas and pull ahead, off of Solano. Parking my Sonata in a strip-mall parking lot, I answer the phone just seconds before my voice mail prompt.

Geo quickly started, "Hey! Clea? Are you seeing this shit?"

"Hi, Geo. What shit?"

"The blob that's gonna wash up on Alaska!"

THE FEW ERRANDS TURNED INTO too many. After the short conversation with Geo, the oil change, the prescription refill, the fuss about the electro bill, and the grocery store, I had to call Asnee to pick up Horus before 6:00. It would be so embarrassing if Asnee could see what I think when I'm not on my meds. As always, I have to tuck these sentiments deep into my vault of secrets. I can never let them out.

He is napping, and we are on our way to Drummer Burger, where there is an indoor slide and monkey bars. The radio still talks about Alaska and whatever is coming toward it. In the last several hours, I've heard the musings of Islamic and Judaic holy men, all postulating apocalypse. I've heard the scientists hashing it out as well. An archaic amoeba, waking from a recent-ly-melted iceberg. Maybe it is something from another world. I do not know who to believe.

At the pharmacy, I had sat in the waiting room, watching footage of the mass extending and protracting itself, whipping with appendages. It all reeked of Lovecraft but also of landfills. The reporters said it was stinky, in any case. I watched with horror as spotlights skimmed the weird and oily creature. I now call it a creature with no speculation otherwise. It is agreed upon. On every network, there is a consensus among all social and political angles: the puddle is a creature.

Dual coverage by KTOO and KQED continued, "And is there any reason to believe that the blob is hostile?" Atkins is gonna get all kinds of awards for this.

"Remember the way it interacted only when threatened? That is clearly a signal of nonaggression," reasons a leading politician.

Another politician jumps in to rebuke him. "Nonsense. We can't wait for it to play the theme from *Close Encounters of the Third Kind*. We need to bolster our military might in the far northwest, and both nations need to dedicate as much firepower as possible. Consider this an official appeal to the United Nations to defend our nations with force. We will not wait for a response. We will not wait for you to dissect and study the abomination."

"Always a hawk in the room," groans another talking head.

Horus is stirring. I do not want him to wake until we get to Drummer Burger. I turn off the radio, but my mind still aches with curiosity. The last rays of a setting sun bounce around on concrete walls. The day is retiring, regardless of the news cycle popping off over the creature.

I am on autopilot. The car will reach its destination safely. Mother mode has been implemented, and I am gazing ahead through the windshield at the businesses and dwellings. They are neon and rusted, bright and burnished, all at once. The sidewalks bustle with students going to late-night lectures. Some of them are inevitably rushing to some event, where people meet in the old-fashioned manner. They are all on the edge of youth, and I have settled on the opposite side of the blade. This old, tired brain needs a dose of lithium and a dose of carbamazepine. After dinner, I remind myself. The flashing marquee of Drummer Burger comes into view. I gently call Horus, in a singsong voice that promises a chocolate malt, once the rest of the meal is finished.

The parking lot is packed. There is a special event occurring all along the block. Vendors are perched every fifteen feet. The makeshift marketplace is bustling with activity, and the sight is enthralling to my little Horus. He points at one canopy that catches his eye. It is selling bargain toys and musical instruments. A blue-and-black Hohner harmonica sits in cheap packaging; they are five dollars even, no tax. I buy one and feel like a good parent. It is short-term satisfaction and a chance to foster creativity.

Another tent has a set of folding tables, placed horizontally and in a horseshoe formation. The tables are covered in real estate magazines. There are listings categorized in different ways. Foreclosed properties are listed on the first table, budget properties on the second. Multiple units and apartments are also being pedaled. A homemade sign rests above these to motivate the aspiring landlord. It says, "Remember, once you buy the properties, you have the right to evict current tenants." One advertisement boasts a listing entitled "freshly-remodeled units, evictions currently pending." The prices are laughable. In a few months, they will double in value as the market reheats.

I have had enough of the swindling caravan of shops. Horus and I walk toward the restaurant entrance, now filled at capacity with people waiting to be seated. On our way, I am stopped by a salesperson. She has magenta hair and alternating shades of white, yellow, and orange painted on her fingernails. With this pattern, her hands look like giant candy corns. The dentist's nightmare and harbinger of Type 2 diabetes. She is pushing data plans and phone upgrades.

"Are you satisfied with your current smartphone? What if I told you that an upgrade was available, free of charge? Are you happy with your hunk of junk?"

I politely smile and answer the question. "I am perfectly happy with my current cell. Thank you for the offer."

Shoving her shoulder into my path, she jokes, "That doesn't sound like the voice of a satisfied customer. Does your phone translate to Spanish, French, and German? Is it even capable of characters and scripts in Mandarin or Hindi? Does it have voice recognition? Are you able to smash fuzzies on the wire with your lad, living in a different state, or even a different country? Aural sex is always better on a next-generation Pixelmate."

"I'll politely point out that I'm with my four-year-old son. Please watch your language."

"Aha! Does your phone have parental controls and censorship software?

The discerning parent cannot own a device without them. You would do well to convert! Convert now! Come to witness the awe-inspiring memory of the next-generation Pixelmate, available in royal blue, lime green, and black."

"Thanks, but no thanks."

I navigate around the annoying merchant. Horus is complaining about being hungry, and I've got to get our name on the waitlist, or we'll be here all night trying to get a turkey club and something from the kid's menu. I love the club at the Drummer. It reminds me of the horrors of childhood when my diet was kosher. As an adult, I am free. I can eat bacon, mix meats with cheeses, partake in the common hot dog.

The hostess comes with good news. Many of the tables are being cleaned for larger parties. We are the only party of two. A small corner booth will be available in five minutes. People all throughout the diner are glued to the television set, or glued to their devices, watching the carnage south of the Aleutians. Sometimes the bodies clear, and the flat-screen is within sight. I distract Horus from the news. I had the foresight to bring a coloring book from the littered back seat of the Sonata. A few crayons had survived the previous summer without melting, slowly congealing over the cold months and settling back into shafts of thin paper. If he loses interest in coloring, I will let him play his new harmonica. It was a game of diverting attention away from the affairs of grownups. I was an expert.

The hostess brings us to a cushy, polyester seat. The bench has rhinestones and other tacky accessories to hide sweat stains and cracked upholstery. My disheveled crayons are supplemented with fresh ones, complimentary of the kid-friendly atmosphere. Horus wants the deep-fried macaroni and cheese clusters. I order a glass of Merlot and let the hubbub of the day wash off of me. Just as I am beginning to relax for dinner with my son, my cell buzzes from the chasms of my purse. Perhaps it is Geo again. He promised to visit me sometime soon, during our discussion earlier. I highly doubt that he meant it.

It is a media file from Maharaj Aten Mazda. I am curious as to what he wants. Based on my experience with men, he is calling to hang out. I shouldn't have given him my number. I am too hard on myself. *It could be fun. Meeting up somewhere to make out.* No. I need distance from the game, from the macho ones that eat up pretty moms like me. Wanting to resolve the suspense and move on, I reluctantly open the media file. It has poor resolution, but the outline is unmistakable. Maharaj Aten Mazda has sent me a dick pic.

IX

Ngome Shammas-Cruz woke up in an awful mood. He pressed the snooze button on his alarm, granting him an extra nine minutes of restlessness. His foot ached. It was aching from the early onset of a diabetic ulcer, courtesy of the maple-bacon taffy he had been eating throughout the week. The disc menu of a DVD, *Johnny Asshands: From Hair to Eternity*, cycled on a fat, tube television. Human methane and the odor of meaty, salty sweat permeated Ngome's bedroom. An automated coffee pot turned on at precisely 6:15. After the second snooze alarm, he reached for his cell and rose from his bed.

The night prior was spent farming experience on the role-playing network known as Khan Muscle. His sorcerer had leveled-up twice, and his dwarf cleric acquired a prism that cures all types of poison. It was also Ngome's night to catch up on *Cannibal Cop*, his favorite program. Supplies were well-stocked: two tall boys of tomato beers, fish crackers, and gummy worms. The bong had spilled over and soaked a dirty pair of pine-green scrubs. A pizza was ordered and delivered from Za Shak. With ample media and snacks digested, he turned in for the night by 10:30, but not before watching the skin flick and rubbing one out. It had been like many other nights in Ngome's past: sedentary, lonely, doped, and satiated.

He fumbled his way out of bed and into the bathroom. He sat on the toilet scrolling through his profile and reading online comics. Everyone was posting pictures from Halloween. Many people had dressed up as Michael Jackson, in honor of his death over the summer.

The cell was plugged into a socket usually reserved for hair dryers and irons. It was the newest model of smartphone. It had a touch-sensitive, silica screen that was partially cracked from overuse. Ngome was proud to have the latest gadget.

He fought and succumbed to the temptation to prowl pics of his ex. Two years out, and she still hadn't found new love, at least not one that would warrant a status change. She had lost weight. She looked healthy. These were conditions of her single life, proof that she no longer smothered the pressures of love in nacho cheese. She no longer took part in the swinish appetites of her mate. Swiping through the most recent photos, it was evident that she had repurposed her sexy pirate costume from two years back. He longed to be in her life in those cropped selfies.

Ngome sat, straining to defecate and browsing aimlessly. Judging from the effort involved, he was dehydrated. Finally, a few nuggets pushed out. He stood to clean himself, replenished the toilet paper roll, and pulled his plaid boxers on. He turned on the shower. Steam filled the small bathroom.

Without thinking to wash his hands, he continued to use his beloved device. He found his favorite playlist, pressed play, and stepped into the shower. The device sat in the steam. Its surface carried streaked fingerprints, covered in Ngome's digestive enzymes and bile. Particles of stool settled into the cracked screen, and baked in the humidity. It could have been anyone else on any other screen. These are common habits among Americans. Entertainment must follow us into every crevice of our story.

Being bored and horny, he considered masturbating in the shower. Many weird memories shot across his mind; all nipples and midriffs. Sometimes he thought about men. Sometimes he thought about women. To be loved in any capacity was far beyond his memory, and he would have preferred a long cuddle to anything else. But the fire never left him. It only rested with spilt seed.

He ejaculates and feels a tinge of embarrassment and self-pity, the loneliness is getting to him. Maybe he will meet someone at the square dance competition. The club does a monthly get-together. It was the last time he got laid. These units of months and years may sound meek to the seasoned, but expectations are high. In the films, you get fucked. In the sitcoms, you get fucked. On the hit pop single, you get fucked.

Stepping out of the shower, Ngome pulled a yellow towel from the rack. Not entirely dried, he once again reached for his filthy smartphone. He stopped the playlist, unwittingly adding semen to the biological stew of his interface. The residues of his body had not been properly cleaned as intended. A black-light investigation would show contamination all throughout his living quarters. Being a healthcare worker, he should know better. Such is the absurdity of a solitary life. No one to watch you or tell you that you can do better.

After airing the bathroom out, he slopped on some black scrubs and gathered his work badge. Front pocket. He made a note to spray deodorizer and pick up trash. In the kitchen, he poured an entire pot of coffee into a massive thermostat and added cream. His wallet sat on the counter near the toaster oven. Front pocket. He grabbed his keys to warm up his car. Outside, the ignition was accompanied by a quick outburst of an electro-cumbia station, preset on the radio. The car was left to defrost, and Ngome went back into his house for one last thing—the most important thing. He re-entered the bathroom to get his cell. Front pocket.

And it sat in his front pocket. The front pocket held everything of importance. It would remain there throughout the day, coming out at times to answer important e-mails. It would come out for boredom. It would come out for tasks. It should have never left his house. Harmless as it seemed, the device was to be a vector. It was a petri dish beaming with gunk, waiting to deliver a plague to the citizens of El Paso.

NOBODY WAS TALKING ABOUT THE recession anymore. Nobody discussed the pensions lost or the lack of full-time jobs. It was already forgotten, because the winners were winning again. Over a span of three decades, the wealth of the nation had been consolidated into a few thriving portfolios. The process was almost entirely complete. The workers of the 47th century were merely waiting for full automation. Then they would no longer be needed, and they could crawl into a damp corner to die.

For Ngome, pay hadn't budged in three years. The cost of medical insurance was becoming too expensive, even for a healthcare worker. The perks of work do not exist for him. Nurses are unionized and support staff are outsourced. It is a blatantly tiered system. The stratification leads to sore feelings and dubious competition. Just last month, corporate was threatening the techs and the nurses with a wage freeze. Meanwhile, the decision-makers doubled and tripled their bonuses. To thrive, one must steal from the mouths of others. The American dream lies at the end of a brick road paved on broken backs and broken spirits.

Housing costs are hard to deal with, as well. Ngome's cramped apartment was twelve hundred a month. He was too afraid to enter the buyer's market. The horrors of Orlando and Sacramento wait inside the pages of every *Realtor World* magazine. Homes for sale in El Paso are decently priced, but only if you know the right agent. And they only rub shoulders with people who drive values higher. An anchor on equity would never do. If the HOA can't handle you, then we don't want you. It's been this way since the Homestead Act. Real estate is an insider's gamble. Repurpose, repackage, and resell the rooms. Rent them if you can. Charge whatever the fuck you want. Landlords beget landlords, ad infinitum.

Cooling can get quite expensive in the summertime. Many people choose to buy non-perishable groceries, a method that allows one to shut off the watt-guzzling refrigerator. By denying the luxury of chilled food, the tenant has freed enough of their budget to sleep in the heat, under the flow of air conditioning. Some resort to ice cubes under a box fan. Others acclimate to the mercury, content to be one less person spewing Freon into the air. On the bright side, heating is not required in the winter. Winters are cool enough to work a second job without passing out from exhaustion.

It is cheaper to buy a processed pile of meat and cheese, slathered with sauce, than it is to buy an apple. Durum wheat is enriched with iron, niacin, thiamine, riboflavin, and folic acid. Otherwise, it is mostly sawdust. Food glues form the dough into any shape imaginable, like dinosaur pastas and pistol-shaped raviolis. Flavors are derived from a laboratory. The chemist was once seen as a saving grace against Malthusian doom. Now they put tacos and fried chicken into tiny vials. Bottled water with hints of vanilla, among other novelty beverages, are manufactured with no clear demand for the product. Fake it until you make it. Something has got to stick.

There is always the effort to cross-market on the palate of the tongue. Peanut butter flavored marshmallows and marshmallow flavored peanut butter. And then, when the people find a food that offers actual nutrition, they pull every ounce of it from the dirt. Ecosystems and economies die for the sake of American variety. It happened with quinoa. The diet fads pushed it as a miracle food, and now the Bolivian man cannot afford the grain that fed his ancestors. Our appetite is monstrous. We force labor upon a variety of mammals, just to craft a decent hot dog.

Ngome considered these realities with a heavy heart. It only saddened him because he was one of the guinea pigs, a data point in the research of mega-corporations. The hunt for basic necessities had become an obstacle course of marketing gimmicks and old-fashioned greed. He merely pushes Pavlov's button at the end of the course. He pulled into a Check-and-Go to buy a sleeve of crackers and some aerosol cheese. Payday wasn't for another three days. In order to cover the purchase, he would have to postdate his payment on a personal check. He smiled and foolishly believed that he had found a way to work the system. It's one of the reasons he loved this franchise. He wrote a check and was on his way. He carried the purchase into his car and continued his commute to work.

A RESTLESS WAITING ROOM FULL of rescheduled surgeries was Ngome's first priority upon arriving. At precisely 7:06, he ducked through and waved his pocketed badge at the chronometer, beating the quarter-hour increment that would have clocked him in at 7:15. Hanging his coat on a hook, he prepared his monologue to the patients. Some of them paced back and forth, forming a long list of grievances as they circled laps around the room. The television was playing a commercial about gold investment, and the magazine rack was recently restocked. Gel Lago graced the cover of *America Weekly*. Ngome took the remote control and muted the television. He took a deep breath and walked into the waiting room.

"I am terribly sorry that you've all been waiting. The providers are on call, and there have been several emergency cases throughout the night. Nothing we can do about that. If your procedure is scheduled with Dr. Asamoah, we should be bringing you back within the next twenty minutes, for she is finishing up an appendectomy as we speak. Unfortunately, if your procedure is scheduled with Dr. Junns-Matsu, we will need to reschedule. We can fit you in later this week. He will be predisposed for the rest of today. All other surgeries and diagnostics are running on time."

Junns-Matsu's 6:30 cholecystectomy shook his finger at Ngome. "I wouldn't have scheduled it for today if I'd known that he would be on call. You never mentioned anything about the call schedule when I made the appointment."

"Sir, I apologize that we did not inform you. It is true that his schedule was clear for today. After Dr. Lewicky's accident, we had to ask the others to fill in for at least two weeks. They are stretched quite thin, and I doubt that you would want a drowsy doctor at the operating table." This is his best bit. Put the perspective back into their selfish mindset. Make it about them. Then, and only then, do they shut up.

"Understood. Do you have anything for Friday?"

"We usually do not schedule procedures on Friday, but I'm positive that we are making an exception for this situation. Let me confirm with our scheduling manager."

"Okay."

"In the unlikely event that I find something later this afternoon, I ask that you continue to refrain from eating or drinking."

"Yep."

And so, the first major fire of the day had been put out. Ngome's calm presence and soft voice had won. He headed to his desk and opened his e-mail. He composed a message for Shanti, the scheduler. Before finishing the message, he noticed that her avatar was shadowed black. He navigated the mouse on to the dark rectangle, hovered over it until a brief status report flashed. She will not be in until 7:30. Not wanting to overwhelm her inbox, he took the most reliable form of inter-office correspondence. He scribbled on a magenta Post-it Note and glued it to her monitor. It contained the simple request: "Overflow on Friday?"

Just then, the office manager walked in from the conference room. "Hey, Ngome. Did you just get here?"

"Yeah. I just spoke with the patients."

"Thanks for calming them down." The manager looked at Shanti's cubicle and focused his eyes on the note. "Oh, yeah. We will definitely be fitting people in on Friday. I'll notify Shanti when she gets here. You can update the patients. You have my permission to offer up anything after noon."

"Thanks."

"There's an inpatient wound-vac that we have to do tonight. He's up in the west wing of 3 south. Would you do your magic and get a consent from him? You might want to go soon; he's in that window between dosages of pain meds."

"You got it. What room?"

"Three oh seven," the office manager said. He patted Ngome on the shoulder and added, "The dude is pretty sick, and his labs results haven't come back yet. You might want to glove up and wear your N95. You've been fitted for one, right?"

Ngome lied. "Yep."

He went into the supply room and pulled three pairs of non-latex disposables from a plastic bin. A series of healthcare masks sat in order from smallest to largest on a shelving unit above the room's door frame. The N95s came in three sizes. He tried on a medium. It pinched on his temples and jaw. The large seemed to fit just fine. A little loose perhaps but just fine. After gathering the mask and the gloves, he grabbed a set of consent forms and a clipboard. He double-checked the sign-in log and left the registrar desk. The hallway to the elevator had portraits of doctors of the year. Dr. Lewicky was the recipient of the 4703 award.

At the elevator, he pressed the service button. As he waited for doors to open, a habitual ting echoed in his mind. The door opened. In the elevator, he pulled out his cell, and harmlessly scrolled through a few updates. The coder from the billing department wants to play *Word Sphere*.

The bell for the third floor rang. Stepping out, Ngome was quickly greeted by the lead nurse on the med-surg floor. "Long time no see, compadre."

"Hi, Spierley. I'm here to get the HIPAA release on three oh seven."

"Suit up, Batman. He's under inhalation precautions."

"Very well." He pulled the mask up and above his chin, forming an almost air-tight seal. The gloves snapped on without mush effort. "Can I go, Commissioner Gordon?"

"Gotham awaits." Spierley was pressing his buttons in a way that would insinuate flirting. She harbored a fleeting crush.

Ngome walked down the hallway and past a gang of mobile charting stations. He stopped at three hundred seven and skimmed over the admission information: patient presents with high fever; consistent coughing, accompanied by the production of thick, black mucus; several samples have been obtained by bronchoscopy; patient presents with many festering wounds, all of which are being treated with cefazolin; the physicians are betting on a combination of valley fever and MRSA; his name is Hagar Von Aboud; resides in Las Vegas, Nevada; on a business trip to Ciudad Juarez.

He peeked into the room, and the patient was awake, watching television, and poking at a lime cube of Jell-O. Thankful that he didn't have to wake the patient, Ngome knocked three times and gently opened the door. Following strict inhalation precaution, he squeezed through and promptly shut the door behind him. Hagar Van Aboud gave him a sour look, a signal of either displeasure or deep, unyielding pain.

The chubby registrar kindly told him, "I am Ngome. As a patient here at Las Palmas Medical Center, you have the right to privacy. You have the right to present advance directives, and we are required to honor them. I have come to ask if you would sign these documents, which explain your rights and responsibilities while under our care. Would you mind looking through them?"

Hagar shook his head. He was familiar with the process. Ngome brought the clipboard, neatly arranged, to the bedside and handed the patient a ball-point pen. Suddenly, Hagar was gripped by a fit of coughing. It sounded like dry heaving. He made no effort to cover the orifices of his face, and droplets of snot filled the room, unseen by the naked eye. He convulsed with each release of the lungs. After the spell had passed, he looked exhausted.

Ngome used his sweet tone of voice, "Take as much time as you need."

Hagar shot him an annoyed look. He grabbed the pen and signed each document, without reading a single sentence. It was obvious he would rather be left alone.

"Thank you, sir. We have your insurance information and will bill them accordingly. I hope you enjoy a speedy recovery." Ngome was pleased that the interaction was over so quickly. He figured he had enough time to grab a smoothie from the on-site coffee stand. After considering his payroll deduct balance, he returned to the elevator and pressed the lobby button.

The lobby's gift shop was already hawking Horus Mass trinkets. Lights were strung up in a display that held wreaths and Coca-Cola polar bears. Red and green adorned everything; from the entrance to the information booth. A seven-foot Thunder Oak stood with triumph over mock presents. The branches were lined with fuzzy metallic twine to reflect light and act as icicles. It was a lot of decoration for the first week of November. The Halloween merchandise sat in a clearance bin.

Standing in line at Heimlich Maneuver Roasters, Ngome once again fidgeted with his device. He was deep in his game of *Word Sphere* with the coder from the billing department. Like many times before, he had too many vowels. *Word Sphere* is a game of diphthongs. There was a pinching sensation in his right flank. It was Spierley. She joked, "I just saw you. We've got to stop meeting like this, you hunk of a man!"

"You practically work a second job here at the Roasters. How many mocha luffas do you drink in a day? We might need to call an intervention in the staff lounge."

Spierley giggled. "I'm glad you got three oh seven's signatures. They're calling a code blue for the floor. It's gonna be under quarantine. I thought I'd get a drink before it officially goes into effect."

"Whoa. Well, good thing I got it done. The pre-op nurse would have had my ass otherwise."

The thought of Ngome's ass excited Spierley. She asked him, "When are you gonna find a girl and get hitched? I can't believe that you're still single. You're too young and handsome for that."

Ngome blushed. He gave his order to the morning barista. "One large mango-pear smoothie." He didn't feel comfortable speaking with Spierley about his romantic life. The topic of love had never come up in any of their cursory conversations. He did not know how to receive a compliment on physical beauty. Instead, he changed the subject. "One of these days, I'll have to try the butterscotch blasters."

Spierley caught the bait. "Oh, they're to die for! I get mine with whipped cream." She looked at the flat-screen on the lobby wall. The television showed a montage of scientists working fervently with a tall Samoan man sporadically giving an explanation of some data set. "I see they are still trying to figure out what Gel Lago is made of."

"It would probably be easier to figure out what it's NOT made of," Ngome jested.

The barista called out, "Mango-pear smoothie."

"That's me." He collected his drink and rushed off before Spierley had a chance to offer another compliment.

Ngome felt guilty for taking the pit stop between duties. After yet another elevator ride, he returned to his office on the second floor. He walked back to the registrar desk and hid his beverage at his feet. He had hardly logged into the network when Shanti came in from around the corner.

She looked happy to see him but in a way that padded bad news. "Hi, Ngome. Thanks for filing those authorizations. Um, boss wants us to stay late today. It seems we're getting an emergency add-on around three."

Ngome groaned at the idea. He asked, "What's the procedure, and why can't it wait until tomorrow?"

Under a chuckle, Shanti answered, "Foreign object removal. Inexperienced lovers once again, I'm afraid."

"Get out of here!"

"Seriously. It's a screwdriver. I just got the CT report on the fax. It's a screwdriver pushed in, handle first."

"Lovely," Ngome said.

Chun-Takuro Industries ordered Mediterranean platters for the physicians and support staff. Between visits to the food, Ngome did his best to wash his hands to industry standards. He remembered Dr. Lewicky's advice: pick an old nursery rhyme and sing it in its entirety. Only then would your hands be safe.

It was a foolish suggestion, as song lengths vary. Ngome's was too short. Too short by a long shot. But the buffet-style lunch did not pose the immediate threat. Neither did Hagar Von Aboud. The food was certainly contaminated; Shanti was known to pick her nose, and the doctors were lax about fixing the malfunctioning steam sterilization unit. But the phone was the problem, and the phone was the means of delivery. It got slathered with more germs every time its owner mindlessly swiped its surface.

Upon aiming for a fifth falafel, Ngome heard a shriek from the waiting room. There were only a few patients on the schedule, and most were waiting for loved ones in recovery or currently under the knife. He wondered what could be going on out there. The scream came from the unisex restroom. Having a strong work ethic, Ngome was the first to check on it. The other office staff stood back and tried to divert attention away from the situation.

After knocking on the door, a woman came out to explain the outburst to Ngome. "I had run out of toilet paper. Now, I wasn't being nosy, I swear. I just assumed that there might be another roll below the sink. You know, where most people keep the cotton puffs and the Fabuloso?"

"Yeah. Was there more toilet paper?" He didn't have the slightest idea. A custodial crew cleans the office at night.

"No! There's a fucking dead skunk in there!" She calmed down and lowered her voice. "Sorry. I'm just a little shaken up. Total barf city. Ew, ew, ew. How do you think it got in there?"

He put on a tone of sarcasm. "Are you sure it was a skunk?"

"Of course, it's a skunk!"

"Did it smell like a skunk?"

She stalled. "Would you please go look for yourself? I'm not lying."

"I'm sorry if I implied that. I believe you." He walked past her and stepped into the restroom. The sink cabinet door was still opened. Shadows blurred the lump in the far corner, but as he moved closer, the fluorescent lights pulled it out of the darkness. It was not a skunk. It was a badger. It was dead. It had been dead for a long time. Ngome wondered how someone could have missed it, or why the office did not stink of something rotten.

He left the corpse and updated the woman who found it. He told his coworkers to watch the front while he cleaned it up. *No use in waiting for the cleaning crew, if they missed it for this long.* Once again, he pulled gloves from the medical stock. He put on a simple mask and carried an empty red biohazard bag into the restroom. Closing the door to avoid any curious gaze, he got on his knees. It dawned on him that he didn't bring a utensil to scrape the guts away. The plunger would have to do. He can bring another one in tomorrow. Pushing and pulling with the rubber lip, the cadaver was stiff enough to move in one piece. After the bulk of it was thrown in the bag, a thin residue was leftover. Ngome tied up the bag and rushed it out to the stairwell behind the office. He opened an employee entrance, walked down a set of concrete steps, and headed toward a nearby dumpster.

On his way back, he felt the buzz of his cell on his breastbone. Without any consideration of his current deed, he checked on it. He could always glove up again. He pulled the device from his front pocket and dabbled in its glory. Not one thought about the silica. It could be smudged, cracked, poked, and prodded. It wasn't supposed to bite back. It sucked up the nasty remnants of this vile death and disease. The badger guts were in there with everything else, and the message was unimportant. It was merely his turn on *Word Sphere*.

With the badger disposed of, it was now Ngome's duty to clean up the remnants and make the restroom look presentable. Winded, he looked under the stairwell and located the bleach. He grabbed a pile of clean linens, doused them in the bleach, and scrubbed the floorboard spotless. Then he disinfected every surface with a grit-cake soaked in Fabuloso. He knew that it would serve him well to take this responsibility on. Someone would mention it to management. The waiting room was probably abuzz with his heroic deed.

It was true. The office congratulated him on taking the initiative. They toasted him with morning coffee reheats. The office manager offered a fresh pair of backup scrubs. He put them on and went back to his desk.

Shanti asked him, "What do you think happened? How long do you think it had been in there?"

Ngome answered, "I'm not an expert, but I would think at least a month. That guess is based on the dry climate. What a weird thing to find."

"Yeah, man."

The feta mess in the lounge was grazed upon until late afternoon. The screwdriver was effectively removed from the lover's rectum in the small examination room that doubled for outpatient procedures. The ER was getting busy, and the staff was filling an already busy call schedule. Around 5:00, a Mongolian family sat waiting for an interpreter phone. Once it was found, Ngome explained the consents. The family signed papers for a man who exhibited symptoms of gangrene on his nose. Prior authorizations were due for the next two weeks. It was a stressful day with no clear end in sight. Sick of dolmas and pepperoncinis, Ngome decided to eat dinner at the hospital cafeteria. His hunger was awake every hour, every day. He left Shanti to cover for him.

His mind itched to plug in an entry on *Word Sphere*. The front pocket. Where the badge and wallet also rest. He unlocked his application. He had three high-scoring letters. Finally, he saw it. Wizard! The word is wizard! Another sphere completed. Now the tiles are seven-by-seven-by-seven.

Suddenly, he sneezed and covered the device with a thin film of mist. He had caught three oh seven's disease, but Ngome did not think of such a possibility. He simply wiped the screen and continued playing. Upon doing so, he lacerated his finger on the cracked display.

"Damn," he said to himself. Finding a tissue at the cafeteria entrance, he swabbed the cut and his smartphone, grabbed a tray, and proceeded to find dinner.

Turkey burgers in Styrofoam. Fruit wrapped in cellophane. Pre-packaged snacks and fifteen varieties of soda. A salad bar with heaping piles of hummus and cottage cheese. Ngome scooped antipasto and syrup peaches onto his paper plate. He also grabbed a high-protein energy bar because the wrapper advocated its use during times of stress. Pulling his plate forward at the cashier's line, he fumbled for his badge. Once again, front pocket. With the germ incubator. He would need his badge to finalize his purchase with payroll deduction. Ngome authorized the transaction through his personalized badge account, to finalize on payday, like his morning snacks from the Check-and-Go.

He touched the plastic card to the scanner. The germs were like little soldiers, island-hopping across Polynesia. The soup that had been cooking in Ngome's phone had jumped to the badge, and now the cashier's scanner was contaminated. It would spread to other surfaces before any first signs of a pandemic. Everyone has a front pocket.

NGOME DROVE TO THE ELK'S Lodge after cleaning up and downing a cup of coffee. He was exhausted from a long and weird day, mistaking his symptoms of congestion and achy muscles as proof of hard work. No sickness could keep him down tonight. He was freshly showered and had been anticipating the square-dancing gala for weeks. It was his only night out in a string of lonely ones indoors. Plus, he had a chance at winning. Like the hospital, he was known and liked. He drove up to the old adobe building and walked in, wearing snakeskin boots and a lively brush popper from Hermosillo.

The caller spat instructions into the microphone. The hot hash was particularly feverish, but Ngome kept perfect tempo. He "do-si-doed" and executed every allemande left. The sickness did not temper his love of the craft, and he was cheered by dozens of attendees. He led two pretty women, one in tight Wranglers and one with even tighter curls. The curly-haired partner kept giving him a fleeting glance, as they swept past each other. It was a flirty look, but he was too naive to ascertain this fact. A star formation was attempted but was not complete due to a few stragglers. After the finals, Ngome and the curly-haired woman received second place, conceding to a Honduran couple. He felt a bit dizzy when the awards were given out, so he took a breather. His curly-haired partner sat next to him on the wooden bench, a few feet away from the children playing in the hay.

She asked him, "Hey there, buddy. Are you feeling okay?"

"Yeah. I'm just winded from the competition. Solid legwork up there."

"Thanks. You were a good partner."

"Anytime."

She fidgeted with her fingernails. "My name is Jyotsna." She extended her hand forward as an official introduction.

He shook her hand and responded, "Ngome. It's nice to meet you, formally. We really kicked ass out there, didn't we?"

"Yep. It was fun. We should have won."

"Agreed."

Jyotsna was just as lonely as Ngome. Like him, she had rarely gone out over the last year. She had not felt the touch of another person since last Horus Mass when she hooked up with a high school crush during winter vacation. She looked Ngome up and down. He had already charmed her on a physical level, dancing and performing the ritual of male chivalry. She was going to make a pass. Ngome was in her league and willing to fool around, she was certain of it. Jyotsna motioned to continue their conversation in a dim part of the dance hall. She pulled him past the mess hall and into a corridor, then cornered him. Placing a hand on his shoulder, she leaned in and whispered, "I'm going to kiss you now. Just shake your head if you're not into it." She pecked his cheek and looked up into his eyes. No movement and no words. She was beginning to doubt her judgment. "Are you okay, Ngome?"

"Yep."

"Good." She tiptoed full force into his lips and snuck a tongue in for good measure. She made her intention obvious. She could already feel him swelling below.

They briefly pulled apart. Ngome boldly stated, "This is fucking awesome."

She nodded her head in agreement. "Let's go to my place. It's just a few blocks of a walk.

He excitedly responded, "Hell, I'll drive you there."

Within five minutes, they were at her driveway. They made out in the front seat for a few minutes. Asses were grabbed and hair was accidentally pulled.

Jyotsna didn't even notice that Ngome was slightly wheezing under his hot and excited breath. They hurried out of the car and into her three-bedroom brick house. She flipped the lights on, and a chihuahua yapped from behind a toddler divider, placed near the rear kitchen exit.

"Get out, Tlaloc!" It ran through the doggy door. "So, this is my place."

Ngome was impressed. He would have been mortified if they had chosen his place to bed down. Pulling her close to him, he looked into her eyes and said, "You're beautiful."

They stood for a few minutes embracing. This would be the best part of the night, although neither realized it. Squeezing each other like some long-lost twins separated at birth. If a slow jam had been playing, they would have swayed until dawn. Then, the limbs started to migrate all over the torsos. Hands swept up hamstrings and into armpits. They split the hot hug and dove in for wet kisses.

The two collapsed into a sagging sofa. Jyotsna fumbled with his belt buckle while he pulled on the hooks of her bra. Moans were exchanged. They were down to their underwear when Ngome thought to ask official consent. "Are you okay, Jyotsna?"

"I am. I want this. You don't have to worry. I really like you. Ever since I saw you at the dance club pot luck."

"I've always really liked you, too."

"Do you have a condom?"

Ngome froze. He wasn't planning on getting lucky anytime soon. It's fine. Either they will make a quick run, or she will have one hiding out in some medicine cabinet. "Uh, no. Do you?"

"No."

"Let's go get a pack at the Check-and-Go."

"Well, I'm clean. You could always pull out," she said.

"Um, that would be fine. Are you sure?"

"Are you clean?"

Ngome sat up straight and answered, "Of course I am."

"Then what's to worry about?"

They ravaged each other over and over again until three in the morning.

The attention was needed for both parties involved. Under normal circumstances, it would have been one of those rare occasions when a one-night stand leads to a meaningful and loving relationship. Sadly, they would not get the chance for a second date. Breakfast would be their last interaction. The romp was the best night and the last night for both of them.

THE PANDEMIC SPREAD VERY QUICKLY. From its epicenter in West Texas, it had covered the American continents within one month. By early 4708, it was devastating Africa, Asia, and Europe. The disease killed within forty-eight hours of infection. Some patients survived the suffocating mucus, only to have their organs liquefied. Clinicians dubbed it *pellem melis speculococcus*. The news called it Glass Badger Lung.

It was not as serious as the Black Death in Europe. It had not leveled populations like smallpox in the Americas. It stopped short of the damage done a century earlier during the Spanish Influenza, but the disease was quick and relentless in its attack. The shock value was quite high. Sidewalk prophets held cardboard warnings once again. Eighty million died before a cure or a vaccine was available.

Ngome was a scapegoat. Patient zero. By the time Jyotsna had drowned in her bile, the federal government had implemented quarantine protocols. Experts tracked down the source of the superbug but could only conclude the place of its birth, not the reason. Las Palmas Medical Center became a hub for viral theorists. Hagar Von Aboud had inhaled a soil-based spore into his lungs; an ice age virus that had been broken up by Gel Lago's settlement on the outskirts of Las Vegas. It was a variant of valley fever, as assumed. But it was through Ngome and his vile smartphone that the organism had mutated into something else.

The link to the smartphone had a larger impact on human society than the dead and the discarded. It was seen as a warning of technology's darker side. People had already been harping on the bad effects. Cells were a drain on our social skills, on our posture, and on our mental health. But to be responsible for a deadly outbreak?

The crisis brought an end to the prominence of personal phones. All devices were burned in giant public bonfires. The smartphone was also a scapegoat. We wanted it all, but the crisis humbled us, and we changed. Thus, the idea of handheld gadgets became extinct. The entertainment and communications industries began to favor larger silica screens, mounted on every wall. The eight and a half by eleven inch was soon available, followed by the full room panel. They became shatterproof, and they were installed everywhere. The individual act of media consumption was now a public affair as well. People purchased, companies produced, the cycle spun once again, and the future continued.

4707 was an important year in American history. Michael Jackson had died. Gel Lago was born. The smartphone pandemic ravaged the world's population. The recession raged on, and '07 was its worst year. The long list of problems warranted yet another scapegoat; one deserving of everyone's angst. Barack Obama was serving his second term as President of the United States and fit the bill just fine. People turned to conspiracy theories, far-right politics, and blind nationalism. It was a response to utter fear, and a warning of things yet to come. Thanks, Obama.

X

riving across the wings of Texas is a full day of travel. Westbound from Houston to the New Mexico border takes at least ten hours. It is a long and sprawling trip, done entirely on Interstate 10. In West Texas, there are few sights between the dead armadillos and gas stations. One must ration petrol accordingly. Food, not so much. The average truck stop platter is the size of a toolbox.

I turn the radio on. I am driving in an old PH-150 pickup, one that has been converted for biofuel. It is howling on the arid strip. The dial stops at 93.5 MHz. "You're listening to KRTS, Marfa Public Radio. Welcome to People's Morning. It is Monday, September 26, 4709. These are today's top stories: Muammar Qaddafi continues his retreat into western Libya, amid violence. Tripoli was captured by rebel groups in August with the assistance of NOTA Air Forces. Global markets are lower on EU anxieties. Greece is requesting additional aid from the IMF and the World Bank. Donald Drumpf is campaigning in Michigan. He is to appear in several town halls throughout the week. I am Pufferdi Palmas. This morning belongs to you, to me, and to everyone. It is People's Morning."

I bite into a piece of elk jerky and roll down the window to gauge the air. Fresh and dry. This road trip is a good idea, and I am reveling in the spontaneity of it. I haven't left Denver in over two years. Last year entailed a nationwide travel ban on account of the cataclysms. Otherwise, I would have visited my friends earlier. We certainly need to see each other more often.

Geo's place was so nice, especially that hot tub on the balcony deck, overlooking downtown Houston. It had LED lights. The lights alternated in hue like a rainbow in the evening as we sipped on iced avocado vodkas. I can't believe how well Geo is doing for himself. And that wife of his; she is amazing. I am proud of my old friend.

Quickly and without warning, I feel a moment of aching distance from that house. This morning, we ate breakfast together. When I packed my belongings, I felt a creeping sadness. Leaving the city limits of Houston, I felt it again. Nothing could deter my plans to see Muhammad and Clea in Caliphornia. I have a strict schedule to adhere to, after promising Clea that we would spend Yom Kippur together. But it was incredibly hard to leave Geo and Mish. Saying goodbye to the Simmermanns, for some reason, pulled at my heart. *I wonder why?*

A conspiracy theorist is talking on the program, "I believe that the Aztecs made the calendar to warn of a coming calamity. Remember, their calculations are as good as anything conceived by NASA. Winter solstice, 4710. That's the end, folks. I won't speculate on whether it will be an asteroid or a solar flare. Perhaps we are already living in the apocalypse? That would make sense. The last two years have felt like the end of days."

"I think many people felt the same about Y4.7K. That wasn't the end of humanity," Pufferdi Palmas retorted.

I laugh at the idea of the Sun Stone. Surely, the Aztecs thought of something better to do when they ended work on the calendar. Doomsday follows every generation and manifests in silly ways. But the current madness is simply preposterous, especially the Planet X theories. The thought of it all amuses Esther as I drive past political billboards in the small, dusty town of Balmorhea.

IT WAS IN 4115 THAT Zheng He met with Chimalpopoca the Tlatoani. This interaction launched an era of wisdom and peace never seen in the history of the world. The meeting was delayed by many months as He intended to make many converts along the way. The first throngs of Mesoamerican Muslims followed him inland. As one version of the story goes, the admiral was given God's tongue and spoke Nahuatl clearly and concisely. In truth, it was a porter from Acapulco, who had learned as much Mandarin as she could in the first months of contact. Hecatl, as she was known, helped navigate He's men to Tenochtitlan. Thanks to her and through her, Zheng He could facilitate the love of Allah. She was an instantly saved soul.

Chimalpopoca embraced the teachings of Muhammad with an open heart. The old gods were relabeled as humans who had done great deeds. Idol worship was frowned upon but allowed. Efforts were made to codify Zheng He's Qu'ran. His officers became spiritual leaders, and they learned the pantheon of Mexica mythology in the process. Gods and goddesses from both sides of the Pacific were weaved into new folklore. It was a miracle akin to Akhenaten's conversion in Egypt, back when gods were shared. And Hecatl was central to every fable and every incantation.

Especially so because she was patient zero. The first to die from the plague that Zheng He had delivered. Millions upon millions, but Hecatl was the first. She had conceived a baby girl with one of He's mariners. After giving birth, she quickly lost the will to live. According to the legend, her wake was visited by many mourners. They all returned home and developed fevers and rashes. Within a week the village was dead, but the baby girl survived. She forgot her mother's name and was raised by nomad coyotes. One haunting tale suggests that Zheng He was her biological father, even though he was a eunuch.

Chimalpopoca gave He's group an estate with which to farm. One of He's men, an acupuncturist and healer-in-general, had the foresight to bring a dried bladder full of seeds and roots. It remained intact throughout the journey, and the contents were planted. They sprouted ginger, peony, turmeric, turnips, soybeans, and a dozen other plants native to China. The crops bolstered the health and happiness of Tenochtitlan and its tributaries. The healer shared his knowledge of medicine and discovered the qualities of cilantro and papaya. He learned how the god, Xipe Totec, was responsible for the spreading illness. *Essential Prescriptions from the Golden Cabinet* was translated into Nahuatl. Bamboo groves grew among the chinampas.

Zheng He would become an adviser to the line of Aztec emperors and was declared high Imam of the capital. His first and only request was to abolish blood sacrifice, and it was granted. There would be no sense in asking Islam to be the state religion. That work was being done without the usual channels of power. Zheng He was also instrumental in the Triple Alliance, which pushed Allah's love even further into the vast corners of the continent. Living to be eighty, He held high position until Moctezuma I. His influence expanded far beyond his post. Within a generation or two, there were Hopis and Yaquis building mosques.

The changes in Tenochtitlan brought a spike in creativity and artistic innovation, much of it associated with the unbending will of the human spirit. Minarets were built in the courtyards of the pyramids. Adobe pagodas, built large and stout along the roadway, carried prayer flags and merchant booths. Leaning on a suggestion from one of He's men, a new paper-making process was discovered. The paper would become canvasses and book pages for the Mixtec Renaissance. The seminal classic, *As Yahweh Wept Chocolate* was written in 4127. The temple of the Five Phases was built in Tlacopan. Murals were painted of Quetzalcoatl embracing a Chinese junk with emerald wings. It was a period of welfare for those who survived the plague. It lasted little more than a century and ended with the coming of Europeans.

Spanish caravans began to line the eastern shore. By the early 4200s, the white-skinned invaders pushed into the capital. They balked at what they saw. They named the empire Tiandalusia, which roughly translated to "Kingdoms at Peace Under Heaven." Still sore from fighting the moors at home, the conquistadors were appalled to find evidence of Islamic thought. They decided to strike and take everything. Tenochtitlan only fell when its citizens starved during the Iberian siege. The Spanish were followed by the Dutch, the French, and the English, until the whole continent was colonized and bled dry.

For them, genocide might have been intentional. But the books never paint Europe as an antagonist. The damage was done with the Chinese expedition. The admiral brought death, not Cortes. The germ, not the aggression, was to blame. It was a free pass for the gold diggers, who aimed for pensions of maravedis. History only remembers Zheng He as the guy who got there first.

This is the extent of my knowledge of the Aztecs. It's entertaining to think about these things while driving along the interlaced telephone poles. In any case, it is relevant to my line of work. Some of my tinctures are derived from the Nahuatl translations of the *Golden Cabinet* recipes. Wen jin tang with culantro is my biggest seller.

The Sun Stone expert continues babbling. He is losing my interest. Interstate 10 is darkening at the end of a long day. I flip on my headlights. I pop another piece of jerky into my mouth and push a tape into the stereo.

TUCSON IS HOT FOR ONE week after autumnal equinox. The temperature hovers above ninety degrees, and a late monsoon rain has left the air muggy, trashy, and sweet. I have found a room right off of the interstate in a cookie-cutter business block complete with a Denny's and a Texaco. After finishing my paperwork with the concierge, I look around for directions to the local gem merchants. The desk clerk was of no help. He just pointed to the information kiosk for assistance. The lobby has a fat desktop PC with Internet connection. At this late hour, it is available.

A bottle of hand sanitizer is mounted above the monitor. A placard warns users to clean up before and after use. I sit down and log on. I locate a few places of interest, including one merchant who claims to have human-sized geodes. I check my e-mail and traffic on my homemade website. I log out. After purchasing a slice of lemon curd pie from the vending machine, I grab my card key and leave the lobby.

I am tired after fifteen hours of travel. I lug my suitcases and notebooks upstairs and into a small palace of tacky wallpaper of goldenrod anchors, lifesavers, and dark blue stripes. It is meant to be naval-themed. What weird roleplay for a bustling desert city. I throw my bags into the corner, remove my sneakers, and sit down. It is still quite hot for late at night. Sweat beads have formed on my smooth, African arms.

On the edge of my bed, I nibble at the pie and watch a late-night monologue. They are still making jokes about Bin Laden. The raid and the assassination seem to be the only bright spot on Obama's record, and it makes for subtle humor. I finish my slice and tidy up. Then, I fall asleep, fully clothed and sugared up.

THE SOUND OF CONSTRUCTION WAKES me. Feeling fully rested, I pop up out of bed and begin my daily ritual. Stretches on a carpeted floor that reeks of cigarette smoke. Local and national news while reading up on botanical properties. Three cups of weak, complimentary coffee. Downstairs, the continental breakfast buffet offers apples, bananas, and graham crackers. I laugh at the sparse menu, but I am happy to have avoided the grease bombs of Denny's.

As I check out of the room, the morning clerk reminds me to stay cool. The computer is swarming with customers, forming a long line of those waiting to use it. They hold paper maps lengthwise and sideways, studying the highway system. Wives and husbands argue about routes. Dashboard GPS units are still too expensive for the common traveler. For this reason, most people are stuck using these kiosks. Like the alcohol-based hand rub, it is a condition of the pandemic.

Two miles down Interstate 10, I find my gem bazaar. While the road trip is strictly meant as a way to reconnect with old friends, the gem industry of Tucson has always been an item of personal interest. I am excited to buy gifts for my friends and for myself. Minerals and crystals make for great gifts.

The repository is busy with activity. Couples holding hands look among the aisles for matching stones to set into engagement rings. Turquoise vendors epoxy their wares into gaudy silver trinkets. A bolo tie shop sells pewter sculptures of Arizona in celebration of the upcoming centennial. I am at peace in this market of stones. The colors and textures remind me of Earth's magnificence. After an hour of window-shopping, my eye is drawn to a collection of fire agate.

Seeing the stones, I immediately think of Mishelle. One of them has been tumbled into a smooth and round teardrop. Layers of brown and red look like waves washing up on a Martian shore. The beauty of the stone keeps me in a trance for over a minute. It reminds me of feelings recently felt, back in Houston, sitting in the neon hot tub. Without questioning my motive, I purchase the agate egg. I want to send it to the Simmermanns, as a nod to our wonderful time together.

After buying a few more gems, I leave the shop with a smile of contentedness. I only have one more chore before leaving for LA, and it should be quick. Looking at some scribbled directions, I plot a course for several practitioners along the interstate. I will drive to each one and hawk my display of tinctures. My menstruation formulas are particularly popular. The first acupuncturist, who has been placing online orders, is happy to meet me in person. His driveway is littered with beer cans.

He looks at the portable medicine cabinet and marvels at new products, not yet available through the website. After mumbling to himself, he asks, "How much for the entire inventory? I have several patients who are hooked on your magic."

I smile with pride. "I was planning on visiting a few other potential customers. Seeing as you're a frequent and special customer, I would be willing to part with everything but the chamomile cocktail. I am visiting LA and San Francisco, and I figure there is a huge market for insomnia."

"Fair enough. How much do you want?"

"Nineteen hundred. You could make payments, if you'd like. I know you're good for it."

"Nonsense. I'll go write up a check right now."

"Thanks."

He pays me and sends me off with a copy of a local pain management brochure. I will deposit the check the next time I find a branch. After getting a bean burrito, I drive around asking a series of restaurants for used fryer oil. A pub gives me seven gallons, free of charge. I enjoy a spliff and two chapters of my novel as the oil sits in a large, homemade reservoir, sifting out burnt bits and other impurities. Within an hour, it is refined for combustion. I jump into my truck and continue west, for Phoenix and eventually Los Angeles. The trip will last about eight hours.

"I wish you weren't leaving town tomorrow."

"Me too," Muhammad replies sweetly.

"Then don't go, dummy."

I arrived the night before. Muhammad introduced Justin, and they joked about the awkwardness of working at Good Sam together. I gifted one of the Tucson gems; a hunk of topaz, splitting to create two columns and representing love's bond. It sits in a velvet-lined box. I pretended to offer it as dowry to Justin for taking my pain-in-the-ass friend.

We spent the day walking through the old neighborhood. We found the concrete slab with the *Mama Zamora* graffiti. We remembered the punk houses. We ran into Hubert Ortegon's mom at an Italian soda stand and made references to Clea's old obsession with her son.

After the long walk, we went out for dinner. The steak house is called Bovinity. It has a surf-and-turf menu for the dining room and a barbecue menu for the bar. Peanut shells snap under the feet of customers who are encouraged to discard the casings like uncouth hillbillies.

Muhammad apologizes, "I know. It's just bad timing. If I'd known you were going to visit, I would have rescheduled. This is really important to us. We've been wanting to see all of the excitement at Zuccotti Park. You could always come with us."

"Yeah. The road trip was pretty short notice. Sorry about that. I promised to spend Yom Kippur with Clea. Otherwise, I would tag along."

"Too bad."

"Seems like a giant camping trip to me." I am pushing his buttons in the playful way that good friends do.

"No, it's more than that. Those people are standing up to the corporations. It's time someone spoke up."

I am not fully convinced. "Yeah, but what are they gonna do about it? It's mostly publicity stunts if you ask me. Protest chants and stoner interviews won't change a thing. Money talks and with a larger vocabulary than those hippies."

"You're such a jerk! You almost sound like one of them!"

"What do you mean?"

Muhammad leans back, "Like some hedge-fund manipulator, or a banker. You know, like Geo!"

"Geo's not a banker, he's a business owner."

"That's not what I meant."

"So, you mean straight?"

Muhammad smiles and throws his napkin at me. "Fuck off!" We laugh and take sips of pilsner spritzers. Muhammad bites into an asparagus, wipes his mouth, and continues, "Occupy is gonna be something. I am certain of it. People are fed up."

"Why can't you be like everyone else and blame Obama?"

"All right." He uses his best miser voice. "Thanks, Obama."

I chuckle through a mouthful of beet salad. This is nice. The feeling of being with friends again. But there is something missing. I can't describe it, but a void sits in my heart. The fire agate. A brief vision of its molten surface comes to me, followed by Mishelle's face. I shake it all off before Muhammad notices anything. I take a breath, dig my elbows into the table, and gossip, "While we're on the subject, have you met Geo's wife?"

"I haven't seen Geo since *South by Southwest* '03. He didn't tell me anything about her until she was halfway through her pregnancy. What's her name again? Was it Mischa?"

"Mishelle. Mish for short." The words roll off of my tongue like a hydrogen zeppelin, flying through a cotton-candy sunset.

"That's right. Mishelle. Do they seem happy together? I never pegged Geo for the type to settle down. How old is his daughter now?"

"Two. Millicent. Millie for short. How come you never remember these things, you oaf?"

"I guess I'm just like all the other dudes," Muhammad jests.

He asks for another round of rosemary biscuits. "So, are they?"

"Are they what?"

"Happy. You know, Geo and Mishelle."

To gauge their happiness is a difficult thing. I saw nothing but smiles for the entirety of the Houston visit. But were they truly happy? It hadn't occurred that they might be faking it. Muhammad's comments are confusing. I entertain the thought of marriage to Geo in my mind. It is not pleasant. The consideration makes me worry for Mish. For some reason, Mish's happiness is the most important thing in the universe, at least for the fleeting moment.

Muhammad interrupts the vision. "Are you alright?"

"Uh, yeah. They are very happy. A perfect little family, those Simmer-manns."

"Well, I'm happy for them."

"Me, too." I change the subject. "I suppose we ought to get together more often. Us and Geo and Clea."

"I would like that. I'm usually too broke to fly out anywhere."

"You know that I would spot you money anytime you need."

"I know, Esther. It is appreciated but not needed. Catch me again after my trip to New York."

We break from our conversation for a few minutes to finish our courses. We had each ordered a heavy slab of rib eye, two side entrees, and a cup of au jus. The dining room plays the schmaltzy trumpets of a classic Bert Kaempfert album. Candlelight creates jittery shadows on every table. Adults roar with laughter and children drink malt shakes. Horse races play in the adjacent bar, where single men eat alone and drink until closing time.

I look up from my food and into Muhammad's brown eyes. "I am really excited to see Clea."

"Yeah. I miss her all the time. In fact, I'm a little jealous that you're gonna hang out. I wish I could be there."

"I'll give her your love, Mo."

"Thanks, Esther."

THE DRIVE TO SAN FRANCISCO was dotted with signs, saying "Congress Gave Us Dust Bowl" and "Remember the Simpson Riots," Muhammad and Justin left early for their plane to Occupy. Before leaving LA, I took a stroll. I walked among the buildings of my past, rebuilt long ago into flashier things. I found an old Nixon Babies cassette at a second-hand market. Growlf, my band back in Denver, covers Nixon Babies' "A Thousand Dead Lawyers" on occasion. It is the first track on the B-side of the tape. It plays as my truck pulls into Berkeley's city limits.

In the late afternoon, I arrive at Carlton Street. After parking in a shady spot, I grab a half-eaten bag of white chocolate wafers and tuck my luggage into my armpit. My door swings open, and dust follows me onto the sidewalk. This is my third visit to Clea's house. It is Clea's prized possession, and the thing she always talks about. I am happy to be here and make note of recent improvements.

There is an addition to the garage. Fresh plywood and tarp jut from the side of it, and the project looks nearly complete. Giant sunflowers and lavender line the walkway to the porch, which holds a tiered succulent garden and a picnic table. On the other side of the porch, there is a plastic turtle sandbox. As if prompted by the image, I can hear Horus. He is singing a toddler's rhyme:

> *"Omen of man,*
> *burning hex,*
> *string the wicker idols*
> *to an X!"*

The doorbell is a MIDI composition of "Night on Bald Mountain"—another solid improvement to the homestead. The jingle ends, and I can hear mother and son. Mother is wrapping up a phone call on the landline. Horus is asking if it is Daddy who has rung the bell. Clea hangs up and answers the door.

"Hey, friend."

Clea beams. "Oh my god! You're here! Honey, Aunt Esther is here! Get in here."

We hug in the doorway, cradling each other and humming like children eating cookies. I softly whisper into her ear, "It's so good to see you, babe."

"You too." Clea looks up and herds me into the living room.

Her boy comes in from the kitchen wearing an orange shirt and acting shy. "Hi, Aunt Esther."

"Horus! Come here and give me some hissy kisses, sugar snake!"

He loosens up and rushes into my arms. I am covered in slobbery kisses. I point at the wafers, and he shrieks with excitement.

"Ask Mom first."

"Mom, can I have a wafer?"

"Of course, honey. As long as she has extra for Mom."

I pull a single cream-colored candy and hand it to Horus. He takes it, thanks me, and runs off to play with his military action figures.

Clea asks, "So, how were the boys?"

"They are all doing well." I pull a leather ottoman from the furniture, sit down, and continue, "Geo is making good money. You should see his place. Mo is still seeing Justin."

"And how about you? How's the clinic?"

"The clinic is busy, but I'm no longer working full-time. I've been concentrating on medicinals. That shit is exploding. I've got customers in seven states."

"Awesome. Good for you, babe."

"Thanks. I see that you've got an addition being built on the garage. What's the plan?"

"Oh, that's our home theater. I've also been doing a lot of research in there. Do you want to see it?"

Giving her a warm look, I answer, "Of course I would."

"Okay. Let's put the wafers in the fridge, so they don't melt."

"Good idea."

Clea grabs the bag and puts it in the butter box. She gets her glass of water and leads me through the garage's indoor entrance. The garage is perfectly kept with cleaning supplies stacked neatly to the side of a washer-dryer combo. The concrete floor is recently repaved and holds no cracks. At the far wall, an entrance is covered by a thick curtain. We walk through it and into a room. In the room, there is a bench holding a half-dozen padded seats. It must have been bought at an auction for an old opera house. A popcorn machine sits in one corner, unused, and in pristine condition. The walls hold giant silica screens.

I ask, "Are those what I think they are?"

"Yep. Full-wall panels. Three walls' worth. Horus and I can watch films in panorama or widescreen on the middle unit. Wireless compatible. Surround sound with dual subwoofers. Seven hundred thirty channels with backup DVR database. Internet connection for work and whatnot."

"Wow. That's fucking rad. I haven't used a screen since the pandemic. They're not touchscreen, right?"

Clea scoffs at the suggestion. "Good God, no. That's still illegal. As it should be."

"I gotta say, this is pretty impressive. How do you find the time?"

"Unlike most of my house projects, I hired a contractor on this one. I'm no good with audio-video."

"Me neither."

"It's one of many projects I've got brewing. This house means the world to me, and I don't think I'll ever be done renovating the thing. It's a lifelong job, and I'll never be done. At least not until I get that nod from *Better Homes and Gardens*."

"I'd vote for you."

Clea takes a deep drink from her water. She looks at the room with pride and satisfaction. "Thanks, Esther."

"So, what are we gonna watch first?"

THE SUN WAS ALMOST GONE when we finally sat down for dinner at the picnic table on the front porch. Clea made Horus's favorite tuna patties. One can of tuna, one egg, and some cornflakes mixed in. Fried in olive oil. Sprinkled with fresh dill and dipped in ketchup. I am amused with the recipe, and satisfied with the results.

I would have eaten cardboard, really. Food is of corollary importance right now. The only important thing is being here, in the company of a good friend. In a reprimanding tone, I mention, "Mo sends his love. He's upset that you never come to see him."

"Well, that's not fair. He could always come here."

"Sure. But it's hard to make ends meet as a nurse. He's broke all the time. This trip to New York is the first vacation he's taken in nearly three years."

"I guess I could step out of my comfort zone," Clea admits.

Horus adds, "Statue of Liberty and Veces Plaza."

"Very good, honey!"

Opening my eyes wide, I exclaim, "Wow, Horus. Are you a world traveler?"

He mumbles through the fish cake, "Yesh."

I turn to Clea and ask, "Why are you so opposed to Los Angeles? If I remember correctly, you haven't been there since high school."

"I don't want to talk about it around Horus." She is serious in tone and in posture.

"Fair enough, but we've all got demons, Clea." As if keen on my cue, Horus pardons himself for the restroom. He goes inside, singing along the way. I continue, "Well, now you've got no excuse."

Clea squirms, "Ugh, You're impossible."

"Yeah, I know. So, what's up with LA?"

"It should be obvious. When I think about the neighborhood, I think about my dad. When I think about the highways, I think about my mom. And it's not just my family. It's the riots too."

"A lot of people hate the city for that very reason. Navigating the trauma of the riots."

"I guess. You know, I did visit Mo once. I had just turned twenty-two. He was still single. All he talked about were the riots. Everywhere we went, he reminded me of the gruesome details of it all, like some history teacher. That was back when you had to have a black friend to walk the streets. He avoided taking me to certain parts of town. I don't mean to sound insensitive, but I can't handle the mood of the city. Everything there reminds me of the riots."

"I don't think you'd feel that way today. It's changed. It's a really great city. You shouldn't let that all that crazy shit define your hometown. I don't."

Clea sighs. "Yeah. But my therapist has told me to avoid triggers of past memories. So, next time you see Muhammad, tell him I'll pay for his ticket here."

"I will."

The phone rings. Clea excuses herself, "That must be the babysitter. Let's find out what our curfew is." She goes inside, zigzags around littered toys and books, and answers, "Hello?"

"Is this Miss SZ?" I can hear the receiver earpiece buzzing through the screen window.

"Hi, Kiki. Are you available to watch Horus tonight?"

"You bet! It's not a school night, so I can work late if you need." Kiki has been babysitting Horus for over a year.

Clea is grateful. "And we're good with ten an hour?"

"Sure thing."

"Okay. Head on over whenever you're free. I'll have sodas in the fridge, and there's those pretzels that you like in the cupboard. You can use the new home theater, if you want."

"That sounds awesome, Miss SZ! See you in a few."

Clea hangs up and locates a refrigerator magnet in the shape of a taxicab. She dials the number and requests a taxi for 9:00. After the reservation is complete, she returns to the picnic table. Horus follows right behind her. The child sits next to me and demands a game of ro-sham-bo.

Horus wins twice with scissors and returns to his seat for another round of green beans. I motion Clea to take a seat on my lap. She sits on my faded blue jeans, and we embrace. My arms envelope her like a seat belt, and I squeeze hard. We are like sisters. We will be like sisters until death.

I release my grip and pivot to the side. "How late can I stay out, Daddy?"

"As late as we want, babe."

"All right! Let's get dolled up."

Clea laughs. "I've got to get things ready for Kiki. I'd also like to start a load of laundry." She is creating a checklist in her mind, wondering what might be put off until morning. "Anyone interested in a fudge pop?"

Horus and I look at each other playfully. He squeals, "Yes! Yes, Mommy! Can Aunt Esther have one?"

"You bet your tuchus she can."

The boy looks confused. "What's a tuchus, Mommy?"

The sweet question makes us laugh. We are amused at the prospect of giving the toddler a crash course in Yiddish. I answer the query, "Well, tuchus means 'butt,' Horus."

"Tuchus means 'butt'?" His eyes widen as the words come out, like Eve biting into the fruit.

WE HAD BEEN RIDING IN the taxi for nearly thirty minutes. Clea leans in and asks, "Are we almost there?"

"It's just down this street and around the corner."

"Okay."

"What are Nefe and Yoshi up to?"

She shrugs. "Nefe is in Redding. She was in an industrial accident, at some paper mill. They say she's got lung damage. In any case, she's getting some settlement money. She recently bought a house. Yoshi . . . I haven't heard from him in three years."

I am utterly shocked. At this point in her life, Clea's brother is probably the only man that she trusts. "I'm so sorry. You were so close."

Clea shudders. "Yeah."

The taxi pulls up to the entrance of Lycanthrope Saloon. Red mist is thinly spread across the windshield. The driver asks for twenty-three dollars and fifty cents. Clea gives thirty with permission to keep the change. As soon as we leave the car, we are thrilled to feel the drizzle. Both Denver and San Francisco had seen little rain throughout the last summer. We coo and complement each other, walking down a flagstone path marked with the occasional sleepy Mexican paver. Lycanthrope Saloon is a hole in the wall. That was the intention. No need to involve some party scene when you're merely trying to catch up. It is the first of eight nights that Clea and I will spend together.

Clea picks a set of stools at the dead end of the bar. We order a drink special called Google Juice. It is rum, lemon Schnapp's, pineapple juice, and hatch chilis from Albuquerque. The bartender mixes the concoction and pours it into plastic tiki tumblers. We clink them in honor of our bond and sip vigorously.

Clea asks, "How is your love life?"

"Non-existent. I never made it a priority before. I don't now."

"Whoa."

I smile and chide her, "Seriously? You think I'm that cold-hearted? No, honey. I just haven't found the right person. I'll know it when I do."

"You know I didn't mean to—"

"I'm just kidding, Clea! Relax. If you'd like to know, I've been hooking up with my bassist, here and there."

Clea giggles. "Okay. You're still playing with Growlf?"

"Yep." How about you? Are you seeing anyone?"

"Uh, nope. I'm over it all."

"Yeah, I'm sure." I stir my puke-colored cocktail and sip through a disposable straw. "What about that teacher? He seemed like a real nice guy."

"Ishmael? No, he was a creep. He put a camera in my bathroom."

"What?" I can feel anger rising within me.

Clea snorts. "Oh, man. That's fucking classic. No, he's a saint. Ishmael moved to Missoula last year. We tried the long-distance thing, but we both ended up seeing other people. No biggie."

"You're a twat, Clea."

"I love you, Esther."

"I love you, too."

Suddenly, Clea retreats in her mannerisms. It almost looks like she is trying to invert her physical presence. She begins, "Geo visited me before the travel restrictions were in place. That was kind of weird."

"How so?"

"Well, he had been planning to visit for a while. He said that there was a Check-and-Go in Durango that he occasionally drove to, to manage the branch and whatnot. Right before the pandemic, he reached out again. He came out for a few days. It was nice catching up with him. But the night before he left, he tried to kiss me."

"And what happened?" I am curious and annoyed.

"I told him that I didn't want him. He stopped and apologized. The rest of the night was awkward. The next morning, he acted like nothing happened. I hadn't noticed until after he left, but he had left a note. It asked me not to tell Mish. Please don't say anything to Mish, Esther. Geo's just the slut we've always known. I don't think it should end his marriage. You won't tell Mish?"

After hesitating, I reply, "Of course not."

"Good. I would be in so much trouble if she found out. He would probably lose half of his fortune."

"Don't worry, Clea. I won't say a thing."

"Thanks, babe."

I am tired of gossip. "Should we put something on the jukebox? I've got a shitload of singles on me."

"Chippendale party again?"

"Ew, gross. What do you want to hear?"

Clea mulls it over. Finally, she makes her suggestion. "Loper and Empanada, *Masks and Games.* And anything by Chris Isaak."

"Got it."

I grab my drink and a fistful of dollar bills from my handbag. Walking past a billiards table, I read the instructions on the jukebox. Three songs for a buck. I set the Google Juice on a table and look through selections. Lots of classic swing and a few newer rockabilly albums. Chris Isaak has a few tracks from a singer-songwriter compilation. I flatten a bill on the corner of the machine. It says, "In Allah We Trust" in a bulky, demanding font. Before putting it in, I notice the cover of a mustached crooner holding a rose. It is Loper and Empanada. I have never heard Clea's main suggestion. I deposit the dollar, enter the song, and use my other credits on the Isaak selections.

Steel drums, soft and like a lullaby, start filling the bar. It is followed by a steady drum beat, indicative of a slow burning love song. A heavily-distorted guitar comes diving into the mix, and then, the angel falsetto of a broken heart. It is articulate and haunting. The singer begins:

> *"The fool can dream away the hours*
> *and never seek the arms of love*
> *The wisest men pretend to flirt*
> *The fool lies dead in the dirt*
> *The mask we wear does not fit right*

The plant we watered wilts
and never forms the words to speak
The fool can dream away the hours
We are the clock by which he reads
The game is played another day
From now until the end of time."

I listen, and inside I weep. I do not pretend to understand the lyrics. Nonetheless, they speak to me. Mishelle Simmermann is on my mind. The song is telling me something.

At this moment, I wish Geo a million mistresses, as long as they aren't Mish. I want Geo to disappear, regardless of the memories and regardless of the friendship. I know what I want, and it is Mish. I have been lying to myself, pretending to be happy for the nuclear family back in Houston.

I pull the fire agate from my pocket. Why have I been lugging it around like some talisman? It is beginning to make sense. The agate is for Mishelle. It will be an innocent gift and a subtle nudge in my direction. I want to keep my name on Mishelle's mind. Certainly, my subconscious had guided my eye back at the Tucson gem market. Sending Mishelle the fire agate will be a great first step in maintaining correspondence. Geo won't suspect a thing.

I whisper to myself, "Mish will be mine."

t first, I was happy to hear that Horus was planning on staying home after graduating high school. The economy was in the early stages of tanking. Kids his age weren't finding reliable work or affordable housing. Moving inland wasn't really an option, either. For most Omega Gen, there is no rent control, and twenty-somethings huddle, a dozen at a time, in tiny studios.

The currency fluctuations have made it impossible to finance mortgages ever since 4719. Keeping my own home has become a struggle. The Bay is the home of the super-wealthy, but there are the few of us who claw and tear to hold on. Some of us treat them as assets. Some of us treat them as homes. All of us will be gone soon. We are in our death throes. The elite have won it all, yet again. This is life in the Third and Fourth Terms. *Yahweh help us.*

My house has a listed value of ninety million, which is modest compared to other Bay neighborhoods. The additions have reclassified my property as custom-built. A power grid backed by solar panels keeps my utility payments low. My pre-arranged mortgage is one of the cheapest items on my budget. Unfortunately, I spend over half of my earnings on property taxes. In any case, it is worth it.

The house is my greatest pride and joy. Last year, I finally finished the octagon planetarium. Last weekend, I retiled the base of my giant, porcelain bathtub. The sunroom has parallel rows of ocotillos and lemon trees that lead to a sauna. The den has a full encyclopedia and a hundred books on American history. On the back deck, there is a canopy for shade, covering an endless waterfall and an energy-cleansing altar. The altar is equipped with sage and candles to burn. The backyard is my favorite part. It has a cobblestone path, which is flanked by sodded mounds covered in perennials and tulips. Near the fence, there is a furnished patio and a fire pit.

And now Horus pisses in the tulips. Now the house is full of pizza boxes and laundry. Horus has sponged for nearly two years, of which he has worked hardly three weeks. Lately, he has been bringing girlfriends over. I guess I am buying groceries for them as well. There is also the credit card. A three-week vacation in the Dutch Antilles, and he returned with fifteen grand in debt. I am still helping him pay that one off.

Did I spoil him through the years? Is this some expectation I have set? My neighbors and coworkers assure me everything is normal and that it happens to them as well. The whole situation makes me fume. I spent this entire morning cleaning up after him.

But now my Sunday can begin. I open the windows and relish in the warm air of July. Cradling a cup of coffee, I stretch across the living room couch, turn on my wall unit, and open an article on environmental racism. There is a class-action lawsuit against several industrial companies. Apparently, they've been dumping by-product into Los Angeles River. I would rather tune out. I should just throw on a slutty rom-com or a dance competition. I should finally get a bit of rest. But it is incumbent upon me to learn about these cases, as our firm may be facilitating payments to victims. I am straining to understand all of the implications.

Suddenly, I hear Horus's console power on. He likes to play games with the volume full blast. I grit my teeth, listening to the orchestral swell of his game. Most days he plays for six hours or more. The soundtracks can get overly repetitive. Horus frequently connects with his friends in the garage theater, where we used to play games of the late-Nintendo era, many years ago. The three walls have been modified to four, with a ceiling screen and shatter-proof floor units. The silica cube can simulate any environment.

Horus's favorite multiplayer game is *Macabre Safari*. It features a gaunt and skinny Englishman, wearing colonial-style khaki shorts that expose his engorged patellae. He looks like Ichabod Crane fighting in the Boer Wars. The Brit assists the players who are various creatures of the savanna in a murder mystery. I remember seeing the commercials years ago. They ended with a silly announcer, screaming:

"It's a big bucket of who-dun-it!"

Horus doesn't understand how serious it's gotten. Hyperinflation is a word that does not exist in his vocabulary. He eats and eats. An apple costs twenty bucks. A pizza delivery is about three hundred. *How am I going to survive with this insatiable man-baby leeching on my retirement account?* I shouldn't think about these things. I'm starting to shake. I need a Xanax.

I walk to the bathroom to find my prescription. The hallway is decorated with hanging mementos; framed photos, curios, and the occasional piece of art. My brow furrows as I catch a glimpse of a family photo with Asnee. It was put up upon Horus's request.

Next to Asnee hangs a tender portrait of Yoshi. It is from our high school years. He and Nefe are posing for the yearbook, as members of the choral club. Back in April, I heard the news of Yoshi's overdose. He had been scraping Fentanyl gel from his pain management patch, and smoking it in punctured tin cans. I hadn't seen him in fifteen years. Now, he is gone forever, and I wish I had made more of an attempt to find him and help him. I was too busy raising a child on my own. Horus didn't even get to meet his uncle.

I look at a picture of the gang. It is from New Year's. Geo is holding two thumbs up, and wearing that crazy adobe polo. Muhammad and Esther are engaged in a tango. It makes me nervous, the thought of seeing them in February. But I always feel this anxiety. Being around Geo reminds me of the secrets. He reminds me of the vault.

I wonder how he and Mishelle are doing. My Divorce Pool bet was a bit of a jab at him and our past. We had argued for an hour in that Phoenix diner. He was defensive about the strength of his marriage and insisted that the game could only include the famous, the wealthy, and the powerful. I shot his argument right back at him. The success of his Check-and Go franchise, and the various trials for misconduct, had made him a well-known name. He had fostered a friendly image of the gas stations by starring in advertisements and promotional materials. And his fame did not end with the downfall of his empire. His lax sentence drew the ire of an entire nation. The late-night shows still use him as a punchline, when writing jokes about corruption and greed. By definition, Geo is a celebrity.

So, he agreed to let me list the Simmermanns as my primary pick. But he insisted on setting the odds. He was gracious with them. He said that the probability of divorce was so low; it was almost non-existent. He set the odds at one-in-one hundred. Seeing as I had put down five hundred, the base payout would be fifty thousand dollars. And that's without the inflation adjustment, which I am guessing is close to two thousand percent. If the Simmermanns file for divorce, by the rules of the game, I am looking at a million. Geo must have great faith in Mishelle to agree to such wild odds.

It doesn't make sense. They are both being unfaithful. They are both committing adultery. Esther and Mish have been continuing their affair. Geo and I still keep our encounter a secret. I wonder if everything, friendships and marriages alike, would fall apart if the truth came out. I don't imagine any relationship could weather such stress.

While looking for my orange bottle of pills in the bathroom, I am reminded of sex with Geo. It is unpleasant. He has been on my mind. Our secret has been on my mind. I need to stop. I can't remember the last time I felt so much shame about it. Back when it first happened.

The first year or two afterwards was hell, hiding it from Esther. Hiding it from the gang. Hiding it from Mish. I was always reminded of my mistake. There were even times in which I questioned my own motives. For a while, I thought I was in love with Geo. I had mistaken my symptoms as some form of being lovesick. I even confessed these thoughts to Geo. He scoffed and quickly convinced me otherwise.

I felt so embarrassed about opening up. He made me so angry and confused. Our one-night-stand has been a real stain on our shared past. It is a struggle maintaining our friendship. *Does it all bother him, too? Why do I give a flying fuck?* I suppose this is why so many people avoid high school reunions. Finally, I find my prescription. I pour a pill into my palm and swallow it dry.

I need to write all of this down in my journal. Horus, Geo, my obsession with the house; I need to let it all out on paper. My journal always helps me return to a safe state of mind. It is the inanimate object that I turn to whenever I can't find access to my therapist. I leave the bathroom and walk toward the master bedroom, where I keep my log of secrets.

I enter the bedroom, open my nightstand drawer, and pull out the thick, leather-bound diary. Holding it, I am already beginning to feel a sense of relief. The journal is such a cathartic process. It helps me to be mindful of my thoughts and mindful of my actions. With the topic of Geo still banging in my temples, I curiously turn the pages back to the entries of years gone by. I am curious as to how I dealt with the guilt, back when we first slept together. I stop on a page inked with a purple pen. The entry reads:

November 4, 4707.

I haven't been keeping this journal as frequently as I should. Dr. Nguyen recommends I make daily entries. I like her. She is better than the last one. I feel better these days. I deal well with the daily challenges, and find joy in the simple things. But not today.

Last night I made a mistake that I pray will have no consequences. My good friend Geo made another move on me. It happened in Los Angeles three or four times, as we grew up. I just shook it off as friendly play, and even succumbed to his goofy charm, once after a Sentinels game, behind a porta-Djinni. But that was before he was married. I want to believe that Geo genuinely wanted to shoot the shit, get stoned, and play video games. I want to believe it was a visit between friends. I hope he did not come here with the intention of creating this tryst.

And so, after rapping about Gel Lago, he pulled the same old stunt. At first, I was pissed. But then I gave into the temptation of possibly getting laid. It's been a long time. And I've been so good, all things considered. I even pushed off that hunky meditation guide.

It started as kissing and stayed kissing for what seemed like hours. I think that we were scared to proceed. It was kind of stressful, wanting to stop while also wanting to push the idea further and further into existence. Someone grabbed an ass cheek, and it escalated quickly. I was allowing my old friend to commit adultery on his wife. And it was fun. That's the part I hate the most. It was almost as if I was basking in the glow of a broken norm, another notch on the belt of my freaky life. I got off on fucking a married guy. Maybe that's the only reason I did it. In any case, I feel gross. Why should I care? Well, I had hardened myself to men. Now I have to start over. Of all the irresistible morsels, with six-pack abs and spry dance moves, why Geo?

And now I have to hide it. I have to keep it to myself. What ended up as a tender exchange must go into the vault. I am sure he loves Mish, but now I've got reason to question that assumption. Perhaps, I've never really known him. Perhaps, he's never really known me. In any case, I sure as hell can't mention this to Mishelle. It would devastate her. I wonder if I'd feel the same if Geo hadn't left the letter. It was leaning on my paisley vase when I woke this morning. It isn't long. It reads:

"What a fun time. I really enjoyed my visit, and it is great to see you and Horus thriving. Asnee was an asshole, and I'm glad you've gotten rid of him. Last night was special. Just so you know, I value our friendship more than any quick-naked romp. I can't wait to see you again sometime soon. I hope it's not too much to ask that you keep this all from Mish. Love ya."

I can't read anymore. The vault feels like it's opening up. It creaks, like the door hinge of a horror film. It opens wider. There is a din inside, increasing in pitch. Behind the rusted and padlocked entryway shines a sick light. Shadows race across the back wall. They are my father and my mother. They are my brother. They are my boyfriends. They are Geo.

And then it hits me—two birds with one stone. Release the weight with confession, help yourself out in the process. You would be doing Esther a favor as well. Another idea is forming. I am beginning to realize that of my many demons, Mr. Simmermann is the only cash cow among them.

I leave the bedroom with a mission in mind: It is time to be the one with power. It is time to be the one who influences the direction of my life. One million will pay off Horus's credit card, the balance on my mortgage, and at least three years' worth of property taxes. I walk back down the hallway of mementos, past the living room, and into the kitchen, where my vintage rotary phone is hooked to my landline. A list of important numbers is pinned onto my bulletin board on the wall. I locate the Simmermann's number and dial it hastily. After two ring tones, a female voice answers. My heart sinks.

Mishelle, in her broad and strong voice, introduces herself, "Hello, this is Mish."

"Hi, Mish. This is Clea. Can we talk?"

XII

r. Bukharov positions the colonoscope above a large polyp and directs me, "Open."

I open the plunger with my right hand, and the nickel-plated snare slowly expands into the shape of a noose. "Open."

"Very good. Now close."

"Close." Pushing the plunger back, the noose closes and rests at the base of the polyp. Dr. Bukharov is very particular about his snared polyps. He likes the base cut slowly. The base of this polyp could contain a blood vessel, so it's important to cauterize carefully. You don't want a bleed, and you don't want to create too much charcoal. I wait for the doctor to give the cue.

"Cut." He presses the pedal that supplies electrical current.

"Cutting, cutting, cutting, through." The polyp bounces to the side of the camera's view, and a wisp of smoke flashes across our monitor. The base has a clean cut. I quickly remove the coiled snare and put it aside. I attach a trap to a suction tube connected to our industrial wall vacuum. Dr. Bukharov presses his suction, and the polyp is sucked into the channel of the colonoscope. We can hear a straining wind as the polyp travels through five feet of scope. It is the sound of a vacuum being blocked. Finally, the polyp is pulled into the trap. I reconnect the suction tubing and empty the trap's contents into a jar of formaldehyde.

Dr. Bukharov is impressed. I am the only endoscopy nurse at Good Samaritan that he trusts. We have fixed many bleeds together. He hates working with Batie, the on-call technician. Batie is clumsy. He once sprayed Bukharov with bile during an air flush.

Bukharov praises me, "Well done, Mo."

"Thanks, Doc. Don't make me blush."

"I'll try not to. Hey, I saw Justin working in ICU the other day. Isn't he starting a new job somewhere else?"

"Yeah. I don't know where, but I've heard he's out by October."

"Well, good riddance. No offense, but that's a cold blow. Dumping you and choosing to keep his job, where you'll see each other and whatnot."

"It hasn't been that bad. He's not weird about anything. To be fair, he lives closer to Good Sam. If anything, I should be packing my bags."

"Nonsense. How long were you together?"

"Twenty-two years," I answer quickly and bluntly.

"Damn. That's heartbreaking, Mo. I'm so sorry. When did he drop the bomb? He was seeing someone else, right?"

This is the most difficult part. It makes me feel worthless, disgusting, and utterly undesirable. "Yeah. He, uh, he . . . told me about it in May. He's been seeing a woman."

"Well, I don't blame him for that," Dr. Bukharov jests.

"You're incorrigible, Doc."

"You'll find another good one, Mo. A better one. I know it."

"Thanks, Doc."

As he pulls the colonoscope past the hepatic flexure, the patient starts to stir. The propofol is beginning to wear off. Andrea, the nurse anesthetist, pushes the milky fluid into the IV, and the squirming slowly stops. She has an on-call contract with Good Sam. I only see her once every couple of months. Andrea has been silent for the entire procedure. She looks up from her syringe and exclaims, "That's a damn good drug, that propofol. If it's good enough for the King of Pop, it's good enough for Sleeping Beauty here."

Dr. Bukharov and I laugh uneasily at her joke. He is curious about Andrea and asks her, "What do you think? Why does love end? Why does it never seem to work out?"

Andrea checks the heart rate and oxygen levels on her monitor. It is unclear if she wants to answer this silly question. She switches to a sullen tone of voice. "It's the world around us that makes love impossible. It's a pile of shit. You have people who hold power over the rest of us. And we must want more stuff, or they will lose control of us. The more goods and services you've gobbled, the better life you've lived. It is this idea that warps the meaning of love. These days, people mistake a healthy bank account for the path to happiness. Romance is tied up with the financial incentives of kinship. Some of us find love organically. But it is easily lost. For most of us, getting fed and housed is enough. These days it's even harder to find firm footing. How can love thrive when we always worry about losing our electricity or our apartment? People are too occupied with surviving this hell."

I let out a long whistle and reply, "Damn!"

"Y'all asked."

"I like you, Andrea."

Dr. Bukharov curves the tip of the colonoscopy into a hook formation. This is to facilitate examination of the rectum and to check for hemorrhoids. After snapping a few shots, he removes the scope and puts it in a plastic bin on top of the processor. We lift the side rails and cover the patient's body with a thick bed sheet. I unplug the colonoscope and bring it to the steam autoclave for disinfection. As I come back into the suite, Andrea is already wheeling the patient out to recovery. I quickly pull off my disposable gown and follow her to help push the bed. Bukharov calls out, "See you all in a few minutes for lunch!"

The patient is letting out the air that we had put in. We park the bed and pull the privacy curtain. Andrea and I give vitals to the post-op nurse. We are careful in explaining medications rendered. That second dose of propofol will probably add a few minutes to recovery time. It is forty-five minutes until the next procedure. Ready to eat, I go to the hand-wash kiosk and lather up with alcohol scrub.

While drying my hands, Andrea comes up behind me and whispers, "I've worked with you before. You're a nice guy, Mo. I'm sorry to hear about your break-up."

"Thanks, Andrea. That means a lot. I'm with you on that stuff you said." We walk down the corridor and to the office. Pok and Chryllis are both on hold, waiting to authorize insurance payments. They wave at us as we head toward the employee lounge. Pok and I just recently started talking to each other. I had ignored her for three years on account of her rampant homophobia.

Andrea asks, "What did you bring today?"

"The same as every day. Government-issued egg and lentils."

"Me, too."

"Thank Allah that Drumpf took control of the chicken farms, so we could all get our daily protein."

Andrea giggles and responds, "Praise Drumpf!"

"Indeed, my friend."

Everything is a nightmare. There's no way one could rationalize the mood, the flavor of this nation today. If anything, it is reminiscent of the fall of empires. I open my heavily-used Pyrex and smash the hard-boiled egg into the lentils. Lentils are the cheapest thing on the food market. Given the situation of most people, it's a pretty good meal. Breakfast and dinner are always some mixture of apples, carrots, and rice. I have been growing my own beans and squash too. Every other Thursday, I treat myself to a burger and fries. Every other Monday, I treat myself to a new record. Today is Monday, and the records are starting to become cheaper than the burgers.

Dr. Bukharov comes in as we are eating our sorry meals. Andrea is resourceful enough to have some spinach in her lentils, but it is obvious that she would rather have filet mignon. As Bukharov navigates around our table and to the fridge, he seems down. I take notice and immediately ask him, "Are you feeling all right, Doc?"

"Yeah. It's just . . . Andrea's little speech got me thinking."

Andrea asks, "How so?"

He scratches his head while looking through the sea of bag lunches. "I don't know. I'm just overwhelmed by it all."

"I hear you, Doc." I feel sympathy for him. It's true. It is all overwhelming. The miniseries reboots. The beauty competitions. Hell, even the fucking Olympics. The screens hide a vicious ghost story, and no one knows what matters anymore. All we can hope for is a full belly and a complete programming schedule. We live in a dual-reality in which we are at war with everyone, and no one cares. No one cares because the other reality is shiny and plot-driven.

Dr. Bukharov sits with us at the folding table. He opens his lunch. It is a bowl of lentils and a government-issued egg.

WINO RECORDS IS WAY OUT on Hollywood Boulevard, but it is worth the drive. I'll have to double back past work to get home to my shared east Los Angeles apartment. Now that the summer heat has settled, construction efforts are in full swing. Highway travel moves like molasses. Driving on the 101, inch by inch on a strip in repair, I am thinking about Justin.

He was always so good to me. We truly understood each other. We spent much of our time in separate quarters. We valued being individuals with the capacity to allocate proper time to one another, without dashing our personal projects and hobbies. He had a deep love for fixed-gear bikes, riding The Strand every morning and evening to see sunrises and sunsets. A few times, I tagged along, riding on a pathetic Huffy hand-me-down. I didn't get it. I couldn't see the appeal, especially when LA life is already a mad dash. Over the years, he made new friends in the bike community. He ditched his sedan for a reliable frame and a tire patch kit. He focused on fitness while I built a little bit of a gut.

It was in those bike communities that he met Foziah. She manages a CrossFit clinic on the boundary between Venice and Marina Del Rey. She also oversees the distribution of a popular energy drink throughout the southwest. She lives in a two-bedroom house on the beachfront. The house was part of a large inheritance, passed down by her family of agricultural barons. Her great-great-grandparents were the first to grow alfalfa in the state of Caliphornia. Between the gym memberships and the beverage sales, she does very well for herself. Compared to the rest of Los Angeles, she lives like a queen.

Over the last few years, as Justin worked on his physical appearance, I assumed it was his mid-life crisis. In a way it was. Our entire adult life had been spent as reflections of each other. Both of us were in need of attention outside of our romantic life. So, I tried to be understanding.

We had spent so many years as social recluses. He deserved a change, and I was supportive. There was no reason not to believe in our contentedness. When the ridged trapezoids and firm thighs appeared, I foolishly thought it was an effort at personal maintenance, an effort at longevity. In reality, he was trying to impress Foziah.

They started seeing each other sometime during the Third Term. That is all he will tell me. It could have been two years or four years. He won't give me the peace of mind of knowing exact details. A few weeks back, I saw them at Good Sam together. They had been hitting the tanning beds and looked like two carrots holding hands.

I imagine his life is much easier now. I am in the same apartment. I have had to find three roommates to cover his portion of rent. The four of us sleep on opposite corners of the small studio. We have a schedule for bathroom use posted on the refrigerator door.

To avoid paying for valet or meter, I park at Rolf's Groceries and walk a half-mile to the record store. It is quite hot out. The Jinghong Minarets jut out into a cloudless sky, and the sun is pointing directly at me. The Fonda Theatre looks the same as it always has. Its marquee is painted red, yellow, and green for an upcoming Bad Brains tribute. Further down the street, a carniceria has a wall covered in masks, all of them styled after the Benin Empire. To my left, two hundred feet of silica. Grunge Revival plays on a video ad. It is about a father and son fishing. Son falls overboard as comic relief. His head emerges from the water, and his father helps him into the boat. The son looks upset and embarrassed until father reaches into the Styrofoam cooler and pulls out an ice-cold Heaven's Head lager. Other screens talk about fall fashion, Celeb Rec, and various offerings of pumpkin spice flavoring. The images are splayed across the urban landscape.

Every other shop is a postal service or currency exchange. Most of Los Angeles has denied federal services, and local merchants have jumped in to fill the niche. Global shipping is relatively cheap, and many make a lifestyle, trading dollars for other notes. In the Fourth Term, it is best to diversify your currencies. Sometimes it helps to have an extra rupee or peso. A few weeks ago, I found myself washing dishes. After my biweekly burger, the restaurant refused to accept US bills.

There are many workarounds. All businesses will cash your paycheck and with very reasonable transaction fees. This is especially helpful as more employers are giving daily and weekly raises. To fight hyperinflation, you've got to think outside the box. Zimbabwe's been doing this shit for two generations. Venezuela had it pretty rough.

A library is holding a special event and handing out bowls of potato stew. It has marble columns that narrow toward the top, ending in an abruptly pointed edge, like a pencil or the obelisks of the Necropolis. The entrance has an intricate geometric pattern on the tiled floor. A man holds a sign that says, "Remember the Simpson Riots!" This city does. It's the reason we run independently of the government in D.C., for the most part. It is one of many reasons. Only in the direst of circumstances, like plague, war, or a Gel Lago attack do we accept assistance. We could never fully disengage from the federalist system. You've got to get your eggs after all.

And if I am living in the end of the American Empire, then LA is the place to be. Petty crime is rampant, but murders and rapes are at the lowest level in our history. You can still get eats on the cheap. Cuisine from every corner of the world, if you look in the right places. Creativity is a highly valued and bartered skill. Every night, when the twilight touches the rooftops, street musicians flood the markets and sidewalks, and they play until dawn. Painters hawk portraits of couples as engagement gifts.

The influence of Tiandalusia is also evident. There are statues and murals of Hecatl, and homages to the Chinese junk. Bookstores have entire sections of material on the spread of Islam in the precolonial era. It is a city of jaguar warriors, pharaohs, vegans, and dragons. Los Angeles is a freak show, and it is heaven on earth.

What better representation of our failures? Hollywood got us hooked on pretty people and captivating monologues. It's been a century-long experiment, turning the moving image into a drug. Our values are compromised by the promise of a sixth season. And while we avoided electing one actor back in 4678, we've had another actor elected four times. I use the term "elected" loosely and with obvious sarcasm.

Wino is brimming with customers, many of them wearing ripped denim, homemade patches, and sleeveless T-shirts. Some new album must have dropped, and everyone is lining up to get it. I guess that was one good thing about the pandemic. The discontinuation of personal smartphones had revived the record companies. Labels have returned to the age-old model of producing albums, and people wait with anticipation to hold physical copies from their favorite artists. I always hated the digital age of music.

The line is moving quickly as I look through the discount vinyl bin. Most of them are 46th century country. Wino also has a rack of tapes that I frequently check. The rack appears to have new additions. Upon closer examination, I find a copy of a Megadeth bootleg for twenty bucks. This will certainly be a gift for Esther when I see her in February. I can consider it repayment for buying my plane tickets.

I grab the tape and continue to peruse. I find it amusing that Britney Spears has a 25th anniversary edition of her freshman album placed next to Tank Krakoa Noir, a blastsynth duo. It appears that many knockoffs are cashing in on the *a cappella* reggae craze. Aggropop is already dated and inundates the bargain racks.

I only have enough money for the gift and one thing for myself. I need to be picky, or I'll give myself grief for the next two weeks. Returns and exchanges are no longer facets of consumerism. The exchange rate is too unreliable to allow people the flexibility of fixing a poor decision. They have to stick with that poor decision and live with it. My eyes glance across the alphabetically-listed names of artists, and I can see one of the customers near the entrance, holding the record that everyone is here for. It is dark green and black with a graffiti-style font. The cover says *The Punks of Los Angeles*.

The title has piqued my interest. I go toward the back of the line to inquire about the album. There is a display that has dozens of copies in vinyl, cassette, and disc. I pick one up and marvel at the cover art, which looks like something from *Mad Magazine*. It depicts a bike gang hanging out. The gang is wearing spiked helmets and sipping from bottles of malt liquor. The subtitle of the album says, "Formative years: 4675–4685."

I turn the album over and make an audible gasp of surprise. The first two tracks on the album are Nixon Babies' "Acid Rain" and Bile Rocket's "Castle of Discarded Limbs." I can hear the songs without any effort. I am imagining the end of Mom's song fading into the introduction of Dad's song. It seems perfect. The other artists are obvious: Black Flag, Circle Jerks, and the like. Perhaps I'm biased because of my heritage, but these first two tracks are a solid cut deep into the history of West Coast punk. I am impressed, filled with pride, and welling with tears.

As if on cue, a patron touches my shoulder and asks, "Hey, are you Muhammad? You know, Abdul and Franka's kid?"

"Yes, I am."

"Oh! That is incredible!" He grabs his friend by the shoulder to show him. He continues, "Are your here for the release of the compilation?"

I flash an embarrassed smile and raise the record. "Truth be told, I didn't know anything about it."

The patron lights up with excitement. Turning around toward the check-out line, he yells into the store, "Hey, everybody! Muhammad Liu-Miller is here! The ACTUAL Nixon Baby!"

FOUR HOURS AFTER GETTING TO Wino Records, they are finally closing shop. After an exciting and busy day, I can go home. The revelation of my royal lineage drew the attention of everyone coming to buy the newly-released punk compilation. The owner asked if I would stay for the promotion and promised me a store credit and hourly pay at the state-mandated minimum wage. I happily accepted. It was nice to be honored. It was nice to think of my parents and share stories of being raised by punk rockers.

I talked about the divorce and I talked about Larry and Tariq. I talked about my father's home and his job at Hyperion. I talked about their waxing and waning beliefs as Muslims. I talked about their activism and I talked about their deaths. I even mentioned the time I apologized to Mom at the cemetery. It was like therapy without the billing statement.

I need these brief reminders of my happier past. Sometimes, in the hustle of earning wages, I forget to cherish the memory of my parents. It's so easy to get wrapped up in the madness of this world; wrapped up with work, wrapped up with friends, and wrapped up with love. Mom and Dad are the foundations of my character. From them, my sense of purpose is defined. They gifted me with concepts about social justice, fairness, and protest. They gifted me with love.

I got a few phone numbers. That was an especially nice part of the evening. I felt adored and wanted. It was something I had needed ever since losing Justin. My self-esteem hasn't been doing well, but today has perked me right up. After today, I am beginning to feel as if everything will be alright.

As the Sufi would say, "This, too, shall pass." It is the small victories that define us, not the melee of the outside world. The silica screens may try and dictate our conceptions of failure and success, but we live on without them and in spite of them. In Los Angeles, I have found ways to hide from the darkness engulfing the world. Many others have done the same. The city is our sanctuary as the storm passes overhead. Donald Drumpf and the political entertainment machine are serving a fourth term in office, and I could care less.

PART THREE

THE WAY WE WILL NEVER BE AGAIN

XIII

It is obvious that Mishelle is feeling tipsy. We have been in the hot tub for nearly an hour. Dehydration is beginning to set in. She excuses herself from the conversation and walks a drippy path to the sliding glass door. I can see her through the door. She fills a tumbler with tap water, chugs it, and positions for another round. She is having fun.

There is that certain charm about Esther that I've never been able to pinpoint. Mishelle has certainly loosened up around her. It is good to see her like this. I can't believe how much we have laughed tonight. My jaw is sore. I hope that these visits become more frequent. I hope that Clea doesn't muck it up with Esther.

Mishelle returns wide-eyed and glowing. She smiles directly at me. For a moment, she loses her balance. She maneuvers onto one knee, puts her drink down on the Jacuzzi's edge, and braces herself. She eases into the water on the plastic, corrugated step. I adore her klutziness.

Esther reaches for her satchel and removes a box of turmeric candies. Each yellow puff has a creamy saffron mousse, stuffed into the center. From this magical satchel, she also pulls a long and ridged spliff. The air immediately reeks of a dusty skunk, lying dead in a pile of pine needles. Before sealing them, Esther had sprinkled some cured eucalyptus on top of the concoction. And she packed about twenty of these cigarillos for the long haul across the West Coast. The menthol flavor is an homage to Clea, whom Esther will see later on this road trip. Their meeting is one of the many things that I am currently worried about.

Esther lights the stinky stick and takes a rip. She asks, "Are you thinking of having any other children?"

I smile widely. "Maybe in a few years."

Mishelle immediately retorts, "I'd like to start having more right away."

Esther laughs heartily, "Well, it looks like you've got your work cut out for you, Geo." She passes the spliff to me.

"Yeah, I guess so."

"Do you feel the same?" Mishelle scoots towards me for a toke. "It sure was fun making the last one."

I wrap my arm around her. "I'm fine with whatever you want, Mish. When do you want to start?"

"Immediately!"

With this comment, a brief shiver of neurons ascends my spine. The sensation crawls through the valley of my trapezoids. Up and up, until finally settling upon my scalp. It feels like a newly-shaven head, smothered in a soft, anise rub. Little forks gently massage my temples and my eyeballs well with tears. The episode is a weird mixture of bliss and nausea.

Esther gloats, "I think it's a splendid idea. How many do you want?"

Without hesitation, Mishelle replies, "At least four."

I can feel my cheekbones turning red. "Whatever you want, babe." I am feeling overwhelmed. I shift into a standing position and make an excuse to leave. "I've got to piss."

"Whatever, Geo." Esther jokes.

Mishelle teases, "The gall of that man." She takes another deep sip from the pea-green martini glass. "What a catch, huh?"

Esther smiles and answers, "You bet. He's a charmer, for sure." She takes a bite of her turmeric snack. After some vigorous chewing, she continues, "The gall of Geo."

"Yep."

I WASH MY HANDS, LOOK into the mirror, and softly wish, "Ugh. I hope Clea doesn't say anything about us fucking."

I have been having a rough run. I don't have the guts to tell Mishelle about the indictment. I am afraid of her seeing my face on the television or the cover of *The Houston Pahayagan*. Check-and-Go, my pride and joy since conceiving the algorithm, is being investigated for fraud and embezzlement. And they are going to find a lot of shady shit in those snack-shack, check-cashing cesspools.

Perhaps I should avoid the fun outside, at least for a little while. As I walk down the hallway of varnished wood and into the den, there are dual monitors and a keyboard waiting for me. I click the flat-screen on and navigate to my favorite futures channel. Trading isn't done at night, but speculation still thrives at all hours. The transiting ticker is categorized alphabetically. CNG is my ticker symbol. The correspondent explains the many reasons to invest in gold. When CNG scrolls across, its numbers are printed in red. A third of its value has been lost in just six hours. If corporations truly are people, mine is now limbless.

The moment is bittersweet. I dumped my CNG shares two weeks ago at a reasonable price. That doesn't temper my mood. I simply don't want the franchise to shut down. Watching it die feels like the end of an era.

But there are reasons to celebrate the death. My lawyer had mentioned something important: defendants that lose their assets during litigation face softer penalties. I know I can avoid prison time with luck and well-placed loopholes. The trick is getting my fines as low as possible. The spiraling failure of Check-and-Go ensures a type of empathy. I feel thankful for this small victory and thankful that my legal troubles are reported in economic terms, and not in headlines.

I click on one of the desktop monitors. It is time to move money to the islands. The website is bookmarked. Brujas Banking Corporation has me registered under an alias name. With a few swift swipes of the mouse, I authorize the transfer, just shy of seven figures. And just like that, the money is resting safe and sound in a tropical home.

Opening my e-mail, I notice a message from my lawyer. It was sent just an hour ago. It describes a patron of the franchise who is filing suit against the company. She claims that Check-and-Go had garnished her paycheck for some NSF fees. This left her unable to pay her auto insurance premium.

She blames Check-and-Go for a whole run of bad luck. On the day after her policy was canceled, she was involved in a head-on collision. Responsible for damages to the other party and drowning in medical bills, she had to declare bankruptcy. Now, she is seeking retribution, given my recent legal woes.

The e-mail assures me that the case will be easily won. My lawyer is assembling a team of representatives for this very situation. In fact, after winning the case, there will be a precedent to avoid future class action. In this light, the suit is a blessing in disguise. The only painful aspect would be the exposure. This suit will bring the court drama to all facets of mass media. Everyone loves a David-versus-Goliath narrative, and the channels will surely eat it up. According to my lawyer, the media coverage will probably catch on within a week. He advises me to talk with Mishelle since she will soon know anyway.

"Shit."

I move the message to a special archive. A receipt of transaction from Brujas Banking Corporation has been sent, and I move the confirmation to yet another archive. I delete a few advertisements for dick pills. A Nigerian prince is still asking for help. I shut off the monitors and power down the motherboard. I grab the remote control and shut off the television.

I am worried about talking with Mishelle. I'm not sure how she will handle the revelation. I am mulling over the possibility of divorce and the possibility of co-parenting Millicent under two different roofs. It is becoming obvious that I will have to do some damage control. Perhaps, I should succumb to another attempt at creating life, to sugarcoat the news for Mishelle.

Wow! I am an asshole. I should definitely tell her before this weekend. Wouldn't want to stress it on my night out at the county fair. I poke my head out of the sliding door and yell, "Hey, dudes! It's almost 9:30! The new episode of *Succubus Shuffle* is on, and I know neither of you would want to miss it!"

Esther asks, "Did Koreah pick Granth?"

Mishelle looks shocked. "Oh, hell, no! She's moved on to Lars, and they are planning to open a cupcake shop." She stands from the hot tub and motions for Esther to do the same. "Come on! We don't want to miss the recap!"

THE SMELLS OF THE HARRIS County Fair are thick enough to have their own caloric value. Variations on cotton candy and pork dominate the fare. Twinkie-style Cornish hens are a popular item as well. They are basted in cream filling and packed with sweet sponge-cake stuffing. Most vendors offer a deep-fried version of everything on their menu. Picnic tables are lined up for acres, each one equipped with mustard, ketchup, and a napkin dispenser. Butter and oil soak the walkways and the dumpsters behind the porta-Djinnis overflow with leftovers. It is a holy event, the eternal ritual of family-sanctioned binge eating.

I walk among the aisles looking for Carl Shapiro. Carl is a friend from the city baseball leagues. Check-and-Go sponsors my team, and Shapiro's Mufflers sponsors Carl's. My team is The Peanuts, and Carl's team is The Allen Wrenches. Once or twice a year, we hang out at Kyoo Matsu brewery. It is a superficial friendship with no basis other than cheap, corporate competition. I can't find him, walking through the confetti madness.

Feeling parched, I look for the shortest line to buy something wet and sugary. There is no wait at Al-Limonana, which boasts fourteen flavors of lemonade. The stand also has horchata, pineapple bouquets, and a blood-red fruit punch. I walk to the counter and place my order.

The throttling of dirt bikes roars in the distance. It reminds me of the advertisements for the fair, promoting a huge motor competition, complete with stunts and monster trucks. I give five bucks to the vendor, grab my strawberry lemonade, and make my way to the bleachers. The large, dirt course is near capacity.

About three rows up, I can see a seat. I position myself into the uncomfortable steel bench, lean back, and look out upon the arena. Advertisements are pasted all along the exterior walls of the track, which rise and fall with the occasional ramp. No doubt, these are put in for freestyle jumping. Each ramp includes flame throwers, mounted at forty-five-degree angles and aimed for dramatic effect.

As more people pile into the stadium, the announcer comes over the loudspeaker. "Ladies and Gentlemen, please welcome the knight in crimson, the scourge of the Viking Age, and the handsome heartthrob, Heimlich the Red!"

The crowd applauds as the monster truck emerges from its corral near the announcer's booth. It is perched on giant and cumbersome shocks, with wheels the size of a compact car. The truck is painted in a deep, red background, covered with orange and pink flames. On its enormous rolling cage, flood headlights are mounted, shining in the eyes of spectators. The windshields are also decorated with decals of skulls and axes. It is all meant to invoke the mood and ferocity of Scandinavian life during the Middle Ages.

Suddenly, the engine lets out a deafening belch, and the vehicle accelerates toward the first berm. Gaining speed, the monster truck spews diesel fumes into the Texas wind. It hits the jump, briefly teeters onto its left side, rebalances itself, and launches into the air. The flame throwers spit at rapid intervals and then hold steady. The behemoth breaks through the wall of fire, accompanied by the squeal of guitar feedback. Setting the mood of masculine action, the stadium speakers play a track from Judas Priest's *Canadian Steel* album. The cheering crowd echoes throughout the entire complex.

The driver rolls her window down and gives a thumbs up to the audience. She speeds up and hits a second jump. After landing, she positions the truck for some cheap stunts. It is all quite enthralling. She drives donuts, poses in hydraulic suspension, and pops a wheelie while driving a second lap.

Then, the engine of Heimlich the Red is joined by another roaring motor. On the opposite end of the arena, a purple-and-sky blue chassis bursts from the shadows. It revs and positions itself face-to-face with Heimlich. The announcer dramatically describes the scene. "Looks like we have a challenge offered by the likes of Blizzardman!"

Blizzardman was a comic book from the Carter Era that has regained some prominence after a recent Hollywood reboot. In the comic, Blizzardman's real name is Harvey Beckman. His superpower is associated with his name; the ability to shoot snow, ice, and sharp sleet from his hands. He was granted this ability after being assigned to an Arctic research expedition in the early years of the Cold War. When the research facility is inundated with the rays of a radioactive Aurora Borealis, engineered by a Soviet scientist gone rogue, Harvey is buried in an avalanche and left for dead. Years later, during a NOTA ice-breaking mission, his frozen body is discovered in a melting glacier. After thawing, he returns to life. He was subjected to a variety of medical experiments to determine the source of his miraculous recovery. It was during these experiments that he discovers his aqua kinetic prowess. He could turn water to ice, merely by touching it. In addition, he was impervious to cold temperatures. Most impressive of all, he could throw bolts of frozen water as a projectile weapon.

In honor of the comic book character, the Blizzardman monster truck carries artificial snow machines, flanking its two front doors. The snow oozes out of its side like a Play-Doh accessory. The speakers fade into Black Sabbath's "Snowblind," and both vehicles rev and throttle. The two trucks face off in what is meant to be a battle between fire and ice.

They dart past one another at full speed. In synchronized form, each truck jumps and twists its way to the opposite end of the track. After turning the last corner, giant Styrofoam lances emerge from each cabin. It is a classic joust, sprinkled with 47th-century adrenaline. They speed toward what seems to be an inevitable collision. Blizzardman and Heimlich the Red hit the dirt mounds, spring toward one another, and the lances smash upon impact. The trucks land and brake into a cloud of dust. The announcer shouts, "What a hot set of wicked jumps, folks!"

I smile at the pageantry. It reminds me of my childhood when I was fond of racing culture. I can remember my Lamborghini posters. I can remember my Hot Wheels. I can remember oil changes with my father. That reminds me. *What about my friend from Shapiro's Mufflers?* I take a sip of my lemonade and figure I should give Carl another chance.

I stand up and make my way down the bleachers. At the base of the aluminum stairs, my ankle is scraped by the metal burr of a handrail. The skin on the bony ball joint turns pale white and then rapidly shifts into deeper and deeper shades of red. I begin to bleed onto my flip flops and into the dirt. I hustle along, finally getting to the food court. I pull a handful of napkins from a dining table. I look back at the dirt walkway while swabbing my laceration. My footsteps are dotted with globules of dusty blood, easily mistaken for ketchup droppings.

AFTER GIVING UP ON CARL, I ordered a bratwurst with bourbon kraut. Its brine runs down my chin, and my mouth makes loud sounds. My mandible clicks, every time I bite down. In the last stages of my meal, I let out groans of satisfaction. I finish the sausage and make my way through the rest of the fairgrounds.

I walk past the toddler area, where teacups and carousels spin at a non-threatening tempo. The carnies have designed them to look like soft, pastoral landscapes. Farm animals with wide and shining eyes graze on puffy grass. The images remind me of Millicent's crib, which is decorated with Mother Goose narratives. Passing the pastel themes, I can hear the complaints of children, waiting to ride.

At the far end of these machines, there are attractions meant for high-adrenaline teenagers. Some of them are classics from my childhood. Like the Zipper, a welded cage that yanks itself to a height of forty feet, spinning its rider on a spindle, upside-down and back again. The Zipper can hold two people at a time and is a popular ride for adolescents in love.

Next, there is the Jo Jo 'Merica, a star-and-striped monstrosity that whips around like a merry-go-round. People, a dozen at a time, sit in repurposed car seats, upholstered in red, white, and blue. A five-point harness is dropped onto the rider. A strobe light descends, and the centrifuge starts. The disc spins fast enough to pull cheeks back, exposing teeth like those cheesy Air Force videos. One time, Jo Jo 'Merica made me throw up in Las Vegas.

Other attractions are strewn about. It is said that our Ferris Wheel is the largest in the Lone Star state. A hot-air balloon vendor offers rides for eighty bucks. The carnies have brought back the million-gallon pool to facilitate Bumper Junks. I pass the pool and marvel at its size. The next ride in my path is something I've never seen. It stands past the 21-plus zone. It is called The Tingle Chamber and is painted a soft yellow.

I am curious and eager to spend my cash. I enter the contraption, which is as large as a rail car. I pull back a quilted curtain, and a narrow passage widens. Air conditioning blasts my face. Doo-wop music fills the room at a low and soothing volume. A receptionist stands behind a fuchsia podium.

With a snaky grin, the receptionist begins, "Welcome to The Tingle Chamber! Three tokens or fifteen USD."

I hand him a wadded ten and five. "What's this all about?"

"It's kind of a form of therapy. Think of seeing your masseuse, your acupuncturist, your chiropractor, and your favorite prostitute, all at the same time."

"OK. That's rich, man."

"You'll want to remove your shoes, socks, and any jewelry. Please leave them in our specialized locker."

I take off my watch. My laceration has finally congealed, but my flip flops are soiled with blood. I remove them with hesitation and embarrassment.

The receptionist takes the items and remarks, "We will have your plastic sandals washed while you bask in the Tingle Chamber. It is an entirely complimentary service. Tips are not required, but expected."

He leads me to the far end of the makeshift lobby. We pass through hanging beads and enter a room with several seats. The seats are modified bicycle thrones. Each has a series of plastic nubs that jut out. Above the seats, a spine of circuitry and wires lead to a platform. This part of the machine rests above the head and is attached to dozens of flexible fingers; some made of synthetic polymer, and some made of natural materials like bamboo. Two of the fingers are made of dried cattail, picked from a swamp. The sides of the chamber have armrests carved into smaller finger rests. The device is slightly creepy, but my curiosity bypasses my fear or disgust.

The receptionist leaves me. "Ten minutes."

"Cool, dude."

The lights dim, and a sliding wall emerges from the armrests. They enclose me, shift to a static image, and flood my eyes with a rainbow of colors. The sliding walls are flat-screens. I am impressed. There is a lot of potential for these things.

The finger rests begin squeezing and rubbing my hand. I can feel thin, little pinpoints, poking the webbed skin between my knuckles. The sensation is weirdly relaxing. I fall into a comfortable position and tilt my head back. The doo-wop softens and fades out. I can hear a whirring in my ears, as if some machinery was crawling toward my temples. A speaker plays the sounds of crinkling paper and tapping fingernails. A gong rings, and the residual tone slowly dies.

Then, the armrests spray a fine mist into the chamber. It is an aerosol product containing synthesized culantro and chamomile. I breathe in the concoction. The platform of fingers above my head give a brief, jarring motion. It lowers until it rests softly on my crown. The mechanical fingers rub my scalp and the base of my skull.

As I settle in, my feet are sprayed with soothing eucalyptus oil. A rubber wheel presses into my arches and slowly moves up and down the bottom of my feet. As if this isn't enough stimulation, the nubs of the bicycle seat begin to vibrate and oscillate. They move in circular motions and then move in zig-zag patterns. The odd protrusions massage my buttocks and my perineum. The speakers switch from crinkles and taps to whispered poems. My head, neck, back, thighs, and feet tingle with overwhelmed nerves. Before I can soak in the experience, I am interrupted, "That's ten minutes!"

The receptionist presses a button. The screens descend, and I open my eyes. I definitely could have done another session. Instead of purchasing another, I decide to check out some more of the fair. That was a nice ten minutes. I feel rejuvenated and strangely hungry. I look at the receptionist and smile. "That was pretty great!"

The receptionist hands me a pair of bleached flip-flops and a Rolex. "I'm glad you liked it." He stares at me.

I quickly get the hint and tip him five dollars. "Here you go, buddy."

"Thank you, sir. Please exit to the lobby, where you can pick up your complimentary marijuana pop."

THE DAY IS WRAPPING UP, and the sun is setting. I am chewing on a double cheeseburger and strolling the last leg of the fairgrounds. A clown convention has brought a mob of colorful performers. They create human pyramids and fall over in slapstick form. Several of the clowns are executing circus stunts. Two of them are perched on stilts. Above them, a tall and lanky hobo walks across a wire. There are even a few mimes, which must be a rare commodity in Texas. One clown, named Uncle Sammy, looks like he is recruiting people to sign up for Afghanistan. The squeak of balloons being bent into animals can be heard among the moving crowds.

Many people are headed to the roller coasters. The darkening sky brings out the neon décor of each ride. Opposite of the neon, in a dusty clearing, a small crowd gathers around a speaker. Just shy of the crowd, at a poorly-crafted booth, sits a man in a red hat. I walk toward the gathering and focus my eyes on the booth. It has a display of various flags from Europe and Southeast Asia. The man sitting at the booth is stout and wide, with a bustling belly resting above his denim jeans. As I approach, I can read the red hat. Embroidered in white letters, it reads, "Make America Grand Again."

The man greets me, "Hello, brother! What brings you this way? Ask me anything about history, or be doomed to repeat it!"

I playfully take the bait, "Well, I'm a bit of a history buff myself. I've read quite a bit on World War II."

The man scoffs at this, "Hell, that's not the whole of history. It's a limited point of view, my friend. You can't just pay attention to the mid-4600s. What else interests you?"

This is great. I'll get a little obscure. "Well, I've always been confused about European history before Judaism. Everything before the third millennium." I am asking with genuine enthusiasm. It is a subject that fascinates me.

"Ah, yes. You must mean the Era of the Wicker Men? You're right to be confused. Nobody knows how long those beliefs had been around. At one time, it was a spiritual tradition that influenced the entire continent. It is rumored that the first idol burners lived on the Iberian Peninsula, somewhere in the Basque region. But to this day, they keep uncovering burning sites in places like Sicily and Saint Petersburg."

"I've always assumed it was just a bunch of crazy monster stories. Witches and werewolves and the like."

He smiles. "There are so many legends about monsters, it's easy to lose count. Prior to Pharaonic-Judeo thought, much of Europe was polytheistic. There were gods, goddesses, and magical creatures, living in different pantheons, varying by region. And you're right about the horror stories, the tales about vampires and werewolves. There were the fertility obelisks in France and England meant to keep away succubi. In Greece, bull semen was a ceremonial drink thought to give the ability to see ghosts. Danish clerics used to shit into ceramic jars to tempt malevolent spirits away from the village."

The man scratches at his jowls. "But gods and monsters are just part of the story. Everything in ancient Europe is tied to nature and the cosmos. And central to every mythology is the Triad. The Triad of Wicker Men. Worship of the Wicker Idols is a homage to the cycles of life and death."

I croon, "Whoa."

"The three wicker idols are named Henjn, Knoovl, and Brachtbart. The idols are meant to represent the Peoples of the Three Planets. The Peoples of the Three Planets are an intergalactic confederation. Each planet has different jobs and responsibilities. Together, they keep an intricate balance between the sun, the moon, and Earth. Everything is governed by alliances and treaties. Orbits, seasons, and other celestial mechanics are affected by these relationships."

"Henjn represents fire and the sun. In fact, Henjn means 'sun' in several languages. It is the root of the modern word 'engine.' The fire people are the bringers of creativity and death. The fire people are muses, tapped for poetry and songcraft. Henjn himself also feeds the crematory fire in the vacuum of space. Once the body dies, the spirit is burnt by this fire, and it is Henjn who plays the shepherd of cremation. One popular belief speaks of cloudy skies. You see, clouds were the smoke of cremated spirits, burning in the sun's flames, fanned by Henjn's breath."

I ask the man, "How do you know all of this stuff?"

"I got a Master's Degree in religious studies from Arizona State University, way back before the Simpson Riots."

"Does that type of knowledge pay off?"

"It does, if you know the right people," the man replies.

I apologize, "I'm sorry, I kind of derailed your train of thought. Please, go on."

"Well, Knoovl represents water and the moon. She is considered to be an ocean planet. The grayish waters are said to be the source of all life in the universe. And so, the water people are the bringers of life. They are associated with mourning—mourning the deaths brought on by the fire people. Rain is seen as tears, leaving the burning smoke of Henjn's fires. Oceans, lakes, and rivers are all tributaries of the moon's brackish surface, which was rumored to have been larger at one time."

"Brachtbart is the third planet, the home planet. The idol of Brachtbart is a symbol of Earth, and the people living here. Humans represent flesh and dirt. Earth people are the bringers of war and inspiration. It is the ideas of those on the planet of flesh and dirt that moves time forward. Flesh and dirt are the source of human initiative, which is dependent upon free will."

I ask, "Wasn't that a Nazi slogan? You know, flesh and dirt?"

"Blood and soil," he replies.

"Oh, yeah. Go on."

He continues, "In the traditions of ancient Europa, every village had a patron god. And every year, idols were built and burnt in their honor. Large cities tended to revere Brachtbart, while smaller villages generally built idols to the sun and the moon. It was a reflection of the rural centers. Farms were reliant on favorable weather and the movement of the heavens. And in the walled citadels, officials and bureaucrats devised bold plans to move mountains and bold plans to move bodies."

"Regardless of patronage, the wicker idols were burned at different times of the season. Smaller ones were burned at equinox or solstice, as The Triad was also represented in seasons. The large offerings were saved for Ra'elthain. Ra'elthain was the yearly gathering in late December. It is generally noted as an influence on our modern Horus Mass. In any case, people would travel for miles to reach these festivals, spotted all throughout the continent. The three idols, some of which were proven to be as high as fifty feet, were burnt to the ground to ward off anyone who would bring ill fortune or widespread misery. It was the burning of the idols that was meant to purify the community of cosmic demons. All evil intent was thought to be purged with the burning of Henjn, Knoovl, and Brachtbart, with the demons being driven away in the process."

I am fascinated with this mythology lesson. I ask, "What kind of demons?"

"They went by many names. The most common description emerges from the French Alps, a creature known as the Glenganger. Glengangers are the malevolent shapeshifters who cast spells to afflict villages and cities. Their magic spells include deadly diseases, economic ruin, and the summoning of giant monsters. Glengangers are essentially human in form, but a second neck extends from the crown of their heads, creating a second head, which is that of a goat."

"And that presents one of the functions of the wicker idols. Burning them helps 'suck up' the magic of the Glengangers. The entire affair is rather cyclical. The old recipes call for taking the ashes of the burnt idols and mixing them into a compost. This would be used to support the growth of vast willow and reed farms. The trees would grow, their wood would be harvested, and the cycle would start again."

"Wow."

He continues, "Yeah, most people don't think about how that early-European thought was appropriated by Islam and Judaism. Rabbis used to wear wicker idols around their neck. Jerusalem has an ancient relic of Olde Romania, a wicker dedication to Knoovl. The use of crucifixion, as a form of punishment, was done on a wicker X. It was meant to burn away the sins of bad people, or even suspected Glengangers. The goat-headed demon is the source of the word "scapegoat,' meaning someone to place blame upon."

People are beginning to crowd around the historian's booth. They file toward a row of patriotic banners. Many of them are wearing red hats. I ask the mythology expert, "What is going on?"

"Oh, my. That's where we're holding a support rally for Donald Drumpf."

"Is he coming to the fairgrounds tonight?"

The man laughs at the suggestion, "Heavens, no. The man is far too busy duking it out for the nomination."

"Do you think he has a chance? I always thought the dude was kind of a buffoon."

"No, sir. He has the pulse of the American heartland, and he's ready to help us out of the rut we've been in. You should go check it out. They should start the lectures and speeches within the next twenty minutes."

I look into the group. People fervently move folded chairs in preparation. They are all wearing shirts with "Drumpf 4710" printed boldly on the front. As they move things around, the subtle twang of modern country music plays on an echoing sound system. I thank the sideshow historian, and excuse myself. "I think I will."

XIV

It was not the Mayan calendar that brought us to our knees, but 4710 was still an end, of sorts. That's when the screens really took hold, howling in lieu of honest speaking. The construction on the house of mirrors. Twin, and then triplet, and then quadruplet realities, all pushed through a dozen different Flipchat filters. Yahweh had either died or gone crazy.

Wall units got cheap, and people had the perception of expendable income. Every partition in America became a means of communication and entertainment. The faces became permanent family members. The faces became models of our tendency to avoid one another. The faces separated us. It was paramount never to touch the silica panels. Only when cleaning by manufacturer's recommendations. Without a way to reciprocate, we were touched. A boom of media jumped in to meet our standards of beauty, boredom, and excess.

It had been a revolution in ad design and screenwriting. It had been a delicate interplay between consumable content and politics. It was masterfully executed. Before 4710, the average American processed about ten hours of media a day. At the onset of the Second Term, it was closer to thirteen.

Product placement got the goods flowing: a can of Flint's Cola with Tom Hanks in *Gullible and Rich*; Whoopi Goldberg in *Chauntfords' Muscle Cream*; the many hot sauces that sponsored Rupert Grint. On top of the programming, there's a suffocating heap of commercials. Most people, if they can afford it, take the bait. The invisible hand feeds the system. Producers and patrons hold hands across the continent. Consumer goods are the new wicker idols, and we sure as hell burn through them.

With this exposure to the screen, another type of madness gripped the

American. Confusion of Tanakh proportions reigned. We became the Tower of Babel in the Western Hemisphere. We became Eris incarnate. Too many words take on too many meanings. It is word salad in the truest sense. And with the coming of the screens comes the specialized programs catering to individual tastes. Every word is customized to our every whim.

The screens are driving people into different camps. Each camp believes a tailored version of the past, present, and future. Each camp believes the other is a threat to democracy. Soon, there will be no middle ground. Venn diagrams need not apply. People are split, right down the middle, on so many issues. The United States is a country becoming permanently divided.

And it was shaken by the election of 4710. It was a sea change in so many ways. As in the past, the spotlight was on the presidency. After all, presidents are the faces of government. They are mascots for the team.

Like a potent television drama, 4710 affected the psyche of those who won and lost their vote. There were only winners and losers. And we performed mitosis, dividing into the camps and fostering the capacity to murder one another. We should know better. 4498, 4558, 4630, and the reelection of Carter in 4678 were particularly visceral and schismatic.

With each uproar, a relationship begins—one of either love or hate for the face of the mascot. As the years have passed, the nature of the relationship has changed. The mode of correspondence has changed. The printed proclamation evolved into the fireside chat and, once again, into a tweet.

Screens were a perfect platform throughout the presidencies of Donald J. Drumpf. He had already proven capable of being entertaining. We had consumed him for years. And so there began an onslaught of performances. Obama did Gel Lago. Obama did Glass Badger Lung. Make America Grand Again.

It was effective in the same way that a popular miniseries is compelling. You wanted to watch as the characters burned one another. You wanted to watch the main character burn it all. For some, the vote for Drumpf was an honest attempt at change for the better. For others, it was a wish for anarchy. Those who did not vote for him were absolutely devastated.

His inauguration was met with massive protests, organized by offshoots of the Occupy movement. To many, it was inconceivable to hand the nuke codes over to a thief billionaire. It seemed that a credible resistance was forming. Occupy had quickly changed; from a loosely-knit band of anar-cho-punkers to an armed resistance. They became freedom fighters in the face of plutocracy and the rule of wealth. Cleveland was effectively taken by Occupy the week after inauguration with a promise to move east and aim for the federal capital. Their political angle was warranted in the eyes of many: stop Drumpf from appeasing banks and mega-corporations; stop Drumpf from dismantling preservation and public safety efforts; stop Drumpf from going to war with someone.

After being evacuated and firebombed, Cleveland was destroyed, and the movement was brushed off. So, they tried the angle of sabotage through information. The new president's financial records were hacked and released to the public. These records did not paint the picture of a man who ingeniously avoided paying taxes, or one who made a fortune in war. They painted the picture of a man who was actually quite broke. The revelations of his net worth made Drumpf a popular pun.

Eventually, the comedic value wore off. The penniless bum, who was our executive, had garnered a type of national pity. It could be said that this sympathy, on a populist level, would help his reelection efforts. The noise brought by Occupy had been effectively muffled. The anger subsided.

Drumpf entered the White House on a wave of economic recovery, and for a while, it swelled and gained speed. Gas was cheaper, and jobs were plentiful. A brief period of prosperity was experienced, beginning in the summer of 4711. That following Horus Mass, the cyclical holiday meant to gauge con-sumer confidence, was a record in household spending. Jet Skis and fondue sets. Vuvuzelas and bean bags. Cars, action figures, and, most importantly, screens. As the people satiated themselves on baubles, they helped assemble the screen scape. And while wall unit sales had been growing before and after the election, they had tripled by 4712.

Keen on the power of the screen, Drumpf issued an executive order to establish an entertainment capital for every state. And to avoid confusion, the capitals would all have the same name. The state governments would decide on which cities produced the most content. Under the order, these cities would be renamed Hollywood. Tempe became Hollywood, Arizona. Arlington became Hollywood, Texas. Fifty "Hollywoods" competed to streamline drama, comedy, and political propaganda on demand. The screens dug in deeper and deeper.

To ensure this vein of economic growth, the deregulation of industry began. Demand for silica led to quartz mines all across the interior. With mining restrictions lifted, another unfortunate blitz for wealth carved into the mountainsides. Pockets of pollution formed in the Appalachians and in Alaska. Quartz mining in the southwest increased as well. One cheap alternative to quartz is sand, and so the beaches are drilled and shoveled. Silica production was like the new gold rush. It was the engine behind the proliferation of entertainment. We binged on it.

And we binged on other things. We binged food, drinks, and drugs. Pornographic attractions and tingle chambers were placed on every other urban block. A unique industry emerged to meet the demand for masturbatory products. Portions got bigger, saltier, and sweeter. One menu has bacon hashish burgers and a thimble of rum. Another has peach milkshakes and hoagies. When people, and in turn, the economy, experience good times, they tend to squander it on cheap satisfaction. We switch our moral compass into autopilot, and anything goes.

As WEIRD AS THOSE FIRST four years were, the Second Term hit like a tilted horizon. Construction on the wall—which would start at the tail of Texas, skirted the US-Mexico border, and then whipped up and around Caliphornia's coastal megalopolis—was the project of the millennium. The idea was to protect the United States from Mexican migrants, and the Chinese navy in one fell swoop. And when the first tracts of cinder block and barbed wire were placed, they were facilitated with screens. By 4717, it had reached the Chihuahuan Desert. It would forge on throughout the next two terms, invalidating dozens of tribal treaties, and confiscating familial properties throughout the southwest. The militarization of this region led to that special type of disregard for human decency, the type that made the history books. Whispers of monstrous acts began to surface.

But no one really cared. As the wall went up, the United States withdrew aid and support to the nations it had once destabilized. One by one, they bled migrants. The natural course was north, at least to Mexico. It was a mad dash to beat the wall. After all, it seemed there was plenty of incentive to go the extra distance to Arizona or Texas. As this migration progressed, the screens whipped us into our old brand of nativism.

Eventually, the Drumpf Administration enacted a policy meant to intimidate those who would seek such pastures. The policy threatened to split families attempting to cross the border. When the poor souls arrived, toddlers and infants were ripped from mothers through blatant trickery. Families were broken up and placed in dozens upon dozens of detention centers. Brothers and sisters were held miles apart from one another, and in many cases, parents were held in a different state. And what a better place to practice such detention, in the desert and mountain states that already held millions in privately-owned prisons.

In the hurried, bureaucratic mess that followed, the children were misplaced. They were sent back to their home countries to die without the warm arms of a mother to comfort them. With media coverage of family separation came a public outcry, but it was short-lived. As detainees were released, people lost interest. The migrants were no longer central characters in a sprawling drama. Families are still torn apart; they just don't hold our attention for any longer than a few episodes.

And people thought there was reason to celebrate. Tax reform was considered a major accomplishment for those holding political power. Everyone bought in on it for the few extra dollars in the paycheck. Nothing else mattered when the thought of disposable income was teased. The wealthiest hoarded their new savings and reinvested them into elaborate bets on the new economy. Banks were deregulated and eager to automate lines of credit to anyone asking. For a while, it seemed as if everyone could have everything.

Then, the financial system was tested by a series of natural disasters and infrastructural failures. The earthquake in Salt Lake City. Hurricanes Harvey,

Maria, Agnes, Agatha, Jermaine, and Jack. The flooding of the Chicago River in 4716. Breaches along the Intercoastal Waterway. Volcanoes in Hawaii and Arizona. Two of the bridges crossing the Mississippi had crumbled, limiting movement from east to west and vice versa. All of this pressure led to increased deficit spending, with no tax revenue to draw from after the lauded reforms. It was all a case of bad timing; the wealthy speculators, the disasters, the reforms. All of the above had wrecked the United States economy by the end of the Second Term.

The hyperinflation and food scarcity that followed was another short-lived backlash against that face in the White House. Anti-Drumpf fervor peaked in those years. People had to cut their consumption of everything they had grown to love. Protests were arranged, and counter-protesters attended with wishes to disrupt. Even those who had voted red were in line to complain about the state of things. They had a taste of the good life, and they wanted it back.

This growing opposition was met with a very direct and detailed response from the offenders in power, martial law, and the temporary shutdown of the government. In the months before the election of 4718, the three branches were merged into one. All powers under the first three constitutional articles resided in one man. The White House became judge, jury, executioner, soldier, and banker. Drumpf had effectively seized control of everything and was happy to announce his executive order to repeal the 22nd Amendment. He would seek election to a third term, and the new governmental structure would not provide a decent contender against him.

THE THIRD TERM WAS PURE misery, invasion, and control. All across the nation, tiny militias sprouted. They supported the hardline tactics of a macho, bully leader. Cultish and hyper-masculine, there was a resurgence of "brotherhood societies," where men would wax philosophical on the state of manhood, beat on drums, and perform acts of physical prowess. On the heels of stories coming from Charlottesville and the border, there was massive appeal to white nationalist groups. Many groups were not shy to push for stratified opportunities, based on race. There were the Lebanese Celts, the

Emirati Aryans, and the Iberian Peninsulares, each group offering ideas on a caste of skin tone. Anti-Semite clubs such as the Goff Von Henjn were common in the old rural communities: Oklahoma, Yuma, Bakersfield. They were easy to spot, with their khakis, red hoods, and red polo shirts. All of these groups, fearful of everything, were heavily armed. Weaponry became a fetish. Gun rights were Commandments sent from God. This ammophilia was quite pervasive, making men feel powerful and whatnot.

There was also a revival of outdated religious norms. Extreme forms of Islam became commonplace. Sharia neighborhood watches were formed. Belief in the prosperity hadith grew. The brand of conservatism appealed to stubborn Muslims who hated the cultural direction of the country. Allah was a path to financial success in a piss-poor economy, where most people go hungry. Only the faithful could rise above obscurity.

Islam wasn't the only religion getting a boost from the insanity of Drumpf's world. A full-fledged return to wicker idol worship occurred among many people of European ancestry. They claimed that the faith was a true representation of their ancestral heritage. In truth, they practiced as another form of xenophobia, racism, and bias. The same bodies that wear the red hoods of the Goff Von Henjn hold tiki torches, wicker, and bent into various positions of The Triad.

There was good reason to become religious. Famine was on the rise by 4720, and there was regular failure in the sustenance crops that had traditionally fed the nation. Commodity prices shot through the roof, and inflation made it difficult for most people to keep up. It was under these conditions that major price controls were enacted—a useless effort to aid people as the economy spiraled further into oblivion. One type of attempted relief was the federal acquisition of the poultry industry. At first, grabbing up the chicken farms was seen as the last straw in an overly intrusive government. But then people saw the immediate benefit, which was a daily egg ration for every American. Now, people could scratch protein off of their list of things to complain about.

And now with the Fourth Term in full swing, these political and spiritual movements have been appropriated by the government in power. Drumpf appeals to these people and does everything in his make them happy. It is a cult of eggs and idolatry. It is how he won the election of 4722, regardless of being seen as a sham mandate. The most vicious appeals are made to his base.

Drumpf's first executive order of 4722 was the abolition of child support. He claimed it was time to end the victimization of fathers across America. There was also the enactment of policies on gender. Forced gender "readjustments" occurred in makeshift clinics across the country. Medical records were seized to determine those citizens that had done anything to address their sex: hormone therapy, gender reassignment, implants, and the like. Those people were rounded up and kept in government facilities until a surgeon or psychiatrist could see them. Many experimental methods were used to convert them back to their biological sex. Most of these patients died while the rest continued to live in agony for daring to live as they wished.

Another form of social control is the crucifix. Along with the famine, there is widespread theft. Crime, in general, thrives. In an effort to dissuade lawbreaking citizens, prosecution by death penalty has expanded from most petty to serious crimes. All along the countryside, people are strung up for little reason at all. To the government, it is a way to save money. The old model of incarcerating everyone doesn't work when the state is bankrupt. See it as population control and respect of authority, all wrapped up in one nice, little package. At times, it is a literal witch hunt.

This is the world now. The screens are still here to make us happy and to sell us things we cannot afford. We still get hooked on sitcoms. We still salivate over cooking programs. We nosh on government eggs while catching up on the latest politics. The talking heads have us nodding and pursing our lips. The relationship will always be there. The screens are our minds. It will never be different; we can never go back. All we can do is hope we are fed and spend time with those we care about.

XV

It is February 17, 4723. Two days before the year of the horse. On a nonstop flight to the City of Sin, the passengers grab their armrests during a fit of turbulence. Below them, McCarran International glows faintly in the night sky. The red-eye flight departed from Los Angeles around midnight. A luxury to most, the ticket had cost nearly eighty-thousand. Reflecting on the high price, I look out of the window and feel lucky. There are not many opportunities to take time off, let alone travel. Esther and Geo pitched in for the fare, insisted that the game was paramount. No faltering world would change that. Four days off sounds like bliss.

I've been thinking about the troubles facing Geo. I see him in the news, once again in a legal battle. I feel pity for him. I wish he didn't have such lofty goals, such insatiable greed. Sometimes, I wonder if he hides a good heart, deep in that macho veneer. His donation to my airfare is especially heartfelt. It will be nice to see him. I yearn to console my friend in his hard times.

The turbulence jolts the cabin violently. To my rear, an unnerving screech bellows out. The noise is followed by a jumbled bang. Someone behind me yells, "Holy shit! A panel just fell off of the wing!"

As if on cue, the plane veers to its left side and shakes the seating quarters. A man in beige, tweed coveralls is jerked from his standing position and slams into the aisle floor. He brushes himself off, hurries to his seat, and fastens his buckle. The plane gives another violent shake, and a steward tumbles into his serving cart, lacerating his forehead in the process. I am getting ready to assist him when I notice several passengers in proximity, eager to help out; one offers a handkerchief for the cut. The steward finally gets to his seat and buckles in. Under his breath, I can hear him mumble, "Fuck this job."

The pilot's voice comes calmly from overhead. "Okay, folks. You've heard about the cuts on maintenance staff. Here's a perfect example of the consequences. Luckily, we've trained for the situation. Please, fasten your belts and assume the crash position listed in your manual."

Damn! I guess I had good reason to be nervous about the flight. I put my head between my knees and say a quick prayer. The cabin is shaking very badly. Babies are crying, and parents are humming to calm them. But no one is screaming or panicking in a way that would make the situation seem particularly dire. It's funny how people can be so reasonable when threatened with death. Our scary descent almost seems like the only order in a world of chaos.

I hear the pressurized release of the landing apparatus. It clicks into place as it would in any other flight. The couple to my left is kissing and giving thanks for a lot of great memories. The cabin jerks right and left and then balances once again. I am squeezing the padded armrest with all of my strength, wondering if this is my last thought.

Then, a hard jolt of kinetic energy rips through my buttocks and into my spine. We hit the tarmac and bounce several feet back into the air. Upon landing again, the plane skids to its right, tilts upward, and grinds on its left wing. Sparks fly, dotting the interior with flickering lights. The luminescent guidance strips fade in and out during the pyrotechnic display.

As the plane slows down, the sparks begin to fade away. The pilot comes back in overhead. "Remain in position, folks. I think we're through the worst of it."

A passenger excitedly adds, "Hell yeah, bro!" He wears a red hood and a wicker necklace.

I am starting to feel at ease when the personal screens come back on: "—will clean ANY stain. And that's a guarantee, or double your money back!"

We come to a full stop, and everyone gives a celebratory round of applause for the captain. I rise from my crouched position and watch as everyone else does the same. A few passengers are checking on the steward and the man in tweed. The couple is hugging. The cleanser commercial ends, and a newsreel begins. It blasts an orchestral hit, followed by syncopated taps on a sharp, treble note. Words flood the screen: banners reading stock prices and commodity values, banners reading a summary on last night's *Succubus Shuffle,* banners reading of war and famine.

A reporter wearing a burlap dress flashes onto the screen. She begins, "Protesters are lining state capitals, demanding the reinstatement of the twenty-second Amendment. They argue that Drumpf's control of the political process has undermined democracy itself."

The screen cuts to a protester. "There's hasn't been a true election since the teens!"

Another pushes his way in and says, "No man or woman is good three times, let alone four!"

The lights that signal a successful landing come on. The pilot gives a last announcement, "Ladies and gentleman, welcome to Las Vegas."

Releasing the buckle on my restraint, I stand up to check my stowed luggage. I had forgotten about my precious cargo; rations of food to last me the entire vacation. I open the bin and unzip my suitcase. Underneath the sweaters and underwear, I find my padded, plastic container. Looking inside, I can see the items I've brought: two carrots, three apples, a bag of lentils, and eight hard-boiled eggs. Those two eggs per day will make this vacation feel extra luxurious. Everything is in pristine condition, thanks to my perfected method of packing. I zip the suitcase, pull it out, and wait for the rest of the passengers to file out.

While waiting, I look out at the neon landscape of Las Vegas, just hours before dawn. It is fiercely lit by the energy of a city seeking fun. It is refuge from the pressures of life in the 47th century. Every interest and urge are met and drawn out, if you can afford it. In the distance, I can see a pyramid and a glowing polygon. Tomorrow, it is New Year's Eve, and I'm certain that the town is gearing up for some serious debauchery.

Looking past the city in the same desert occupied by a blob, the landscape is dotted with the occasional execution. Every half mile or so is a fiery "X" with a corpse burnt long ago. Some of the fires have gone out recently, but others burn bright. I've heard that the bodies are pulled down every week or so. If there's nothing left to burn, the message doesn't seem as strong. At least that's the reasoning.

Who are the punished? It's hard to know. Most are never given a trial. In some parts of the country, they are suspected warlocks and witches. Some of them are accused of being Glengangers in disguise. A modern adaptation of past evils. The nation is brimming with superstition.

The last passenger walks down the aisle, and I follow them to the exit. A nurse waits to tend to any injuries from the landing. The pilot looks at me and says, "Thanks for flying Pharaoh."

INSIDE MCCARRAN, THE SCREENS ARE deafening. One of them plays courtroom coverage of *Monsanto v. Nintendo*. It is a fight over the meaning of intellectual property. Another screen bleeds electro-dub ballads in Portuguese. Emma Watson has given birth to triplets. Tokyo is irradiated, and Tenochtitlan is flooded. Drumpf's face dominates many of the screens. It speaks praise of his actions and appeals to his base.

A kiosk sells taurine drinks and muscle powders. The canned and carbonated beverages are sold in three flavors: Lava Apple, Iceberg Blueberry, and Tar Pit Root Beer. The powders are generally laced with anabolic steroids. Their wrappers carry warnings of erectile dysfunction and moodiness. Some of them are even cut with cocaine to get the workout going. Deregulation of the pharmaceutical industry has led to some interesting products, that's for sure.

Magazines are sold in another kiosk, some of which have pornographic illustrations of major celebrities performing sex acts. At the far end of one moving walkway, a tingle chamber invites travelers to relax. Next to a combo burger/pizza shop, a masturbation parlor is available for two-hundred bucks a tug.

I am amused to see so many opportunities to tour Gel Lago. The slimy monster seems to be a huge source of income for Las Vegas. Some of the tours are in the winter, trekking out into the slime when it hard enough to hold weight. The winter tours are controversial, especially after a few jeeps were accidentally eaten. Summer tours offer a chance to peep the grand majesty of the entity. Little bottles, holding chunks of the bluish-greenish plasma, are sold to those who want bragging rights.

I feel pretty good. The dire circumstances of the landing turned my train of thought toward general thankfulness. I am getting eager to see the crew. As far as the game is concerned, I am excited to boast one win. My first pick did not pan out, as much as I wanted to see Melania leave Donald. But the Liangs had filed for divorce back in August. This will earn me a cool six hundred. Adjusted for inflation and taking out the loans on my airfare, I should make out with a grand. Not bad for a shot in the dark.

I walk past the luggage carousel and toward the taxi curb. On the screens, a public service announcement warns against theft, trickery, and sorcery. There is footage showing miles and miles of crucified offenders. Like those on the outskirts of the city, some burn, and some have burnt out.

Outside, the air is cool and smoky. A forest fire burning in Flagstaff has pushed smoke into the basins of the Mojave Desert, producing a thin haze as far as the eye can see. The smoke does not offend me, and neither do the busy sounds of the airport. I look up at the signs. Esther and I had planned on meeting at 2:25 at the south curb. I am on the south curb, and it is 2:23.

In the distance, I can see a pair of headlights, shining dimmer than the rest. This is a certain sign of Esther's old truck. Sure enough, a roar of biodiesel echoes through the airport, followed by a sharp bang from the exhaust pipe. As soon as I raise my hand to wave at her, Esther honks at me in acknowledgment. She pulls into the curbside, and I can hear classic gutter thrash blaring from her speakers. She rolls down her window and flashes a smile at me with eyes that look bloodshot and skin that carries a grayish complexion. Knowing that she is an early riser, I can only assume that this is way past her bedtime.

"Hey, Mo."

Running to the door, I kiss her on the cheek and whisper, "Hey, Esther. You look tired. Let's get my shit in the back and head out." I lift my suitcase into the bed and secure it with two bungees.

"You've lost weight," she tells me as I get into the passenger seat. The volume has been turned off, and the cab smells like lemon peel.

"What do you expect? I give credit to the Third Term diet, as the kids are calling it nowadays. I can fit into all of my old shirts again. Looking pretty good, huh? I gotta say, I—"

Esther looks at me with furled eyebrows and interrupts with a question. "What do you think?"

"What do I think about what?"

"Haven't you seen?" She gives me a confused scowl. "I mean, surely you saw something on the flight."

"What do you mean? We were powerless for a little bit. The 747 was a jalopy. The left wing was shredded to pieces."

Esther looks down and seems to be laughing and crying at the same time. "Damn. That must have been frightening."

"Yeah, it was."

Returning to the original subject, she softly quips, "Well, I'm sure you'll hear about it sooner or later."

This is surely a prank. "Oh, will I?"

"I'm not joking, Mo." She looks up, and her pupils dilate to focus on something behind me. She laughs and points to the airport. "Look for yourself."

I am getting annoyed playing this game when I turn around and look into the glass walls of the airport. They are riddled with silica displays. The main screen, consuming an entire partition near the information desk, shows a photograph of my good friend, Geo Simmermann. The banner underneath his bust reads: "Simmermann Wife Files for Divorce."

Freezing, my mind is brimming with a thousand thoughts. I am struck with anxiety and fear. I look into Esther's face and ask, "Is he at the hotel?"

She answers, "He and Clea got in earlier this evening. We spent the evening consoling him. It's a little complicated."

DRIVING DOWN LAKE MEAD BOULEVARD, the city seems asleep. I remember coming here for the first Death Pool. Back then, the city was screaming. With everything that has happened, the fun times seem irrelevant. One thing has changed: there are more screens.

My mind is still recovering from the shock of Geo's divorce. Once again, I feel pity for him. When I first saw the headline, I figured it was due to the scandal at Capitcorp, his investment firm. Geo, with his hard-earned reputation, had been the company scapegoat throughout its short history. The scandal also placed blame directly on him. While Capitcorp had made a fatal mistake by investing in personal tech, Geo's troubles were not about image or practicality. They were about breaking the law. Insider trading laws, to be precise.

Now Esther is telling me it's because of cheating and lying. She explains as she drives, "Mishelle filed, citing Geo's numerous affairs. I'm sure you remember that time he got caught with the cleaning lady."

I purse my lips. "Yeah. I do. Well, I can't say I'm not in support of her leaving such a situation. How is Geo taking it?"

"Pretty hard. Especially, since seeing Clea."

"Clea?"

Esther sighs and continues, "Clea had slept with Geo too."

Upon hearing this, I am less surprised and more upset. The two used to have these weird episodes of flirting all throughout high school. If I remember correctly, they hooked up once or twice. But to do this when he's married? I can't decide who I am more upset with. I whisper, "Damn."

"It really pisses me off too. It happened such a long time ago. And she had been giving this front, like Geo was being a creep. Turns out, she was eating that shit up."

"I'm sorry to hear, Esther."

She chokes back and adds, "Um, there's a lot of other context to consider."

"How so?"

She takes a deep breath and begins, "Truth is, I haven't been acting in the best interests of my friends either." The night sky is orange-yellow, and the windshield reflects the passing streetlights. Esther seems anxious. She reaches into the center console and pulls out a joint and a lighter. With a manual, spinning handle, she rolls down the window. The lighter sparks and ignites the paper. Esther sucks it in, holds her breath, and releases a fog into the dead streets. She continues, "While Clea and Geo may have had their little fling, Mish and I have been having an affair for years. We are in love and plan to elope after the divorce is final."

There is silence for what seems like an hour. It was only a second. But in that second, I felt like a friend eternally out of the loop. I ask her, "And you didn't think to tell Geo?"

"That's the thing, Mo. I've never told him, and I can't tell him. To tell him about Mish and I . . . it might affect the divorce settlement."

"Oh. I see."

"It's not like that. All that she wants is the house. But since her lawyer has the leverage of Geo's affair, I can't let anyone in on Mish's infidelity. She would lose the house, and for all intents and purposes, be homeless. She's never held down a job, other than reception and tending bar."

I ask in an increasingly angry tone, "And what about Geo?"

"Really? You think that he's the victim? He'll be fine. You know that. These legal problems will wash off of him like the ones from Check-and-Go."

"I guess you've got a point." I am trying to calm down while feeling discouraged by the behavior and secrecy of what I thought were my closest friends.

Esther continues, "Plus, I don't think you understand the kind of shit Clea's pulling right now."

"What do you mean?"

"It was Clea who told Mishelle about her night with Geo. She called her a few months ago and confessed. She said something about repressing those memories and having them resurface after reading some diary entry. I think it's all bullshit. I think she called it in so she could cash in on the game."

"Wait a minute. You think that Clea is plotting this divorce for her own financial gain?"

"I wouldn't put it past her. Apparently, I've never known the real Clea."

"Okay. This is way too heavy." I hold my tongue and soak up the vast, romantic conspiracy. My friends in L.A. gossip about homewreckers, mistresses, and trysts with the maintenance man. I would not have expected my closest friends to engage in such petty behavior. After hanging my head for a few moments, I look up and ask, "Should we consider canceling Divorce Pool?"

Esther laughs and replies, "Are you kidding? You would miss out on that sweet prize for the Liangs."

I laugh out loud as well. The humor does not last long. I encourage Esther,

"Don't you think it would be best to lay it all out in the open? Doesn't Geo deserve to know the truth?"

"I wouldn't make that decision without the presence of Mish, and I've already explained the consequences. I really hate to ask you this, but I need you to keep the relationship between Mish and me a secret."

"You want me to keep it from Geo and Clea?"

Esther blushes as she answers, "Actually, Clea already knows. I told her about it last year. But she made a promise not to mention it."

"You don't think she would tell him? I mean, if you really think that Clea's doing all of this to win the game, then wouldn't she relay that information to Geo as a way to ensure the divorce?"

"I pleaded with Clea and asked her not to mention the affair."

"Which affair?"

"You're the worst. Me and Mish, of course."

"And?"

"She promised to keep our secret."

THE HOTEL IS ONE OF many budget options along the strip. The prices look reasonable considering the close proximity to the action. There are six-figure rates at Vegas staples like Palacio de Caesar and the Luxor. Ours is called The Red Henry. It sits next to a twenty-four-hour Xiao's Chicken franchise. Esther's truck pulls into the parking lot, and her headlights shine into the darkened lobby.

Packed with my food and my clothes is a folding tent and sleeping bag. Since my friends had already covered my airfare, I wanted options in the event there was limited sleeping space. According to Esther, they have rented a two-bed suite, and there is plenty of room on the floor. If management asks, I am a one-night-stand, or an old boyfriend. Anything but a freeloading friend.

The engine dies down, and the headlights turn off. I am feeling exhausted from travel. The conversation with Esther has also drained me. I feel as if we should connect on a level that avoids the current drama. Before opening my door to get my luggage, I ask her, "Aside from Clea and the Simmermanns, how is everything else treating you, Marigold?"

She smiles and quickly answers, "Things are good, Mo."

"Are you still seeing clients?"

"No. There's no need to anymore. The clinic has five times as many thera-pists as when I worked there. I would make too many cooks in the kitchen."

"So, it's just the tincture hustle now?"

"Yeah. The herbals have been quite lucrative for me."

My curiosity is piqued. "How so?"

"I've got a contract with the manufacturers of those tingle chambers. They buy a few of my formulas, and make them into aerosol sprays."

"Seriously?" I am having difficulty imagining Esther participating in such cheap thrills.

"Yeah. They're pretty great. You should try one sometime."

"I guess I'll have to."

Esther's face loosens. "I have a friend who got a blow job in one. Said it was the best thing he's ever tried."

"I'll keep that in mind."

We open the doors and get out. I undo the bungees in the back and fling my suitcase across my shoulder. The parking lot is alternately lit with various flickering lights. A flashing construction sign across the street mixes with the dull neon of Red Henry's marquee to show smoke in the atmosphere. The faint, pine smell is vaguely overwhelmed by a reeking dumpster on the far end of the lobby. Palm trees sway along the street and in the shoddy landscaping. Their fronds whip and make the sound of hay being shoveled. Balls of paper and plastic bounce along the pavement. Their shadows thicken and elongate until it looks like a scene of animals at the local zoo.

I follow Esther up the stairs and to our room. I can hear the sound of someone practicing trombone, and I can smell freshly-smoked cigarettes. The drywall is stained with tar, ash, and the occasional display of graffiti. As we head down the cement walkway of the third floor, I see a large scorpion. It dismounts from the wall and lands on the coarse, horizontal surface. Before I can point it out to Esther, she steps forward and shoos it away. Looking closer, I can see that the insect has a half-dozen baby scorpions, tiny and egg-white, hanging onto the exoskeleton. Apparently, this is a mother.

Esther croons, "Would you look at that! Mommy's feeling cocky!" She moves closer and skids her shoes across the cement. The sound effectively scares the mother scorpion, and it scurries off into another dark corner.

We get to the room, trying to be quiet as we open the door. As we enter, florescent lights pour into the suite. I put my suitcase down and make a run for an unoccupied piece of floor. On my way there, I look into the two beds. One holds Clea. The other holds Geo. Tomorrow is going to be a long day.

XVI

The wall unit feeds a signal into my earbud at precisely 6:00. It recites, "Good morning, Clea Socorro-Zamora! What a fine day it's going to be! Weather in Las Vegas predicts a sunny day with a ninety percent chance of rain in the Clark County region later tonight. Do you wish to start your day with some classical music?"

I whisper, "No."

I open my eyes, raise my head from my pillow, and scout the room for anyone who might be awake. The others are sleeping soundly, especially Mo and Esther, who came in late. Esther is curled next to me, softly snoring. If memory serves me, Geo is a bit of a late riser. I might have a solid hour to myself.

I desperately need to get some work in, as the organization is shutting its doors. It had been in a tailspin ever since Ephra left the group two months ago. It was foolish to think that we could ever continue without her. Unable to manage the caravan of lawyers needed to run the operation, it was decided to end the project. There were too many countersuits filed against us. Just another crappy reminder of Drumpfism. All of those fraternal monsters, as pale as cave salamanders, waving their wicker tiki torches. They switched the victim narrative. Now, they seek retribution and have the lawyers to prove it.

All I am trying to do is find my small piece of the pie before it is eaten. I must find a way to incentivize this sad ending. I have sold most of my stock holdings. Next, I have to move money between retirement accounts. I have already floated the idea of acquisition with a few law firms and non-profits. No one has taken the bait.

After sanitizing my hands, I navigate the wall unit and whisper, "Take me to my accounts."

The screen pulls up my 401K and a half-dozen mutual funds. Everything seems in order. Now that Horus has finally found a job, he's not sponging anymore. He pays a small, conciliatory amount of rent. After the ass-chewing I gave him in December, it's a wonder he stayed. In the few months that he's been employed, I was able to stash away some extra contributions, knowing that the end was nigh.

Without prompting it to do so, the upper corner of the screen switches to a news feed. It cuts into my earbuds, "—be a great New Year's Eve for the citizens of America. Wholesale production of foodstuffs has increased by fifteen percent. Commodity prices on the world market are rapidly speeding toward parity. Melania has opened a food kitchen in Baltimore. Please take time to complete our loyalty survey being broadcast tonight at 5:00 EST. Times Square will be broadcasting the countdown to midnight with performances by Usher, Kimbo Kathy, and The Ghents. Come join us, wearing only the BEST in sixth-sense technology. You'll feel like you're actually rubbing shoulders with the crowd!"

I motion the corner console to reduce and file itself away. *Yahweh, I hate this world. I never hear anything about what's actually happening, down here on the streets. What about the famines, the upsurge in Badger Lung, the fact that Gel Lago never hardens anymore? It's too hot for the big fella. It's getting to be too hot for the rest of us.*

I hear a rustling from one of the queen beds. It seems that I have woken Geo. He rises, rubs his eyes, and looks directly at me. His face is cold, rigid, and bears no expression. He puts his index finger and his thumb on his forehead and groans, "Ugh. Is there any coffee?"

THE LOBBY SMELLS OF OATMEAL. The complimentary continental breakfast has a boiling pot and fixings of butter, cinnamon, and brown sugar. I grab a bruised apple from the fruit basket and a wheat crisp from the buffet. With my meal in tow, I approach the concierge to ask for more coffee. The others are awake and thirsty for caffeine.

When I left, Mo was consoling Geo over the divorce. He reminded him of his new responsibilities in co-parenting. Muhammad Liu-Miller is an exemplary case of dual custody. Mo knows the difficulties facing Millicent, Chet, and Stanley. He is such a good friend. So selfless and caring.

I grab the grounds and filters. On my way to the exit, a screen flashes the latest news in entertainment. Justin Timberlake was found dead in an apparent suicide by hanging. He joins a long list of male vocalists who choose this method of death. It would be a fine time to be playing Death Pool. Just two months ago, Tamarah Jackson killed her husband and herself at a gruesome bridal shower. The networks are still getting some mileage out of that one.

Outside, the desert air is cleared of smoke. I can feel the ozone collecting to deliver the rainstorm forecast for tonight. A country waltz plays in a unit on the first floor. It is a familiar song that describes romantic loss. I can hear the wavering voice of an older lady, singing along at the top of her lungs.

The stairs are littered with a freshly broken bottle of malt liquor. It is a dynamic setting with brokers in fine suits renting among crack addicts. It is the reality of a broken currency. Lines of class are blurred and redrawn. At the top of the stairs, I can hear the voice of Mo, still tending to his hurt friend.

Opening the door, the crew looks up at me. They perk up at the prospect of a second round of coffee. Geo is crying again. Nervously, I come to him and put a hand on his shoulder. I softly tell him, "Let's get some more coffee in you, honey."

He looks at me with red eyes and nods, "Sure."

This will be a visit full of anxiety and lies. I had been very clear with Mish. I asked her to keep my confession a secret. I don't know if she is keen on the bet I had made last year. I certainly hope not. I need this money. While I don't feel great about the deception, I need this. Divorce Pool holds great potential to change my life for the better.

Yahweh only knows what Geo would do if he found out about Esther and Mish. He would not take the news of Mish's affair well. Perhaps Esther plans on telling him while we're together. Leave it all out on the table, and start anew. That's up to her. I wouldn't dare mention it.

The coffee is starting to brew. Mo stands from crouching and looks at me. He holds his coffee cup, as if calling dibs on the first cup. With a scowl, he asks me, "How do you feel about yourself, Clea? Are you sad for your friend, or happy for your bank account?"

"THAT'S NOT FAIR, Mo. I'M just as shocked as the rest of you," I answer defensively.

"Are you?"

I can tell that the conservative seeds of his father's influence are sprouting to meet this situation. In this moment, marriage and friendship are sacred. I offer an explanation, "It was a freak circumstance. Never should have happened. And I don't believe I should get all of the blame for his cheating ways. There were other women, after all."

Geo jumps in, "She's got a point there, Mo. Clea wasn't the only one I fooled around with."

Mo is quick to defend his train of thought. "That doesn't matter. You must have foreseen the situation you would create."

I look down at the carpeting in a poorly-rehearsed display of shame. "Honestly, Mo. I didn't think of it at the time. There were a lot of emotions at play. I would never intentionally do anything to hurt him, or you, or Esther."

"Well, what is it that you do? What kind of friend do you consider yourself?"

Esther warns, "Now is not the best time, Mo."

"I don't care. I am tired of giving to these friendships that give nothing in return."

I am getting quite nervous. It seems that the focus has shifted from Geo's divorce to its catalyst: the night in my bed. Or perhaps they've been told of my call to Mrs. Simmermann? *Good God!* Today will not end well; I can just feel it. I am afraid to lose these friends.

Mo continues, "When have you ever visited? I raked up enough cash to come see you every other year. I even did that bike ride with Justin, going up there to spend the week."

"You know how I feel about L.A., Mo. There's too many raw feelings."

"About what?"

I scratch at the nape of my neck and respond, "It is Good Sam. It is the 101. It is our old neighborhood. Everything is a reminder of something fucked up from my past. Even that cement scratch, *Mama Zamora*, makes me want to cry. I've told you before, my therapist doesn't want me around triggers. I just can't do it, Mo. I'm sorry that it has been an obstacle in our relationship."

Mo paces to the closet and back. "It's more than that, Clea. Sure, there are things that I shouldn't expect from you. But I've never seen you act out of love or compassion. Not even once." He takes a deep breath and continues, "Where were you when the agency started filing all of those claims for the Simpson Riots? Surely, you must have thought of me?"

I am floored by the implication that I ignored his needs. "I'm sorry, Mo. I was trying not to arouse suspicion by helping someone close to me. The firm would have seen favoritism as a compromise to our integrity. Not to mention, you always seemed like you were doing fine."

"Not compared to the rest of you. I don't need much in my life, but some sort of compensation would have been nice." Mo looks at the ceiling. "Ugh. Sometimes I wonder if Justin would have stuck around if I had made more money. I wish I could have been more to him. I wish I could have given more."

"Oh, Mo."

"I'm sorry, Clea. I am feeling a lot of anger, especially after hearing about you and Geo. I would have expected better from you."

He storms off toward the bathroom vanity. I am hurting after hearing his thoughts. Thankfully, no one has mentioned my call to Mish. In a soft and emotionless voice, Geo hints, "He's been in and out of moods all morning. The divorce has really got him thinking about some stuff."

I look at the sad face behind the voice. "How are you holding up, man?"

"I'm okay. I'm kind of frustrated with the kids. It's like they have turned on me, under the advice of their mother."

"How so?"

"Millie doesn't even talk to me anymore. Chet and Stanley are also ignoring me."

"Do they know about us?"

"I don't know."

Esther comments, "They are at that age, Geo. Teens get like that with their parents. I'm sure you remember what it was like, back when we were going to Belmont."

"No. The three of them are spending plenty of time with Mishelle. They idolize their mother. They go on family outings when I'm at work. I've seen pictures from the circus, the zoo, and the gulf beaches. Esther, you know how much the kids adore her. You're on half of those trips."

Esther clears her throat and reassures him, "That's true, but I've heard them speak fondly of you on many occasions."

This exchange is making me very uncomfortable. Do the kids even know about Mish and Esther? She hasn't discussed anything of the sort with me. It's been a balancing act between what I know and what I don't know. Keeping their secret has been a fucking nightmare. I wish I could shrink into a tiny cavern and be unseen in this moment. I wish I could go to the vault.

Geo interrupts my thought. "The kids really seem to love you, Esther. They always ask when you're visiting again. I guess I'm gonna have to share custody with you as well? Ha!"

He smiles, but the joke is not well received. "I've been so absent lately. I hope they can forgive me. I want a fresh start after the divorce is final. I just want to be with them."

He cries and continues, "You know, it's more than cheating. She's been slowly falling out of love with me. If she had found out about Clea, back when it happened, she would have forgiven me. I just know it. There were other signs. Over the summer, we vacationed in Niagara Falls. I asked her to renew our vows. She said no. She said it was unnecessary and that I was trying too hard. I thought she didn't want to burden friends and family. Just another thing to plan for and worry about. Now that she's leaving me, I know why she wouldn't do it." His crying intensifies into sobbing, and he draws his head between his knees.

Esther scoots overs to soothe him. "Aw, honey."

From the other room, I can hear a sigh of annoyance. Muhammad comes back into the bedroom. He looks pissed. In a loud voice, he yells, "Cut the bullshit, Esther!" He raises his coffee to his lips with a shaky hand, spilling some in the process. Taking a deep sip and then placing the cup down on the nightstand, he adds, "Why don't you tell him why you've been spending so much time with the kids?"

Esther pleads, "Mo, don't."

"No, Esther! This is all coming to a head now. If you want to keep me in the loop, you need to fess up to the rest of us."

Geo looks confused and worried. "What are you talking about, Mo?"

I can't believe what I'm seeing. This is going to be a shit show. Trying to diffuse the situation, I mention, "The kids have always loved Esther, Mo. What's the big deal?"

"I am tired of seeing you all lie to each other. I care about you all. You're being destructive. The deceit is killing me. Look, Geo. Esther and Mish are in love with each other. That may be the source of your suspicion about the kids."

Geo asks, "What do you mean Esther and Mish are—"

Like lightning, Esther jumps up, looks squarely into Muhammad's face, and slaps him. The clap against his cheek is loud and sharp. "You fucker! Didn't I ask you not to bring it up?"

I stand with the intention of playing peacemaker but quickly realize that I am at a loss for words. It seems that if I were to approach the conflict, I would be shut down.

Geo chimes in, "Did you say that Mish is into Esther? Uh, I don't think you're equipped with the kind of hardware that she's into," he laughs. Then, a look comes across his face. The ideas are forming. Geo's face curls inward as he makes sense of recent events. I can see every dawning: the time with the kids, Mishelle's sudden interest in acupuncture, the impending divorce.

Esther whispers, "Geo."

"You've gotta be fucking kidding me."

Muhammad answers, "It's true. She told me about it last night when we drove in."

Geo yells. "What the fuck, Esther? Seriously? You'd screw around like that behind my back? You, fucking bitch!"

"Oh, come on," Esther screams in frustration. "You didn't expect a jewel like her to stick around with someone like you? Always focused on work. All of that faux machismo. You're a tool, Geo." Esther's chest heaves with excitement. She continues, "Not to mention all of that shit you're into these days."

Geo perks up defensively. "Like what?"

Esther turns her face. "I've been talking with Mishelle, Geo. She says that you have changed in a big way." She faces Muhammad and explains, "I'm fed up with his shit, Mo! It's all lies. He's been dipping out and getting political. He's a fucking Drumpf supporter!"

MUHAMMAD IS COILING. I HAVE never seen his posture change like this. A chord is struck. As he processes information, Geo and Esther continue to argue.

Geo snaps. "There you go. You're just like all of the others. You're unable to accept something that you don't understand. Quit trying to change the subject. Let's focus on how you've been fucking my wife!"

"I am not just changing the subject. I'm calling you out."

"Whatever. How could you do such a thing to me, Esther? I thought we were close.

"You can be kind of a turd. Maybe I wouldn't have fallen in love with Mish if she weren't drowning in an unhappy marriage."

"I've done nothing but work hard to provide for my family."

Esther scoffs, "Money isn't everything, Geo. Not to mention, you've been spending most of your time attending those stupid Drumpf rallies."

"They're called Drumpf Riots."

"Oh, forgive me! I forgot that you all were trying to take back the term 'riot.' You freaks feel like Los Angeles has a monopoly on the word."

Geo looks frustrated, realizing that he cannot defend his political beliefs. Judging from the look on Mo's face, he is disgusted. I've only heard Mo talk about politics once or twice. I am certain that Drumpfism is a trend that he despises. He has good reason to worry about it, with recent talks about an invasion of Los Angeles.

Geo yells, "Fuck you, Esther!"

"Geo, you've changed over the years. True, you were a little shit back in high school. But as we've grown, your priorities have become twisted. You're just another venture capitalist vulture. Your success is based on the suffering of other people. It always has been. You are morally bankrupt. Your political affiliations are confirmation."

After a few seconds of mulling Esther's words, Geo responds, "I'm the morally bankrupt one? You've been sneaking around with Mishelle behind my back! How long has this been going on?"

Without an ounce of embarrassment or shame, Esther tells him, "Since the beginning of the First Term."

"Fucking hell, Esther. You've got some fucking nerve. Thanks for ruining my life."

"I think you've done a fine job doing that yourself."

All of this is making me queasy. I would very much like to leave this argument and walk the streets of Las Vegas, but I have to stay and monitor any mention of the phone call. I have to protect my own interests.

Mo pivots himself and screams, "I should have known you'd be one of those fucking idiots! Why do I bother giving you the benefit of the doubt?" He paces and slaps his thighs. "You're just another Drumpfhead? Good God, man! You make me sick, Geo. You deserve this divorce. You deserve failure."

"Mo, I—"

"Shove it, Geo. You know how I feel about this shit. You align yourself with the white power bloc and expect me to be fine with it? You know, most of those crucifixions are people of color. Flying into Las Vegas, I feared for my life. I have to sit with the red hoods. I have to worry about mob violence. Just last month, a coworker of mine visited St. Louis and never returned. They suspect it's either a flaming chi or a hangman's noose. How could you associate yourself with such madness, such hate?"

Esther comments, "That's the problem. Those types don't have to declare their allegiance. They do it all in secret. Why risk your reputation when you can attend a riot in a red hood?"

"Wow, Esther. I wonder where you find time to be political when you're not finger-banging my wife," Geo says in defiance.

"Maybe if you had done a better job keeping her—"

Before Esther can finish her sentence, Geo grabs a coffee cup and throws it in her direction. "Go away, you, cunt!"

The cup smashes against the wall. It leaves a brown splotch, inches from her head. Her eyes widen with anxiety. "Fuck this." She turns and heads for the bathroom. The door slams behind her. I can hear her choke up in a fit of sobbing, followed by the sound of linoleum flooring being punched. She screams something unintelligible.

This is escalating quickly. I should check on Esther, but I have spent a lifetime learning of her toughness. She is unbreakable. Muhammad's face wears a dumbfounded glaze. His eyes remain tender, like the day that I met him in Ochoa's Arcade, so many years ago. *What is going through his mind right now?*

Geo tries to explain himself. "This is a giant pile of shit. Mo, you don't get it. I have a reputation to maintain. My political beliefs shouldn't dictate my life and my career. There have been many people I've had to hide it from. Truth be told, I'm surprised Mish didn't leave me earlier. It's definitely been a sore point in our marriage. And there are the clients and the lenders. If I wore my politics on my sleeve, I'd be out of business. I'm a victim of discrimination. Just like you, but different."

Mo shakes his head in disappointment. "Bullshit. You're just saving face. I can see why you'd keep it a secret. Most people have to, so they don't become social outcasts. How did it come to this, man? Was the money and fame not enough for you?"

"It's just that he's doing so much for our country right now."

"That's rich. You don't get it, do you? Yeah, there's plenty happening right now. A caste system based on race. Torture. Tyranny. Hyperinflation. There's plenty of things being done, but only for the people who already have it all. You're blind to how it affects other people. That or you simply don't care. I'm willing to bet it's the latter. And it's never enough, is it? You and your stupid fortunes, your overnight jackpot schemes. Forget the president. YOU'RE the problem."

Geo replies with a stern voice, "Hey, that's going a bit too far."

"Is it? Have you been to Los Angeles in the last decade? Do you have to ration your eggs for a twelve-hour shift? I used to think you were an exception to the rule. But you're no better than the other scumbags."

Mo is shaking. I'm feeling sorry for Geo and step in to defend him. "You don't suppose it's the culture of corporate life? People get trapped into these things, like some form of peer pressure."

"Clea, don't pretend like you're not part of the problem," Mo shoots back.

"What do you mean?"

"Aren't you down the street from Silicon Valley? What is the average income for someone living in the Bay? You may not see big money every day, but you sit on an asset that most people will never have the luxury of knowing. It's all the same thing. You perch yourself on your little, golden egg. You make it impossible for others to afford housing. Our rents are tied to the value of your homes. Most of those from the coast have had to move inland. That's on you, Clea."

My eyebrows furrow at this suggestion. I snap back. "You're being ridiculous. I get that you're pissed at Geo. But why bring me into the picture? I'm sorry that it's been a struggle for you, but your suggestion is hurtful. The market affects me too. My property taxes are completely unmanageable. It's a wonder I haven't been forced out. You have no idea what I've been through, Mo."

"Well, how has Asnee fared throughout the last few years?"

Geo suggests, "Hey, Mo. That's off-limits. You know that."

"Apparently, nothing is off-limits anymore! Tell me, Clea. How is Horus's dad?"

"I have no clue. Am I supposed to?"

He smiles. I can tell that he has made a connection. My divorced life mirrors that of his own parents. His father scrambled to make ends meet after his divorce. Mo blames his mother for those hardships. He used to call her a gold digger. Mo answers, "I guess not."

"Look, I understand. You feel a certain way about divorced mothers."

My cynicism seems to sting. He explains, "I used to feel that way. I don't anymore. Perhaps, if you visited, you'd know that about me. I'm sorry I asked, Clea."

I reply with a flat sigh, "It's okay, honey."

Geo interrupts, "Isn't that sweet? I guess I'm the only bad guy in this story."

The toilet flushes, and Esther opens the door. Her eyes are red. Instantly, I can read her intention. She has information that has been withheld. I know precisely what it is. It was foolish of me to think that Mish would keep our secret. After all, they are the star-crossed lovers. I am just a minor character in their drama. She raises her voice and screams, "Clea is always our sweetheart, isn't she? Well, she's the one who tattled on Geo! She's the one who called Mish to confess. It wouldn't surprise me one bit if she did it for the Divorce Pool payout."

With one last shot at feigning ignorance, I ask her, "What do you mean?"

"Mish told me all about it. You called her a few months back and admitted to sleeping with Geo back in '07. As one of my closest friends, I figured you were trying to make things right. Then I remembered our conversations during the road trip when I spent Yom Kippur with you. You seemed really upset that Geo would make a move on you like that. Turns out, you were fooling around with him, and you didn't want to tell me about it. My feelings for Mish were developing at the time, and it was torture keeping a secret from her. I wanted to tell her that her husband was screwing around. But I made a promise to you. If I'd known that you had hooked up, we might have been able to start our life together. Why did I bother keeping your secret for twelve years?"

"You're one to talk about keeping secrets, Esther. Keeping your relationship under wraps for the last year? It drove me fucking crazy. You're just as much to blame. You fell in love. You seduced her. I just had one regrettable night. I was dealing with the loneliness, like I always do."

"Give me a break," she mocks.

Geo cuts in, "What do you all have against me? I can't believe my ears. I'm so confused."

I plead, "Believe me, Esther. I was too embarrassed to tell you about the night with Geo. I'm sorry."

"That's not the issue. Not anymore. The question remains: what motivated you to mention it to Mish?"

"I—I don't know. It was bugging me. I had recently come across a diary entry, written when it happened. I was trying to hash out my emotions."

"You had mentioned."

"Well, my therapist says that I—"

She interrupts, "Are you sure that's why?"

Mo looks at me. He adds, "It really doesn't look good, Clea."

I can feel the tears building in my ducts. I back into the wall and slump into a fetal position. I whisper, "I don't know. I don't know anything these days."

Geo suddenly bellows, "Cunts! How could you? What kind of conspiracy is this?"

"It's not all about you, Geo. Let her work it out," Muhammad requests.

Geo paces toward the wall unit and then to the nightstand. "Were you trying to orchestrate this divorce, Clea? I could fucking kill you!"

He looks ready to pounce on anyone and anything. I guess I can't blame him. I really have fucked everything up. "Geo, I don't know what to say. It's just that your marriage didn't seem like it was—"

"Shut your fucking mouth, Clea!"

He rushes across the room toward me. I am reminded of the incident at my father's house, where I assaulted him with a TV dinner. Where's my exit? My reflexes tighten, and I put my arms up to protect my face. Crouched in the corner, I am unable to move away from the approaching tantrum. I close my eyes in anticipation of being beaten by my childhood friend. Suddenly, I can hear the rustling of clothes to my side. I look up, and Mo and Esther have restrained the angry divorcee.

They lean back and forth, trying to break his momentum. Geo breaks Esther's hold and throws her onto the corner of a bed frame. Her shoulder connects with a wooden knob and makes an unpleasant sound. As I try to stand to help her, Geo swings Mo into the wall behind me, pinning me to the floorboard. He screams, "Mind your own damned business!"

I crawl to the side of the writhing bodies and scramble up the wall into a standing position. Sidestepping the quarrel, I rush to Esther to check on her. She is rubbing her blunt trauma. She looks up and peers into my soul. She wears the emotion I am feeling. We are contributors to this ugly spat.

Geo slams Mo into the wall again. Esther bolts up and out, to strike him in the neck. Her fist smacks like a floor tom. Stumbling and out of breath, Geo falls to one knee. He regains his balance and then stands again.

Esther warns, "Back off, Geo!"

He winds up his arm and punches Mo squarely in the temple. Upon his second attempt, his fist is intercepted and pulled down toward his torso. In a split second of opportunity, Mo slips free and swings wildly at Geo's jaw. It connects and makes a vicious sound. Geo stumbles backward, trips over my briefcase, and lands on his tailbone. Without hesitation, Mo pounces on him. He punches him over and over. He is experiencing some sort of bloodlust.

I look at Esther and see worry written on her face. She sprints toward the men. Unexpectedly, one of Mo's elbows comes up, right into her groin. She lets out a groan and collapses onto all fours. Quickly pulling her up, she shakes it off. We grab Mo from behind and try to restrain him. His arms are impossible to stop. Blood and bruises are covering Geo's face. It seems like we might be witnessing his death.

Their bodies sway to the left and right. Geo tries to pull Muhammad to his side. He fails in the effort. The punches continue to land. Geo's limbs go limp. He has accepted losing the fight and is trying to signal his surrender through submissive body language. No longer blocking the fists, he waits for the spell to subside.

In a frantic attempt to stop this melee, Esther screams, "Don't make me go Zangief on your ass, Mo!"

Through the blood and the sweat, Geo gurgles a weak laugh. Upon hearing this, Mo stops punching. He turns his head and looks at me with bloodshot eyes. His expression is one of wonder and horror. He looks down at Geo and releases him.

The laughter from Geo builds. Wiping his mouth, he weakly comments, "Zangief is the worst character in that game. He doesn't shoot fireballs, and he's slow as hell. And if I remember correctly, Esther always picked Chun Li."

The room is quiet for a moment. We are all processing this absurd turn of emotion. Is it all over? Was that supposed to be a joke? Everything is happening so fast. It is confusing. Esther sits on the bed in exhaustion.

Mo looks absolutely terrified at what he has done. He backs away from the coagulating mess and falls down onto his knees. He is beginning to choke up at the thought of his violent outburst. His tears mix with the sweat from his brow. They drip onto the floor. Esther and I offer to help Geo up. Once he is upright, I grab my suitcase, open it, and offer him a clean blouse to wipe his face with. He dabs it and reveals a deep cut on his left brow.

Esther asks, "Are you okay?"

"Yeah." He continues to clean his face and jokes, "Forget about your scissor kick. I think I've fallen victim to E. Honda's hundred-hand slap."

Mo shudders. "What have I done?"

I put my arm around Mo and tell him, "Everything is going to be alright, honey. We just had some secrets to spill, and the worst is over."

"Okay, Clea. Damn, I could use a drink."

Geo agrees. "That sounds like a splendid idea."

Esther laughs and admits, "Good thing I picked up a bottle of discount whiskey last night. It's in my toiletries. Anyone willing to make a run for the ice machine? I'm sure Geo could use some for his forehead."

We laugh in what can only be described as a collective defense mechanism.

GEO SITS IN THE RECLINER in the corner of the room. The rest of us are leaning against the foot of an unmade bed. The "Do Not Disturb" sign is hanging from the doorknob, and we sip from plastic tumblers of ice and rye. Esther was kind enough to order a pizza for lunch. For the last several hours, we have been trying to make sense of our soap opera. The tone is one of apology, an attempt to make things normal again. Just like that, we are the four friends, getting drunk like we used to. Geo seems to have accepted the reality of Esther and Mish's love. It is obvious that he wants to move forward without completely ruining his relationship with his children. It is largely uncharacteristic of him, and I feel cautiously proud of his effort.

Taking a sip from the whiskey, Esther calmly reminds me, "I wish you would have told me about what happened. But I get it. And I shouldn't have asked you to keep my own secret. That was too much of a demand on you."

"It's fine."

Muhammad adds, "You all are worse than a telenovela."

Orange-tinted light pours in from the blinds. The sun is setting on The Red Henry, peering through gathering clouds. The smell of rain is building in the air. We discussed cruising the strip like we did on that first run of Death Pool. Given the earlier drama, it seemed like a bad idea. The attractions of Las Vegas are too expensive anyway. Sure enough, venues and casinos have jacked up their prices on everything in the hope of making big money on the holiday. The rain is just another reason not to go out. We have decided to celebrate on our own terms. We have enough whiskey. Hopefully, we can rebuild our friendship in the process.

Looking into his tumbler, Geo shyly admits, "You know, there was a period of time where I thought, deep in my heart, that I was in love with Clea." He looks at me. "I mean, I've been flirting with you since we were kids. It's not a crazy notion."

"You do have a certain charm, Geo."

Esther jokes, "Like a lizard in a two-piece suit."

We chuckle in the hazy sunlight.

"I'm getting a little drunk," Mo flatly states.

I giggle and admit, "Me, too. I think I might have to turn in early tonight."

"I think that's a great idea. We can wake up early and have a full day tomorrow," Esther says with a yawn. "I am exhausted."

Geo sits up straight. "That is a great idea, but we still have the game to discuss. You can't go to bed just yet."

I am surprised that he would bring this up. I figured that Divorce Pool was canceled, due to our arguments and altercations. It certainly seemed inappropriate, given the Simmermann's split. His suggestion reminds me of why we are here and of my financial needs. The payout on my pick is crucial. It is the only way I can keep my treasured home. If I go home empty-handed, I will have to start looking for something inland. I once again have hope that I can cash in on Geo's misfortunes. It is a disgusting thought that borders on dual themes of villainy and self-preservation. I ask him, "Are you sure this is something you want to discuss?"

"Of course! A bet is a bet, Clea. We have never shied away from it before, right?"

Esther suggests, "This is quite different."

"Well, it's my fault for putting such favorable odds on the table. Plus, we wouldn't want to deny Mo his prize for the juicy divorce of the Liangs, right?"

With excitement, Muhammad exclaims, "Right!"

"Okay," Esther concedes. "Have any of you worked the math on the Liangs?"

Geo perks up and announces, "I have! According to inflation and the original antes, each of us owes him about nineteen hundred dollars."

Muhammad smiles and turns red. "Wow. Not bad."

Esther asks, "Okay, Mo. Do you mind if I wait until tomorrow to hit the ATM?"

"Not at all."

"I'll have to do the same," I admit.

Geo pulls out his wallet, rifles through a pile of bills, and hands them over. "Maybe you can help cover my medical bills after beating the crap out of me."

"Uh, yeah. You got it, dude."

"That leaves the issue of Clea's top pick." He fixes his eyes on me.

My spirits are lifted, but my stomach drops. *What kind of person have I become to make such a bet on an old friend? Is he really considering paying me? Before Esther mentioned my conversation with Mish, I was half-heartedly expecting it. If anyone can cover such a payout, it is Geo. But given the fight, I had considered it a lost cause.* I tell him, "I don't know if that's necessary, Geo."

"Don't be silly, Clea. Like I said, a bet is a bet. To back out now would kill the game dead in its tracks. It's our first year, and I sure as hell want to play this again."

"As long as you feel that way. Do you know the numbers?" I am asking him but faking my ignorance. I have done the calculations over and over. I just want to hear him say it to avoid looking greedier than I've already come across.

"I haven't crunched all of the data, but I've estimated just over one million," he explains.

"Oh, Yahweh. That's a lot of money, Geo."

"Not anymore. It used to be a lot of money."

Esther jokes, "Damn, Clea! That's a surefire record! You're making out like a bandit."

"Yeah, I guess so."

Geo continues, "I don't have that kind of money on me right now."

"Of course not. Who would?"

"Do you mind if I write a check?"

XVII

In earlier years, the din of Las Vegas fun could be heard and seen from the rooms of The Red Henry. Weeknights raged alongside weekends. Even during the Third Term, the party spirit maintained. People tend to howl and dance when the end is near. Now that the end is here, the streets are silent. Gone are the days of the foot-long hot dog, bought with pocket change. Gone are the days of the nickel slots. It is all out of reach. People are too busy feeding themselves and their families to think of such things.

As promised by the local forecast, rain started falling just shy of midnight. The downpour waxed and waned in intensity. It was continual. Puddles of standing water, deep at crosswalks and at intersections, spotted the landscape like a Dalmatian in profile. Streams carried escort fliers and tin cans. Lightning occasionally flashed through the windows of the hotel.

There were many reasons that the friends had tucked in early. It had been tradition to whoop it up on New Year's Eve. This time, it seemed like an unrealistic gesture. They were exhausted from a day of fighting. Nerves had been deep-fried. They nursed the pain of fisticuffs. Not to mention, it was just too damn expensive to spend a night out.

Clea and Esther rested on a queen-size mattress, made with periwinkle sheets and a matching comforter. Esther snored in the first stages of COPD, sprawled out on her back with limbs akimbo. The nightstand held an empty whiskey bottle. It stood there as a reminder. Things are and will always be awkward, from here on in. Booze was the necessary crutch to get through the night.

Clea drifted in and out of sleep. She was affected by insomnia on most nights and had been given an official diagnosis by her therapist. Even the safety and security of her dream home could not assuage the problem. Like many others, she turned to pharmaceutical assistance. The cost of over-the-counter sleeping pills had increased twenty-fold in the ruined American economy. For the last year or so, she had substituted with dirt weed. Weed is a commodity with a relatively stable price.

She had offered her entire stash to the crew. It was meant as a buffer after screaming and clawing at one another. Now, the effects of the last joint were rapidly wearing off. She wore her earbuds and listened to a track of Tibetan bells. They rang out and held their tones while a wind chime softly jingled.

Unpleasant dreams also plagued Clea's mind. They painted her as an amoral and ruthless manipulator. Her sleep was restless, marked with periodic bouts of guilt and worry. She tried not to rustle the bedding or wake her roommates in her personal struggle. At times, she merely laid there and stared at the ceiling in the darkness of the night.

Sometime after midnight, she felt the pressure of a full bladder. She tried to ignore the sensation. Slowly, the urge overpowered her sleepiness. Bracing her hands upon the mattress, she pushed her torso up to sit at a ninety-degree angle. Then, she carefully pivoted to sit upright on the edge of the bed. The earbuds were pulled from each side and placed onto the nightstand. The Tibetan bells played on repeat with no ears to hear them.

Cracks and pops from the spring coils followed her as she stood up. Esther slept in a lump of bedding. One of the boys slept on the floor; she couldn't tell who. Clea snuck her hand into her pajamas, scratched vigorously at her pubic hairs, and pulled her bunched underwear out of her buttocks.

As she focused her eyes on the floor, a lightning strike filled the room with white. It helped her envision a suitable walkway to the bathroom. She took a step, and then another, and was relieved to find a quiet, squeak-free floor supporting her feet. She continued on her path and felt the onset of a mild hangover creeping into her brain.

Leaving the main bedroom, she turned into the vanity that held the coffee maker, the hairdryer, and various toiletries. The mirror reflected the outline of her silhouette. The path to the bathroom was dark and disorienting. She was confused, trying to locate the light switch. Unable to find it, she decided to risk a slow dash directly to the bathroom door.

Clea used the faux marble countertop to steady herself as she tiptoed. Her fingers came across a miniature bottle of lotion as she navigated the dark corridor. It fell into the sink without making much noise. She could faintly see the shine of silica screens in the mirror. With adequate light, this would have created the illusion of infinite reflection.

She passed the small walk-in closet that held her jacket and a complimentary ironing board. Finding the bathroom door, she turned the knob and opened it carefully. A window near the shower was aimed right at downtown Las Vegas. The sight was aesthetically pleasing. Behind her, the door to the walk-in closet creaked open. She disregarded the sound, mistaking it for her own footsteps.

HE HAD BEEN WAITING IN the cramped closet for over an hour. For a budget hotel, the jacket depository was surprisingly roomy. It was large enough to fit a grown man. Nevertheless, his legs were starting to ache from being stationary for so long. In his knees, an irritating sensation bordered on numbness. The ironing board was at his back, supporting him while he waited. His eyes could not see through the tiny crack of the door hinge. He relied solely on his ability to hear movement. He was unwavering in his dedication to the task.

Geo was desperately hoping for Esther to wake up and make a visit to the bathroom. His plan was contingent on her waking to perform a bodily function, or rising before the others. It was a rushed plan, put together in his mind in the last minutes of the hectic day. He had watched as they went to sleep, one by one. Esther was the first to nod off, and Clea was the last. He had quietly tiptoed to the closet to set his trap. Now, as he waited with the jackets and the hangers, he doubted whether everything would work out in his favor.

The task would be committed regardless. Geo had already made the promise unto himself. With everything else closing in on him, it felt necessary to lash out at something. The affair between Esther and Mish was a huge blow to his ego. While he maintained a veneer of cool, he was screaming inside. Nothing short of Esther's death would make him feel better. He could have waited it out, see how he felt in the morning, or even gone to therapy. But given his legal woes, he truly felt like vengeance was the only solution.

His plan was cold-blooded and simple. In his hands, he held his thin, leather belt. He would wait for a moment of opportunity and attack her from behind. He would use the belt to strangle her. With any luck, he would be able to get it around Esther's neck. If the belt failed, he would resort to using his hands.

There was the possibility of Muhammad using the restroom instead. But Mo had chosen to sleep on the floor. Geo could use the sound of the box spring as proper notification. The cue would tell him to be ready to strike. The snoring was bugging him. He wished he could discern who it was.

He reflected on a life brimming with potential and personal victory. His notions of success were an entirely American thing. His mantra had no precise words but carried an obvious theme: get yours and fuck everyone else. His cutthroat approach had provided a stable and pleasant life for his family. His children were well-adjusted, and his wife had everything she could ever ask for. But in his heart, he knew that he was not a good provider. Money was always available. But his attention and his love were not. He thought about these things with a mixture of regret and unquenchable fury.

Geo wondered how things could have gotten so bad. He could not pinpoint the moment when he lost Mishelle. He knew that it had started over a decade ago. She may have never been in love with him. He might not even have the capacity for love. In this moment, he could not remember why he ever took interest in his soon-to-be ex. The reason was either lost in his memory banks or never existed at all.

In these thoughts, he heard the box spring jumble. His grip tightened around the belt as he remembered the gravity of the situation. He asked himself one last time if he was prepared to murder someone. The answer was a resounding yes. There was no turning back. This would be a difficult task, one that certainly carried a sentence of crucifixion. It did not matter. Everything had been lost. His life was in shambles. And now, Esther must pay for her contribution.

The footsteps came closer. He could tell there was an effort not to wake the others, based on the slow and calculated pace of walking. He stood there, sweating buckets and tightening every muscle. Lightning struck and filled the vanity closet with a tiny slit of luminescence. Geo felt as if he could be seen, even though he knew otherwise. A rush of vulnerability passed over him, and then was gone. He gathered his thoughts and waited. The figure stopped shy of the vanity mirror. Geo desperately wanted to open the door and look upon his prey. The slow walk continued toward the bathroom door. He took a deep breath in anticipation of the cruel and irreversible act he was about to commit.

Once the shadow passed the closet door, he grabbed the handle and slowly turned it downward. As Geo pushed the door open, it gently creaked, and he was immediately filled with the dread of being seen before he had a chance to ambush Esther. He hurried his pace, figuring that his element of surprise had been compromised. Then, as he started to sneak out from his hiding spot, the bathroom light came on, and he could see what stood ahead of him. It was Clea.

He rapidly processed his mistake in judgment. He had sworn unto himself to kill Esther for her secret affair with Mishelle. She was still sleeping soundly in bed, and he was forced to make a decision. He could do one of three things: he could play it cool; he could retire back into the closet unnoticed and eventually make his way back to the living room, giving up on retribution; or, he could also follow through with his original intention, making a racket as he stumbled toward the bed to kill Esther in her sleep. This was an unsavory and messy thought. He was certain that Muhammad or Clea would foil his attempt. Lastly, he could kill the other component of his recent problems. In his mind, Clea also deserved some form of pain. After all, it was Clea who had snitched on his bad ways. It was Clea cashing in on the divorce.

He chose the third option. As the bathroom door started to close on him, he blocked it. Pushing the door wide open, he shoved Clea into the lit bathroom. With both hands, he lassoed the leather belt around her head and across her throat. He pulled up and back with all of his force. Once he had decent leverage, he held the slack with his right hand. Then, in an effort to avoid being caught, he used his left hand to close and lock the door. After the entrance was secured, he cupped his free hand across Clea's mouth. She began to struggle. He considered her a suitable death in lieu of Esther.

He whispered into her left ear, "You, fucking Glenganger. No one will be a victim to your witchcraft ever again."

IT DIDN'T TAKE LONG FOR Clea's shock to turn into confusion and then into crystal-clear understanding. The bathroom lights were on, but she could not see her assailant. At first, she figured it was some low-level street thief or maybe a random pervert breaking in to take what he could from her. Then, she recalled the events of the day. Within seconds, and without clear sight of the fiend, she knew it was Geo. The gross whisper along the lobe of her ear confirmed her suspicion.

Almost instantly, she was unable to breathe. She fought to break free from the makeshift noose. Her hands tried to pry the belt away from her chin. As she struggled, her mind wondered how Geo could be driven to such a low impulse. She experienced a flash of memories; she worried that they might be her last. She remembered seeing Geo at his bedside on the day of her mother's death. She imagined him at a Drumpf riot and in combat with Mo. Her emotions bordered on hatred and pity, with the latter rapidly fading away. These memories hardened her spirit and lit a fire in her bones. Adrenaline gathered in every molecule. She refused to let this creep get away with killing her.

She tried to lift him up and over her shoulders. He anchored his body with a toe under the cabinet. Next, she tried to kick backward. His positioning made this impossible. She jerked him from left to right, but he didn't budge. Her elbows flailed, praying for hard contact. She was starting to see floaters in her vision and was quickly losing the energy to fight back. She realized the depth of Geo's intent and that overpowering him might be impossible. Releasing her grasp of the belt, she let her arms go limp in an effort to build a quick jolt of strength. Then, she shot her hands back and dug her fingernails into the first piece of flesh she could find. This happened to be Geo's temples. She pulled her fingers forward. She could feel the wetness of blood building on her talons.

To deal with his pain, Geo lessened his grip by a small fraction. It was enough. Clea pivoted to her left side and shoved him with her shoulder. This maneuver gave more slack to the belt. She turned again, this time to face her murderer. Looking into his eyes, she could not find any sign of her friend. His face read confusion, as it seemed that his plan was being foiled. He lunged at her, dropping the belt and reaching for her neck. Trying to avoid the attack, Clea was caught off guard. She fell backwards and hit her head on the toilet bowl. Geo followed suit and tumbled with her onto the floor.

What happened next was a flurry of hands. Clea's hands clawed and punched their way upward, fighting back and trying to survive this betrayal. Geo's hands reached down toward her throat, trying to finish what his belt was unable to. The bodies thrashed and twisted on the floor, making plenty of noise. Their fight was no longer muted from the living room.

Seizing upon a clear path, Geo punched Clea on the right side of her jaw. She was stunned and swaying. He shoved his hands forward and formed a grip around her neck. Once again, she was unable to breathe. She had hardly recovered from the first bout of strangulation.

Geo squeezed with ferocity. He relished in the thought of soon having retribution. His heart beat wildly, and his chest heaved while trying to catch his breath. The ordeal was exhausting. He wanted to fall to one side. He wanted to rest and celebrate a plan well-executed. It all seemed to be coming to a close. As Clea's face lost complexion, he whispered, "Should have minded your own fucking business. I hope you rot in—"

His lecture was cut short by a loud rapping on the bathroom door. It was Muhammad. After knocking, he called out, "Is everything all right in there?" There was a short pause. He continued, "Don't tell me you guys are hooking up again!" Clea kicked her foot against the cabinet of the bathroom sink. It made muted thumps, but carried the weight of desperation. With a more urgent tone, Muhammad yelled, "What's going on in there?"

This new element in Geo's plan triggered a deep fear of being thwarted. For a fleeting moment, he became distracted. Clea picked up on the confusion and thrashed about. She reached for something to use as a blunt weapon. Her hands found the toilet plunger, rubbery and useless. Grabbing the tool from the bottom of the wooden handle, she managed it out of the small opening between the sink and the porcelain base of the urinal. With a quick motion, she jabbed the handle into Geo's abdomen. He let out a sharp groan and a wheeze. He released his grip. Clea planted her feet on him and pushed him back.

She screamed, "Mo! Help me!"

Muhammad began heaving his body onto the door. Geo wavered on his knees, trying to recover. Once steadied, he leaped at Clea. She pivoted to avoid the maniac, but he grasped a handful of her blouse and pulled her inward. They both fell into the glass partition of the shower. The wall broke into many pieces: most fell to the floor, and some larger remnants remained lodged within the caulked seal.

Muhammad screamed with worry, "I'm trying, Clea!" The door thudded with the rhythm of his body being used as a battering ram.

Gasping for air, she replied, "He's trying to kill me!" Free from his claws, she had just enough strength to twist herself out of the bathtub. She stood and inched her way to the door, to unlock it for Muhammad.

Geo planted his hands on the rim of the bathtub and positioned his posture for one last try at killing his friend. He was furious about being overpowered by his victim. His brow furrowed, and his nose pushed upward, making his face a cluttered replica of his normal profile. As he pulled his weight up and forward, his palms were cut by tiny pieces of glass. Sweat and blood dripped onto the slip-proof mat and dotted the complimentary soaps used earlier in the day. He stumbled up and looked Clea squarely in the eye. "Come here, you fucking twat."

As he lunged forward, Clea intertwined her fingers and made a double fist. She swung it with one wild burst of adrenaline, like a baseball bat made of flesh and bone. It hit him with a wet, slapping sound. The force of the impact sent him back into the shower. He fell to his side and made contact with a large, jagged edge of the broken partition. Quickly and completely, it lodged itself fully into his neck, making contact with his jugular vein. The shard was large enough to fully impale his throat. The red and glistening point jutted out from an exit wound opposite of its entry. Blood immediately began to pour down from his collarbone. His eyes rolled around as he lost consciousness. The shard was pulled from its frame, and remained stuck in Geo's esophagus as he fell.

Clea observed in horror as her friend's body collapsed into the tub. She could see the color fade away from his cheek. The amount of blood filling the bathtub was obscene, reminiscent of a Tarantino film. Geo reached his hand out as if asking for help. Clea's first instinct now that she was safe was to help him. She thought of dialing emergency assistance, then, she reconsidered.

It was hard not to think of her father and the many times he had attacked her. In a weird mixture of past and present memory, she stood there and watched Geo die. She never broke eye contact as he drifted off and bled out. It was a cold reminder to herself that she was in control. The shard of glass was merely another incarnation of a steaming Kid's Cuisine platter.

Finally, Muhammad broke through the door. It startled Clea as she stared into the crimson bathtub. As if waking from a dream, she broke away from the gruesome sight and rushed into her friend's arms. His eyes were bleach-white discs of panic and disbelief. He could not believe the scene he had stumbled upon. He embraced her uneasily and asked, "Are you okay?"

She did not answer. Her tense body was beginning to release itself. The fear and the fascination turned into tears as she began to cry into Muhammad's chest. As she sobbed, the crumpled body in the bathtub took its final, gurgled breath.

Muhammad asked, "Should we call the police?"

Collecting herself, she looked up at him with red eyes. They widened with a realization. After a few painful seconds of silence, she replied, "No. God, no. Don't you get it? We can't call the police."

ESTHER HAD SLEPT THROUGH THE entire ordeal. Eventually, she woke from the sound of Clea crying sometime after the attempted murder. As she rose, she noticed that Clea was not in bed. The crying came from the bathroom.

She figured that the coming day was going to be another round of arguing and finger-pointing. She had no idea of the heavier context.

She turned on the bedroom light. Outside, the rain continued. A car honked as it was cut off by someone leaving The Red Henry. In the adjacent suite, a screen played recaps of New Year's celebrations from around the world. Dirty clothes were haphazardly placed along the carpeted floor. The million-dollar check sat on the bureau. It would never be cashed. Even if it was, it would bounce.

Esther stood from the bed and let out a deep and satisfying yawn. She could now hear several voices coming from the bathroom. The crying was mixed with sighs. She called out to her friends, "What's going on in there?"

From the scene of the crime, Muhammad's voice responded, "Don't come into the bathroom."

Frustrated, she took a deep breath and said, "But I've got to piss." She disregarded Muhammad's request and made her way to the bathroom.

Clea yelled, "No! Please, Esther!"

"What's going on in there?"

After a few seconds, Clea answered, "You don't want to see this." She resumed and intensified her sobbing.

"See what?" She could hear them having a whispered conversation, which piqued her interest even more. She walked past the vanity sink and opened the door to the bathroom. Her stomach dropped, and goosebumps formed on every inch of her skin. She saw Muhammad and Clea, picking up pieces of glass and cleaning up the blood. Geo was in the bathtub, dead and with eyes wide open.

Clea shuddered, "Esther!"

"Oh, dear Yahweh. Is he . . ."

Muhammad finished her thought and answered her question. "Yes. Why don't you grab a chair so we can explain?"

She didn't move. She just stood and stared at the corpse.

"All right. I'll get one for you," Muhammad said. He got up and washed his hands in the sink. After drying them, he walked past Esther and into the bedroom. He grabbed an upholstered chair, lifted it, and side-stepped his way through the corridor to where his shocked friend stood. He set it behind her. She sat down and took a deep breath.

Clea stopped what she was doing. She apologized, "I'm so sorry, Esther. I was just defending myself."

"Are the police coming? Did you at least call an ambulance?"

The two looked at each other. Clea spoke first. "No. We haven't called anyone. We've agreed that we shouldn't."

"What?"

Clea explained, "Mo and I discussed it. There are many motives for either of you to have done this. I may not have any motive to kill him, but I've got a fucking check signed by him. The whole thing looks bad."

Muhammad cut in, "We're thinking about dumping the body in Gel Lago. The rental car is in his name, and the room is in his name. He did not list any guests, because that would have cost him more. Is that right, Esther?"

"Yeah. There's nothing with our name on it." She paused to consider the situation, and then continued, "You never told me what happened."

"He tried to kill me, Marigold. The fucker tried to choke me out in the bathroom." She tilted her head up to reveal her neck, fresh with friction marks from the leather belt.

Esther looked at her in disbelief. "Did you see this, Mo?"

"No, but I heard it. I heard them wrestling with each other. From what Clea described, he stumbled into that shard after she clocked him. The door was locked, and I had to bust through. By the time I got in, he had already bled out."

"I can't believe it."

Clea agreed, "Yeah, me neither. If I could have it my way, he'd be alive, and we'd be waiting for the police. But it's our word against a mile of evidence against us."

"Explain what you mean by that."

Muhammad started, "Think about the fistfight we were in earlier. He's already beaten up from that. It wouldn't take too long to find my DNA all over his face." He lifted his right hand, and his knuckles were marked with several gashes. He continued, "They would probably find his blood on me as well. I'm not crazy to think that the police would assume this as the doing of some angry, black guy. I've seen it too many times before. I refuse to be blamed for this. The odds are already stacked against me, and I don't even have a motive."

"I get your point. I suppose that I have a motive because of my affair with Mishelle."

Clea nodded and replied, "The news was all over about their divorce. It wouldn't take long for them to get wind of your relationship. There's plenty of photo evidence in any case. To be honest, I think they would blame you first and foremost."

"Ugh. This is fucking complicated."

Muhammad agreed, "It is. Clea could be implicated too. It wouldn't be a far stretch to think that those belt marks were self-inflicted. I don't want any of us to face the crucifix. We have to get rid of the body. We have to clean up too."

Esther advised, "You have to do it before daybreak. You don't have that much time left. Three or four hours. And I agree. You should get him to Gel Lago. It hasn't been solidifying as of late. They will never find the body there. It will dissolve, quickly and fully."

"That's what we were thinking," Clea said. "We were also considering driving the rental into the slime as well. We could store any other evidence in the car."

"Wow, Clea. You really missed you're calling as a clean-up contact for the Mafia."

"Shut up."

Muhammad noted, "We gotta keep working, if we're going to beat the sunrise. Clea, did you get the keys to the Chevy Crucero?"

"Yep."

Esther asked, "Why don't you guys wrap up the body and get it in the car without anyone seeing you. Go on. You have to clean up all of this blood. You also have to get the body to Gel Lago. You don't have enough time to do both. I can clean up this mess and split afterwards. I parked just down the street."

Clea asked, "You would be willing to do that?"

"It's my problem too, honey. You said so yourself."

Muhammad walked into the bedroom and grabbed a handful of clothes from Geo's luggage. He handed them to Esther. "You can use these as rags." He turned to Clea and added, "You can go pick up some bleach from the gas station down the street. Hurry up."

"Okay." Clea pulled the keys to the rental and headed straight for the door. Before leaving, she looked at Esther and said, "Thank you, my sweet Marigold. I'm sorry I lied to you."

"It's fine. Let's fix this mess."

As Clea left, Muhammad returned to the living room and pulled out his sleeping bag. It would make a good gurney to carry the body. He told Esther, "We have to hurry. I don't know when we'll have another chance to see you after we split. I just want to say that I love you. You mean the world to me. The fact that you're helping us is everything."

"Don't forget, you're also helping, Clea. You're a good man, Mo. I love you too."

"Are you going to tell Mish about this?"

"I haven't decided yet. Your story makes sense. I always knew that Geo was capable of something like murder. I have a feeling that Mish is keen on that as well. Don't worry. If I do tell her, I'll make sure to corroborate with you and Clea."

"Okay. Well, let's get to work."

Esther bent over and started to pick up bloody pieces of the shower partition.

XVIII

"I could have died," Clea noted.

"Be thankful that it was him and not you."

The cabin to the Chevy Crucero rental was silent, driving on the northbound passage of US-90. The radio was off, and the windows were closed. The heater did not blow air. Clea and Muhammad, too tired and frightened to exchange anything in terms of words, were focused only on beating the sun. Their minds swam in the horror of the day.

One issue, other than the dead body in the backseat, had presented itself: They would have no means of returning to Las Vegas after ditching the car. It was a contingency not planned in the rush to leave The Red Henry. Worst case scenario was a walk back to Cactus Springs, to find a payphone and hail a taxi. The fare would most likely be astronomical. They could also hitchhike. Both had flights departing from McCarran late in the evening.

Over the last seventeen years, Gel Lago had grown. It nibbled on the southern outskirts of the military outpost known as Mercury. This cut the drive time by a few minutes. It was unclear how many miles remained between them and Gel Lago, but they were getting close. The Chevy Crucero had been driving for nearly an hour. The digital, dashboard clock inched toward 6:00.

"I'm sorry that you were brought into this nonsense, Mo."

He sighed and replied, "It couldn't have been helped. We have to place our blame on Geo. He brought the violence. I wrestled with him as well. Obviously, he had gone off the deep end. You were just defending yourself."

"I still can't believe that he would do such a thing. All of these years, he was my friend. Something about him never felt quite right," Clea said in contemplation, staring out of the window.

"I was always hopeful, Clea. I had nothing but love for that man for so many years. But he was just another fragile, white dude." Muhammad measured his next words before saying them. He added, "If there's one thing I've learned about guys like Geo, they will fight tooth and nail to keep things in their favor."

The road ahead glistened with a layer of fresh rain. The glare of the headlights reflected off of the wet surface and dispersed into dozens of sparkling points, like coins in a fountain. In the immediate distance, a billboard approached. The bottom of its frame was lined with powerful floodlights. As the Chevy Crucero sped toward the sign, its picture came clearly into view. It featured a background of blue sky and a young girl as the central and sole character. Her eyes were a striking, emerald green, and her hair was a bold red. Freckles dotted her cheekbones. She wore a silvery, knitted sweater and smiled wide. In orange letters, the sign read, "Keep Her Safe."

Muhammad accelerated. He and Clea found a little solace in the general emptiness of the highway. During their drive, they had seen only one other vehicle leaving the city limits of Las Vegas. The absence of traffic would make things a little easier. It might make hitchhiking back to the city difficult.

The rain surely wouldn't help them. The cold air of February was a nuisance, even in the upper stretches of the Mojave Desert. A mix of wind and precipitation made for unpleasant weather. They didn't want to leave the heat of the car, especially for such a morbid chore. The walk to Cactus Springs would be frigid, and their umbrellas would provide little or no haven from the elements. Only the sun could do that, the dreaded sun that was rapidly coming their way.

Muhammad asked, "Do you mind if I turn the radio on?"

"Not at all."

"Thanks. I didn't want to be inappropriate, but I need something to lighten the mood."

He clicked the FM channel on. It began with a low buzz of white noise, the voices of the cosmos coming through a low-fidelity mouth. The dial was parked on higher frequencies, which were generally reserved for contemporary country, Norteño corridos, and UFO-themed talk shows. He twisted the tuning dial and could not find a clear channel. Radio stations have lost funding over the years, and most have been forced to shut down. Being well outside the Vegas sprawl did not help in the effort. Finally, the speakers chimed in on the frequency of 95.1. It played Dusty Springfield, the featured artist for the five o'clock hour on KNYE, Nye County.

Clea hummed along to "I Can't Make It Alone." She put her hand on Muhammad's thigh and patted it. It was meant as a sign of affection and trust. She was grateful for him. She faced a grim and unfortunate reality; most of the men in her life were violent in nature. Muhammad was the only exception. She let out a sigh.

A lightning strike briefly consumed the sky of the coming dawn. It gave a quick sight of the desert landscape. On the northeast horizon, there was a mirage of something that looked like a hillside. It carried a faint glow, fading in and out like a pair of expanding and contracting lungs. Gel Lago was coming into sight. Once the flash passed, the sick, neon green held its outline on the background of stars.

"Finally," Clea commented.

Muhammad joined her in a sense of relief. "Thank Allah. We are almost there. I can't quite remember; Is there a road that leads us to the edge?"

"I don't know."

"I'm sure we'll see something soon."

The radio station shuffled to the last song of the hour, closing out the Springfield repertoire. It was the classic "Son of an Imam." The blues guitar faded into Dusty's signature voice and mixed with a subtle horn section. Any other day and in any other mood, Clea and Muhammad would have replaced the original lyrics with those of the stoner song from their high school years. They absolutely loved Cypress Hill, back in the day.

As the song played, another roadside sign came into view. Unlike the imposing billboard, there was no lighting apparatus. Once the car was close enough, the shape and purpose became clear. The sign was nearly five feet high and shaped like an arrow. It pointed into the cactus-laden fields of dust and away from the highway. Judging from the rot on the wood and the rust in the frame, upkeep had been abandoned. The words slowly came into focus. They read, "Road to Gel Lago!"

The directions mildly lightened their heavy hearts. They passed the sign. There was a poorly-maintained dirt road on the right side of the highway. The car slowed down and turned into the path. It was wet, rickety, and littered with potholes. Another old sign came into view, claiming an additional twenty-five miles of driving. The view from within the Chevy Crucero said otherwise. Gel Lago was straight ahead, and the race against sunrise was won.

CLEA AND MUHAMMAD HAD TO drive off-road to reach the beast. They had driven through cholla and yucca clusters before finally arriving at Geo's grave. Up close, it occupied the entire horizon. The vast desert and distant hills were replaced by swaths of wreckage, collected over the generations. It consumed the peripheral corners of vision, so that the world was only slime and sky. Gel Lago was a sight to behold.

The black rental faced the living mass. It sat on a layer of frothy foam, slowly wobbling and making a long, drawn-out sound of suction. After all of these years, the creature still fed on the waste of the test site. It sponged radioactivity like a drunken uncle who only visits to borrow cash. Soon, it would be sucking on a man of low-moral compass.

The doors opened, and the passengers got out. At their feet, the dirt was soft and wet. A nearby palo verde tree buzzed with the giant beetles that eat upon their roots. The sound mixed eerily with the falling precipitation. Creosote bushes carried a sweet and pleasant aroma. Raindrops shined in the headlights of the Chevy Crucero and pelted the viscous mess ahead. The car would be abandoned, cast off into the gunk, to destroy all evidence of Geo's accident.

The two friends stood there, mourning the death of a friend while cursing his name. A wave of sorrow hit them like a brick. Clea started crying uncontrollably and Muhammad rushed around the front bumper to embrace her. He joined her in weeping. They had faced the terror of a man turned murderer. Now they were flooded with memories of childhood and youth.

The basement parties. The video game marathons. Walking along Temple Street. Romantic comedies and the raw emotion of pogo-jumping while a shitty band played.

Clea looked up from Muhammad's bosom and muttered, "This is all happening too fast. I wish we could just grieve a little."

"As do I, Clea. As do I."

"Do you think we're gonna get caught?"

Through tears and clogged sinuses, Muhammad answered, "It's too early to know. Something tells me that there will be an investigation. He's too high-profile to go missing without being noticed."

"Yeah. But I doubt anyone will get a detective on the case. Look at what's happening in Seattle. The police department packed up and left, once the payroll was cut."

"That's a good point."

"I can't help but feel like this could have been avoided."

He looked at her and asked, "How so?"

Once again, the tears welled, and she choked on her words. With difficulty, she explained, "I made that call to Mish . . . for selfish reasons. I suppose you and Esther had already figured that out. I—I didn't think things would get this bad." She put her hands up to her temple and rubbed at them. In between sobs, she added, "I was only looking out for myself. Things were getting really hard to deal with on the home front and—"

"Stop, Clea. You don't have to explain. Come here, honey." He brought her head back into his collarbone, put his fingers into her scalp, and gently massaged her head.

Clea sighed and continued, "Good God. What about Mish and the kids?"

"I'm sure everything will work itself out."

"I hope so."

Muhammad pulled away from her and saw a face soiled with phlegm and salty tears. He leaned over and dug into his backpack, which lay at his feet on the soggy ground. He pulled a handkerchief from the side pocket and offered it to Clea. "Here. Your face is a damned mess."

She giggled and took the smoothly-folded square of cotton. It had a checkered pattern of beige and maroon. She wiped her cheeks and her chin. Then, she heartily blew her nose into the thin fabric. "Thanks, Mo."

"Anytime."

"Yahweh, I can't wait to get outta here."

Muhammad looked into her eyes. With newfound seriousness, he mentioned, "Speaking of which, we better get going."

Clea agreed. "Yeah." Stepping away from Muhammad, she began to search the immediate area. It was still quite dark, so she walked toward the glare of the headlights. Kneeling down, she pried an oblong stone from the base of a prickly pear. It was big enough to require both hands to lift it to her abdomen. "This should do," she said.

Muhammad squinted and eyeballed the stone for a second. "Yep. That will definitely do the trick. I'll shift into gear, and you can put it on the gas. You'll want to jump back as soon as you drop it. The car might jolt forward pretty violently. I can release the emergency brake before it revs up too much."

"Okay." She lugged the rock over to the car, waddling like a penguin to support its weight. She stood ready to do the task.

"Are you ready?"

With confidence, she answered, "Yes."

Muhammad looked at the positioning of the front wheels to make sure they were pointed toward Gel Lago. He was satisfied that the car would veer directly into the froth. He opened the door and pulled the lever for the emergency brake. He pivoted to let Clea in under his armpit. She squeezed in, holding the stone in her hand. She craned her head, looked into the back seat and whispered, "Goodbye, Geo."

She looked up at Muhammad to get a look of approval. It was given to her with a smile. With one quick and fluid movement, she placed the rock on the gas pedal, jerked backward, and tumbled into the slushy dirt. She crab-walked away from the Chevy Crucero. The motor began to purr with anticipation of leaving its stationary position. Then, Muhammad released the emergency brake and stepped back. The car moved forward at a steady rate until it made contact with the blob.

The car made a sick, slapping sound. Its wheels peeled out at the base of the massive, kinetic broth. Slowly, it inched further and further into the creature. There was a crackle of paints and chemicals meeting with gastric acids. The rubber bumper and wheels began to melt. Then, the slime thinned out and reached itself over and under the car to reel it in, like a hybrid between squid and angler fish. It was a terrifying sight to see. Clea and Muhammad could not look away. They were too fascinated with the process.

It slurped at the front end. A wicked crashing of gears and belts ensued, as the interior machinery was compromised. The engine spat and slowly died out. As the tentacles reached the chassis, a fire broke out. The fire burned a haunted aquamarine, like copper over a Bunsen burner in a high school chemistry class. It was a reaction between Gel Lago and leaking gasoline. The flames did not last long as the gas tank was quickly sucked dry. The car continued its sluggish entry into the abyss.

As the back seat was being eaten, Muhammad walked to Clea and helped her up. They looked at each other in recognition of the obvious. This was their last goodbye to someone they did not understand. They felt sorrow, but they also felt a sense of relief. Geo Simmermann was a friend. He was also a lying sack of shit. They thought back on their time with him and felt disappointment. They had tried to win his heart, to make room for him, for three decades. But he represented too many evils in this world. He aligned with the nastiest elements of American culture. He was a sex addict who sought his fix at the expense of others. He was capable of murder. Muhammad and Clea said their final goodbye with a mix of heartache and disdain.

Within five minutes, the entire car had been consumed. It could be seen, floating and sizzling in the transparent, gelatinous goop. It was gradually imploding under the massive pressure. After watching with a sense of dread, Muhammad turned to Clea, took a deep breath, and asked, "Do you mind if I offer a quick prayer for our comrade?"

"Not at all. After you're done, we should probably start walking back. We've got a long day ahead of us."

"You bet." He began a recitation, learned many years ago, when his aunt spoke at his parents' funeral. It began:

"Creator of all thought,
prime mover of the heavens,
and architect of sin:
Every drop of wine upon our lips,
Every wisp of air within our lungs,
Every lover held between our arms,
These things are contingent,
upon our humility unto you.
We plead of you to trade flesh for insight.
We plead of you to acknowledge,
the brothers and sisters,
taken into the wings of darkness;
past, present, and future.
We climb the ladder of stars,
to meet you with level brow,
and plead of you to foster fair judgment.
We plead of you to craft a chariot,
carved from the ether,
to send them where you will.
We plead of you,
to make sense of it all,
or leave us in ignorance,
if that best suits our lot."

Clea nodded her head and commented, "Well said, Mo."

"Thanks. It's all up to the cosmos now."

"Let's just hope he doesn't have to weigh his heart against a feather. I don't think that would work out in his favor."

They laughed for a brief moment. Muhammad lifted his backpack and strapped it on. Clea released the handle on her wheeled luggage, preparing to trudge it through the tire marks left by the Chevy Crucero. The tracks would be washed away within an hour.

As they turned to leave, Clea noted, "The gall of Geo."

Muhammad repeated the inside joke that was a fixture of friendly conversation ever since grade school. "Yeah, I'll say. The gall of Geo."

They walked away from Gel Lago, heading toward the dirt road that would take them to US-90 and, ultimately, Cactus Springs. The rain continued to fall. It would fall for another two days. Clea and Muhammad picked up their pace and fled the scene. Behind them, the sun was hiding in a screen of stormy clouds. It was an ugly sunrise that deserved to be ignored.

XIX

I am a learner of languages. Over the years, I've accrued many. I have learned living languages and dead languages. I can read them, translate them, and think them in my mind. Unfortunately, I cannot write them or speak them, but that setback is of minor importance. What truly thrills me is the application of words as a form of reality. When a language dies, a constructed universe passes along with it.

I can pick up any variation or dialect easily and quickly. I can "portmanteau" them into something odd, like a Tagalog valley girl or a Dutch cowboy. I absolutely love the process. In another existence, I might have been a writer, or maybe a professor of linguistics. Words are my favorite thing in this world. One could say they are my only hobby, aside from eating. Curiously, those two activities are intimately tied, or at least they are in my case. Everything I eat, I osmose its tongue. This miracle is instantaneous and complete. It is total.

At the subatomic level, inanimate and animate objects speak the same language. They cannot afford to do otherwise. Communication must be quick and efficient when traversing the large stretches of dark, empty ether. It is chaos and order in the same stroke. It pleases me to see the language become varied as the scale become larger. Confusion grows as one climbs the spiral staircase. I can dampen the confusion. I can make sense of it, for the most part. It is this quality that makes me the ideal narrator.

I also absorb the experiences of the things that I eat. Their pasts are rolled out like a dusty carpet—an accessory or decoration to their present lives. Some match and some clash. I can recall infancy or childhood on the spot. Sometimes, I can even make use of their talents, at least those limited to the brain. It is a gift that Stoker's Renfield would have wished for. I doubt that his broken mind, or any human mind, could manage such a burden. If I practiced the response known as emotion, I might feel the burden as well. I know the highs and lows of physical existence, but only as onlooker. I do not absorb the raw drama. I am passive. I am not a judge. I am not a creature of morals.

My first memory was shared with a hodgepodge of elements. At birth, the ether itself. Then, larger themes like hydrogen, oxygen, sodium, and chlorine. The atmosphere came next, and it carried the aftertaste of lead. The composition of things became weirder and more complicated as I squeezed into existence: sandy shores, a makeshift bridge, wooden boxes and munitions.

Then, I tasted my first samples of living mass: a. A lizard in the white sands. Albatross eggs just shy of hatching. There were goats, swine, and a variety of rodents. As I took their memories, it became clear to me that some of them were brought unwillingly to my birthplace. I still do not understand why. Perhaps, one of these days I will eat something or someone that knows the purpose of bringing these animals to the South Pacific. Until then, I will cherish them as my first introduction to true consciousness.

Although they were quickly vaporized, there were signs of marine life as well. Krill, mollusks, and the tiny tardigrade were among my favorites. These smaller lifeforms are not as self-centered as the predators of the sea. Nor do they live in fear of being eaten. They simply wait for the tide to bring them somewhere else, much like I did after breaking free from my nursery, so many months after coming into the world.

It does not take much of a physical trace to synthesize other, more complex experiences. For instance, Marshallese was my first human language. The former residents were long gone; moved to another island, deemed haunted by a malevolent demon. But their fingerprints, left hastily on abandoned homesteads, remained. The Bikini were relocated, but they left oily residues, shed skin cells, and generations of everyday waste as a sample. I swam in their dreams and nightmares. I frolicked in their deepest secrets.

I remember being on the verge of starvation and making that first anxious leap into the currents of the Pacific. If I'd known how long it would take to find nourishment, I might have stayed there to die. Luckily, the people of this world were doing a fine job irradiating every blue sky. Knowing what I do now, it seems that men have weird fetishes—trying the bomb on every type of surface in every type of scenario. These isotopes would be slim pickings but suitable enough to keep chugging along.

There were the massive coral reefs, living the last years of an ancient existence. That was my first brush with English. Odd how I didn't pick it up in the atoll. I also came across the occasional dead and bloated blobfish, which I had mistaken for a human ancestor. Easy to assume so when the face resembles that of a cheery, Eurasian grandfather.

On my way to the Antarctic, I stumbled upon a rare and exciting artifact: a piece of floating pumice brushed across my underbelly. It turns out that this igneous stone was discarded from one of the vessels of Zheng He centuries ago. It was used as a natural loofah whenever the mariners needed to clean themselves. Although the human cells had washed away long ago, the stone shared fond memories of its time on the voyage. It helped me understand that quadrant of the South Pacific and my adherence to the flowing currents. I eventually went north.

After sweeping the American continents, I continued on my massive figure eight. I flirted with the hot and humid waters of Earth's waistline. I ached to eat radiation. Many years had passed when I finally saw the Old World that Zheng He's pumice spoke of. As I approached the giant islands of Asia, everything carried the slight taste of nutmeg, like some meal at Horus Mass.

On the way back to the Americas, I encountered the trash heap. This was my osmosis of American culture. Tin cans spoke of their insatiable appetite. Copper wires spoke of their addiction to electronic devices. Other substances spoke of their tendency to discard anything and everything. They worshiped the miracle of single-use. It was not gross nor entirely pleasant to eat such material. In any case, it gave me strength.

Landfall was exciting. I remember the taste of dirt and the crazy languages coming from its layers. It was then that I realized how so many species and cultures have come and gone. Cruising into and past the coastline was my first lesson in the mind-numbing expanse of time and space. It was also my first lesson in human fear. They were so afraid of me!

Finally, I got to the Nevada Test Site, and my wildest dreams had come true. After the fuss of my presence, and when it was obvious that I posed no threat, people from all over the world came to see me. In time, they even walked upon my surface. At least they did before the winters got warmer, and my glop stopped hardening. The tourists brought odd things: margaritas, contraceptives, crack pipes, and hot dog water. My fascination with human culture deepened as I made more contact with them. They spoke every language in the world. So, as I ate to my heart's content, I learned more and more about this world. It was becoming a very happy existence for me.

Over the years, I eventually met the four friends that grew up in Los Angeles. Muhammad, Esther, Clea, and Geo were well into mid-life when I made contact and pieced together their tale. Esther pissed on me, on a pit stop of her road trip. I was captivated. She was falling in love at the time. It was a fascinating story that lacked some vital context.

I had also eaten that cigarette butt, the one that touched Clea's lips in transit to Phoenix. A lot has changed in one year. In 4723, she was just another human story. She was mixed in with a myriad of other stories, packed into the database of my consciousness.

Now, there is deceit. Now there is scandal. And now, there is the morsel of deadly regret. It is the high drama that fuels the American interest. It is the stuff of novels and sleeper films. And that is why I choose to tell it.

Did I migrate to the four, or was it the other way around? I suppose it doesn't matter. Sometimes, after a large meal, I flirt with this idea of fate. I can't help but consider some cosmic thread pulling us together. There are so many connections. The four are drawn to me, and I am drawn to them. Perhaps, I will never know the reason why. In any case, their story is, by far, my favorite. It is telling of a moment. It is telling of many moments combined.

What is the purpose of any movement, away from one thing and toward another? Migration is defined as the movement of animals, but it doesn't apply only to herons or humans. So many things carry the feel of migration: politics, spirituality, power, and love. Like when one takes inventory of opinion and puts forth the effort to change. Undeniably, the mind moves.

A sense of rightness or wrongness just packs up and heads to another state. What a miracle. Stubbornness is not eternal. No, the synapses shift to meet the demands of an environment.

The theme of migration is most evident in relationships, financial or friendly. The elevator to the penthouse is built parallel to the ladder of success. Move up and move down until the demand for your labor shadows its supply. Kiss up to the boss. Fire her at the first opportunity to do so. Do not merely keep up with the Joneses. Obliterate them.

And faith is never sedentary. It bounces between gods. Sometimes, it is dampened entirely. The heavens are shitting on us. The heavens are smiling on us. Pick one and move on.

From what I've gathered, true affection travels quickly and freely. The doting toddler becomes the unappreciative burden. Adoration of the bard, in time, spawns a critic's column in the arts section. A parent rejects the very existence of their child. Love comes and goes, and it turns into hate. Head over heels quickly becomes the boot.

I am thankful to be below such sentiment, content in the heat of Nevada.

ABOUT THE AUTHOR

PHILIP BRENT BUCKMAN is an educator, musician, and author. An avid fan of science fiction, Philip's work focuses on the uncanny relationship between emotions and technology. He received a BA in History from Northern Arizona University and currently researches the impact of agriculture on the American Southwest. He also harbors a deep love for punk rock, having toured in the early 2000s as the one-man band I Hate You When You're Pregnant. Philip puts peanut butter on nearly everything and lives in Phoenix, Arizona with his two daughters, Gemma and Ashley.